WHITE WOLF
STEWARD'S WORLD, BOOK 2

MICHELLE L. LEVIGNE

www.YeOldeDragonBooks.com

Ye Olde Dragon Books
6909 Ackley Rd.
Parma, OH 44129

www.YeOldeDragonBooks.com

2OldeDragons@gmail.com

ISBN 13: 978-1-961129-69-6

Published in the United States of America
Publication Date: August 1, 2024

Foreword

Like *Plantwise* before it, *White Wolf* is a massive revision of a previously published novel, with earlier changes in characters and storyline causing even more changes in this book, like a ripple effect from a rather sizable stone thrown into a pond.

In the original novel, *The Wolf That Was*, Fiera was a spoiled brat princess named Sorcha, who was the perfect bride for evil King Fallon (now known as Maddix). When they married, the world held its breath, anticipating a lot of trouble when those two teamed up. Originally, they were both conflicted and miserable, attracted to each other, and positive that the moment Sorcha gave Fallon his longed-for heir, one of them would kill the other. Either he would kill her and use their son to try to take over her father's kingdom, or she would kill him and rule Stonemount through their son. A lot of their scheming and working their way into an uneasy alliance and understanding, of course, had to be cut out of this book. Not that those two deserved even a hint of possible happiness before they got their comeuppance, but I wanted the happily-ever-after reserved for my heroine, Taran, and her man-wolf companion, Bard.

Besides, I certainly couldn't let good Princess Fiera marry the evil king, could I? She was nothing like snotty Princess Sorcha at the end of *Plantwise*, and she proves herself wise and brave and devoted to Yeshen's service in this story, even though she isn't a main character.

Instead, Fiera knows when she is forced by political expediency to go to Stonemount that she is on a dangerous mission, a diplomatic dance that could end in disaster. For the sake of an innocent life, she is willing to go into the enemy's den.

In *The Wolf That Was*, Princess Sorcha ends up very badly off, with a curse put on her as punishment for all her schemes and lies. What's funny is that I did write her story, a sequel to *The Wolf That Was*, to have her forcibly reformed. That book was originally accepted by the publisher at the time, but just as the book was to go into edits, my rights were returned to me. The publisher later closed its doors, returning all the books in the series, which led to revisions and creating this new series, *Steward's World*. What could I do with a perfectly good book? I didn't want to waste all that work and all the fun I had fracturing fairytales. Massive rewrites, again, ending up with a totally new fantasy series. Maybe you've read the book, or at least seen it? It's now called *The Kindness Curse*, Book 1 of *Magic to Spare*. Book 2, **Majjian Springs**, released earlier this year. I had a lot of fun fracturing fairytales to give my reformed princess lots of challenges and puzzles to solve.

There is also more to Taran and Bard's story in this story, more growth and introspection, and a strong hint of future books in the series.

I discovered that the children introduced in this book need to have their story told. Ivy needs to do some growing up and learning how to control her massive magical heritage. Maxin needs to learn some important lessons to become the strong, brave, wise king who can reverse all the damage his father did to their kingdom. And Princess Violet deserves a chance to shine and find some happily-ever-after of her own.

What's going to happen as these three children grow up?

I'm still brainstorming as this book goes to press, but I hope you're interested enough to check back in from time to time, to my blog and website, and the Ye Olde Dragon's Library storytelling podcast, to find out! Look for **Violet and Ivy** (tentative title) late in 2025.

Thanks for reading!

Chapter One

Taran was the daughter of Eyrian, a wise woman who tended the five villages along the river flowing through the Aerbach Valley in the Swordtop Mountains of Brentonwald.

At the full moon, in the late fall after she turned sixteen, Taran came home from a night roaming with the wolves and found her mother's cottage filled with the bitter smell of anger. When she looked for Eyrian, she wasn't in her bed or sitting by the fire or working in her stillroom, brewing another healing tonic against the winter coughs and sweats. Taran shuddered at the prickling of hairs rising on her arms and the back of her neck in silent warning of trouble. She paused to grip the silver amulet she had worn since infancy, whispered a prayer for Yeshen's protection, and slipped outside again to look for her mother.

She followed the scent trail that drifted on the wind. The sour metal smell of angry male stranger mixed with the rancid stink of repressed magic made her head throb. She found Eyrian standing by the spring pool that provided their water and allowed her to speak with other Gifted folk who served Yeshen with magic in many kingdoms.

A stranger dressed all in black and purple, his hood pulled low over his face, stood on the other side of the pool. Taran wished she could call the wolves, her friends, to come protect her mother. She had no magic, except the knife-sharp senses and grace that let her slip through the forest like a shadow. She could smell magic, though, and this man stank of it. Powerful and twisted and sour. He was an enchanter, full of magic born into him, but he had submitted and enslaved his power to evil.

The stink of Durmad was all over him, like a sickly-sweet fog of corruption. Taran knew the smell from others who had come against her mother over the years, thinking to steal her magic gifts or frighten her into serving Durmad. Or when Eyrian helped to free the minds of those who had been tricked into serving Durmad and found out almost too late the bitter truth behind his promises and rewards.

Taran fought not to run away when the stink seemed to reach for her, like the prickly poisoned tendrils of a creeper vine. She prayed silently to Yeshen and moved out of the reach of those invisible tentacles.

"If you do not give it to me," the stranger said, his voice a cruel, cold rumble, "I will take your child and tear her in two to learn your secret."

"Doing that will hide the secret forever, and seal Yeshen's curse on you," Eyrian said, her voice a weary sigh. "You come here in arrogance and the false promises of Durmad. He has no power here."

"He has power because I give him a foothold, and I will be rewarded when he overcomes the last barrier and takes all this land." The enchanter let out a low rumble of laughter. "Just imagine how rich you will be with power, when the springs of magic flow free and wild, instead of guided and reined in, and all those who please Durmad can drink freely."

"I can imagine, and I stand with Steward to keep those springs not just restrained, but hidden from rebellious, cruel children like you."

"Fool!" He stepped forward.

A flash of heat and light made him stagger backward two steps. A brief, scorched smell oozed through the air.

"In the ancient writings, fools weren't silly, childish souls, but those who rebelled and made selfish, cruel choices. I am Yeshen's servant."

"Slave."

"Gladly." Eyrian smiled.

"The child Durmad requires has been born. Her parents foolishly think they are free to come and go. They will learn the truth quickly enough. You should change your allegiance before you have to learn the same bitter lesson. Are you so foolish as to think your child is the defense and the receptacle for magic that was promised?"

"I think no such thing. You are the one who declared her such, when she is my gift and my reward, and dedicated to Yeshen's service. That is more than enough."

"Durmad's chosen child is a weapon, not a tool." The enchanter raised his hands, and again, that sensation of heat. Purple-black sparks danced on his fingertips. He hissed and took another step backward. "Give me the key, the binding spell, and my warriors will spare you when Durmad sets them loose across the land."

"No. Never. Be you gone. This land is held for Yeshen's service and in his power and authority I declare you a violation and abomination and cast you out." Eyrian raised her hands and sparks of magic glittered on her fingertips, blue and green and silver, swirling up in the air like dancing fireflies. The triangular amulet resting at the base of Taran's throat warmed, the enchanted silver reacting to the touch of magic in the air. *Taran*, she said, her voice touching her daughter's soul.

I'm here. I'm ready. Taran rested her hand on the long knife at her belt.

No. This is not your battle. Return to our cottage. Now. Blue and silver sparks spun through the air to swirl around Taran's head and nip at her nose and chin, stopping the girl from protesting or stepping out of hiding.

A growl rumbled silently in Taran's throat, but she obeyed and ran home, as light on her feet as the wolves who sang to her at moonrise. Her ears strained for the slightest sound, her muscles ached to turn back, to ensure the enchanter did not prove stronger than Eyrian and attack her with corrupted magic.

Her fears were proven groundless. Eyrian triumphed and returned to their cottage a short time later, serene and untouched. The moon had barely descended any further in the sky.

"What did he want?" Taran asked, when Eyrian settled in front of the fire with a mug of water sprinkled with tonic herbs, and still said nothing.

"He wanted what he has always wanted, to turn magic from healing to profit. There was a time, long ago, when all magic-users, no matter their level of strength, no matter their expertise, were bound to the land. They served the land, protected the people, and lived to heal, guide and guard. They lived for knowledge and for life. They were bound to the land that they tamed, in Yeshen's service and to protect the people who came into their territories to settle. Durmad scoffed at Yeshen's laws and declared the sensible things to be foolish. Despite his defeat at the hands of Steward, in Yeshen's power, Durmad's teachings still trickle through the barrier of the Cascade Mountains and infect those who believe their inborn magic makes them better than all other people. More powerful and wiser than kings. Some magic wielders believe their magic makes them free of Yeshen, and declare they are not answerable to anyone. Not Steward. Not Yeshen. Such foolish arrogance makes them vain and cruel."

"But what did he want?" Taran settled at her mother's feet and rested one hand on Eyrian's knee. She tried to read the answer in her deep, silver eyes. "He thinks he will find his answers in me. What is it? Did you hide magic in my amulet?" She tugged on the triangle of silver and the magic buzzed against her fingertips like lazy bees.

"No, there is no magic *hidden* there. It solely exists to keep you whole and safe."

"Solely?" Taran snorted and earned a weary smile from her. "What did he want?"

"I will not speak of it. Some wizards can reach into others' domains and catch the sound of our words." Eyrian rested her hand on Taran's head. "What was done for the sake of life and love, he would turn to profit and power. I will not give it to him, even if it cost me my life."

Three months later, when the winter storms slashed the mountain valleys with razors of ice, Taran remembered her mother's words.

Lagan, headman of Sweetdeep, the largest of the five villages, came to Eyrian with word that a stranger stalked through the village, flinging fire at thatched roofs and muttering curses so that the cattle fought to break free of their shelters. In the face of magic, the villagers turned to Eyrian.

Taran rarely felt the cold, but a shiver ran up her back when Lagan said the stranger hid inside a cloak of deep purple like clotted blood.

Eyrian calmly continued packing her supplies.

The stranger had moved on when Eyrian and Taran followed Lagan back to Sweetdeep. Taran found his tracks, nearly obliterated by blowing snow. The smell of anger and sour magic bit at her nose and she rocked back on her heels, wishing she hadn't bent to catch his scent.

"It's him," she said, glancing back over her shoulder at her mother.

Eyrian held still for ten long heartbeats, then the silver of her healing magic filled her eyes and spilled out, enfolding her so the whipping winds didn't stir her pale green cloak or tug on one white strand of her hip-length hair.

"Mother?" Taran choked on the cold that filled her. She had never before seen Eyrian wrap herself in magic so completely. Not even when the black vomit ran through three of their five villages had Eyrian needed to call up her magic to such an extreme.

"Taran, gather all the villagers and take them to the Whispering Caves."

"We can't go in there!" Lagan blurted, fear crackling in his voice.

"My daughter's presence will protect you and drive back the magic hiding in the shadows. You will be safe. I do promise on my soul and my service to Yeshen." Eyrian's smile stretched, thin and grim. "Have I ever lied to you or failed you, in all my years of service?"

"No," he grumbled, and glanced at Taran, doubt in his eyes, before turning back to Eyrian and shaking his head. "You have always given us your best wisdom and strength. Even when it cost you too much."

Taran held still, despite the shuddering, the brief slash of hot anger in her chest. Her father had paid the steep price of Eyrian's devotion and loyalty. He had been traveling, alone, when bandits attacked him.

"You will be safe there. I do swear. If everyone obeys my instructions. Lagan, you and all the headmen must join the talismans I gave you, once everyone is inside. The magic will hide you. Do not come out until the battle is finished." Eyrian turned and strode off in the nearly invisible tracks of the angry enchanter.

"How will we know when the battle is over?" Taran dug her booted feet into the snow, wanting to follow her mother, knowing she had to obey.

The villagers would likely stay at the pillars carved with warning symbols and freeze to death in the oncoming storm, if Taran wasn't there to guide them into Whispering Caves. The tales of strange beasts and voices out of the darkness and echoes from the past were woven by the wise women who had served the villages for more than a dozen generations, to protect those caves and what they held. The fearful imaginations of the villagers and the stories they wove around the fires on stormy nights added to that protection. Eyrian stored herbs and medicines there, and the record books of all the wise women of the five villages.

"I will come for you when the battle is done," Eyrian called back without pausing. "And if I don't—"

"You will," she insisted.

"Always remember that I love you, my child. You are my treasure, my joy, and my greatest triumph."

"Mother." Taran's feet barely touched the ground as she ran to Eyrian and threw her arms around her. "Why can't you hide until he tires of looking and goes away?"

"There is a time to run from your enemies, my dearest, and a time when the only choice is to fight. There is a time when the wisest choice is to face death, because the alternative is so much more dreadful." Eyrian gently gripped Taran by her shoulders and moved her back so they stared into each other's eyes, green-gray meeting silver. She stroked her long fingers through her daughter's tangled, silver-white ringlets, and smiled sadly, serenely. "There is so much more than this world that we know. Remember that, my child. Now, you are responsible for the villages."

"I have no magic," Taran protested.

"No, my darling, you *are* magic, through and through." Eyrian kissed her forehead, embraced her tight and hard for one brief heartbeat, and released her. "My duty is now yours." She turned and strode away into the storm.

Taran gritted her teeth when swirls of snow blinded her, so she didn't see Eyrian before she entered the shadows of the trees.

All the villagers knew Taran and didn't hesitate when she gave them orders in her mother's name. The night grew thicker, blacker, and the snow piled up nearly to her knees before she knew every villager, every dog and cat, was safely inside Whispering Caves. And all their cattle, sheep, goats, chickens and horses safely inside several adjoining caves, sleeping under one of her mother's many defensive spells.

She double-checked, by scent, and counted every face. Then she nodded to Lagan and the other four headmen. They stood in the mouth of the cave with the storm yanking on their cloaks and held out their talismans. Blue and silver sparks of magic burst through the cave when the five pieces touched, merged, and solidified into one piece. When the headmen let go, the talisman hung in the air, spinning slowly and blocking the opening.

Taran went to her knees, shoulders hunched, as she felt the web of magic woven into the walls and ceiling of the caves thicken and grow into one unbroken sheet. All the villagers and their goods were now enclosed in a bag of magic that no one but its weaver could find.

She didn't like being enclosed. The sound of the wind couldn't penetrate. A thick, muffled feeling wrapped around everything. The villagers took comfort from it. Taran heard their voices sweeten and soften, and the tightness in the air relaxed. She stayed in the blocked mouth of the cave, with the magic buzzing against the soles of her feet and her fingertips and tingling in her scalp. Everyone else could relax and talk and laugh and let their children run loose to play games. She had to keep watch.

Eyrian would feel that the magic woven into the caves had awakened and everyone under her charge was safe now. Did that help her, make it easier to focus everything into the battle with the enchanter?

"Blessed Yeshen," Taran whispered. "Protect her. Strengthen her. Give her victory."

The world turned upside down. All her senses blanked, tossing Taran into an aching abyss. For a moment, she was a toddler again, dying of a fever that melted the flesh from her bones. Her mother's face hung far above her in the blackness of delirium. Eyrian's face glistened with tears as she begged Yeshen for her child's life.

Taran choked on a howl of pain when it felt as if claws of magic tried to separate her skin from her flesh from her bones. She couldn't move, couldn't breathe, couldn't hear or speak. The magic around her strained and twisted, searing the soles of her feet, stabbing her fingertips and scorching the roots of her hair. Her gorge rose in agony that paralyzed her, numbed her senses, and sucked the marrow from her bones.

She blinked, and her senses slammed back to normal, like the bolt of a lock clicking home. Taran slumped, barely managing to brace herself with her arms before her face hit the cave floor. Around her, the villagers talked and laughed and played. The five headmen chatted about spring planting, and the winter fevers and chills.

Silently, Taran mourned, her heart bruised and stumbling in her chest. She closed her eyes and saw the place where Eyrian's body lay, curled up in the snow as if asleep, all the blue sparks and shimmers of her magic evaporating in the swirling snow and ice. The enchanter stood over her, his bloody purple cloak whipping in the storm gales. He shouted fury, his fists raised to the uncaring skies as Eyrian's magic and all her gathered wisdom, generations of practice and learning and service, slipped through his fingers. They evaded his grasp and pulled away streamers of bloody purple magic wherever the mist touched him.

Taran concentrated on his enraged face, bared to the storm. She etched his iron-gray beard and gray eyes and his broken nose, blunt cheekbones, and the ruby stud in his left earlobe, into her memory. She knew his scent and now she knew his face. She had no magic of her own, though she was descended from a long line of wise women, but she swore someday she would gather the strength, the magic, the allies necessary, and she would claim justice for her mother.

No, be honest, she scolded herself. *Not justice, but revenge.*

~~~~~

The enemy's name, Taran learned when King Egis's messengers made their thrice-yearly survey of the land that following spring, was Nueroch. The messenger who came to the five river villages wasn't a gossipy sort of man, but rather someone who liked to share good news. The news someone so cruel and arrogant had met his comeuppance was good. Nueroch had closed off the valleys around his mountain fortress. No one could get in to ask for help that he only granted after demanding jewels and gold, furs and exotic foodstuffs. Magic-users who were friends to King Egis investigated, tested Nueroch's magic, and declared it had been seriously damaged. He was sleeping and recovering.

Lagan and the other headmen said nothing of the battle between Eyrian and Nueroch, but they turned to Taran as one person, questions in their eyes. The messenger wasn't a stupid man. The king of Brentonwald didn't send stupid men to communicate with the far-flung, outlying territories and their villages. He turned to Taran, who sat in front of the well in the village square in her mother's place and gave her a bow of respect. He had been nothing but respectful from the moment the headmen and Taran met him in the village square of Shadesong, though he had been startled to see her in Eyrian's place.

"Do you know what happened, Wise Woman?"

"You did not ask why my mother is not here to send greetings to the king." Taran clasped her hands tightly in her lap, hiding them under the heather-brown shawl Eyrian always wore to such meetings. "She died in a battle of magic this past winter, with an evil wizard who matches your description of Nueroch."

"Yeshen rot his soul," the messenger snarled, and spewed a string of foul words. The hairs stood up on the back of Taran's neck, but she smiled because this man honored her mother, and her death angered him. "Be sure, the king will express his displeasure to Nueroch. Our king values all magic wielders through Brentonwald, no matter their gifts."

"Let the king know that we are well cared for in Taran, Eyrian's daughter," Lagan said.

Taran maintained a calm mask, though inside she wanted to leap to her feet and run fast and far. She had no magic. In the months since her mother's death, she had been able to meet all their needs with simple remedies, the many tonics and pastes and powders she had learned to make since childhood. Someday, the villagers would need magic from her, and then what would she do?

~~~~~

Taran did not inherit her mother's magical gifts, but the villagers who depended on her as their wise woman and healer didn't listen when she said so. She was Eyrian's daughter, so of course she had magical gifts. If they weren't the same gifts as her mother, that didn't matter to them. She was their wise woman, though she wasn't quite seventeen.

After all, she kept the mountain wolves from ravaging the flocks and herds. No child feared to go into the forest, to play, pick berries, or gather roots and herbs and firewood. They knew if they became lost or injured, Taran would always find them when no one else could. They knew she loved them, and anyone she loved, the wolves never harmed.

Taran had only told Eyrian that she understood the cries of the wolves, and sometimes tried to sing to them in their own tongue. Only Eyrian knew that from half-moon through full and back to half, Taran roamed the forests with the pack. She could hunt and track with her eyes, ears, and nose, as if she were a four-footed beast herself.

As the months trickled by like a slow stream of fall honey, no crisis arose to force the people to accept that Taran lacked her mother's magic. Eyrian's understanding of illness and injuries came through magical touch. Taran learned by watching her mother, and her senses helped her reach similar understanding. In a way, she supposed it was magic, but she couldn't give some of her own body's strength and health to heal others, as her mother had done.

Eyrian had died too far from her daughter to Gift her healing magic to Taran. She had willed her magic to dissipate in the storm, so Nueroch couldn't claim it and ransack her accumulated knowledge. Even in her death, Eyrian had defeated and denied him. The people of the five river villages believed that when Eyrian died, Taran inherited her magic, as well as her secluded forest cottage and her duty to the five villages.

Taran understood those duties in her blood and bones. She kept her counsel to herself, played with the children, helped find lost sheep and cows and children, listened to the gossip around the village wells, soothed the dying and helped bring babies into the world. Despite her longing for just a touch of magic, so she wouldn't fail the villages, she was content. Most of the time.

Chapter Two

Sometimes Taran ached with a loneliness that gnawed at her vitals. She could usually ignore that complaint in the light of day. Young and old welcomed her with smiles when she entered a village on her duty rounds. They pressed gifts of honey and flour into her hands when she left each village and made sure she was provided a slab of fresh meat when the men went hunting.

In the dark of the moon, when the wolves howled and her feet ached to run, Taran dreamed she ran on four feet, and wished for something she could never put into words.

She still ached with her moon dark sorrows when the village of Holding Green held its spring dance. Taran went to watch the dancing.

No one asked her to dance. As usual. That sense of being set apart ached a little more. Taran watched from the sidelines as long as she could bear it. She didn't stand with the giggling, blushing, whispering maidens, and didn't sit in the corner with the children who thought dancing and kissing were silly, or with the mothers and grandmothers. She contemplated going to the far side of the village square to listen to the talk among the fathers and grandfathers, and the young men who didn't have the courage to ask a girl to dance. Instead, she wandered around the far edge of the torchlight, her empty smile fixed and steady, and met no one's gaze. Her mother had taught her how vitally important it was for the villagers to believe their wise woman never felt doubts or pain, loneliness or fear. Not even a shadow of it in her eyes.

Then, when she couldn't withstand the lure of the thick, cool shadows of the forest, she considered her duty done and melted into the darkness to wander home. Still aching.

No one ever asked her to dance. No one ever brought her courting gifts. How was she ever to marry and birth a child to carry on her duties if a young man didn't dare to touch her hand or stammer compliments? The villages would have fought each other for the honor of hosting her wedding feast. A wise woman with children was a double blessing on any village.

Yet no man pursued Taran. She encouraged no one because no man in any of the villages interested her. She wondered if the long illness of her childhood affected her heart and soul. Any other wise woman of her age would have been besieged with suitors. She wasn't ugly, and neither was she plain, though no one could say she was beautiful, either. One old granny described her as "strong," with her long face and pointed nose, high cheekbones and thick, silvery-white hair. She was sleek and agile, able to carry heavy burdens and go long distances swiftly. Her green-gray eyes were a challenge to any poet or lovelorn young man to describe as enchanting. Yet the children of the villages found nothing frightening or hideous about her, so what was the difficulty?

Taran vowed she would never take a husband unless he wanted her as a woman, for herself, not for prestige or honor, or because no other maiden would have him. Still, in the moon dark when her loneliness clawed at her soul, Taran wondered if she would take a man as her husband simply because he was there.

She didn't go straight home that night, after fleeing the dance, but climbed the mountainside to the sentinel rock at the head of the main pass into the valley. From there, she could see the shining silver length of the river and the blurs of firelight and lantern light that marked each of the five villages. She lay on the flat slab of rock, larger than her cottage, and studied the stars, wishing for something she couldn't put into words. Not even in her dreams.

<center>~~~~~</center>

"Father?" Fiera paused on the doorstep of her father's office in the palace of Caer Aerys, capitol of Brentonwald.

King Egis wasn't visible immediately. The shadows in the massive, book-lined room worried her. Usually the curtains and shutters were pulled back in the morning, letting light flood the room. Her mother often teased her father that he drank energy directly from the rising sun.

"Back here," he called. A hand appeared from behind a bookshelf that hid a nook tucked in an odd corner of the room. A moment later he stepped out, cradling several scrolls against his chest. He gestured with a tip of his head for her to follow him.

He led her across his office to the other side, where low couches sprawled in a wide horseshoe in front of the deep fireplace. Fiera hesitated again, seeing the deep bed of coals in the fireplace. This early in the fall, fires weren't necessary yet. Was her father ill, to have the servants build a fire?

Then she saw the people sitting on the couches, half-hidden in shadows. She didn't know the young man, with the shaggy head of sandy hair, dressed in simple browns and greens, leather and broadcloth, what her nursemaid had always referred to as traveling clothes. The woman who shared the four-seater couch with him was somewhat familiar. Fiera had seen the seeress, Aireen, several times over the years, but had never spoken directly to her.

The third figure was Shepherd Chyrion, priest and counselor, a

10

friend to her father, and something of a surrogate grandfather to the royal children. Fiera had never seen the white-haired, red-cheeked man look so somber. That whispering voice inside that she hoped was a gift from Yeshen advised her to be especially cautious of what she said and did and even thought among these people.

"Princess Fiera." Aireen smiled and beckoned for her to come, gesturing at the low hassock that was the girl's favorite perch when visiting her father's office. "Come. I've so looked forward to meeting you at long last." Her sweet, grandmotherly smile softened, saddened, just enough for Fiera to notice. "I wish the circumstances were more joyous. However, taking into consideration all the good things I have heard about you ... perhaps this conversation will be a favorite memory, in years to come."

"Thank you, Lady Aireen," Fiera murmured, and dropped a deep curtsey before settling on the hassock. "I hope I will not disappoint you."

"Ah, dear child, my feelings do not matter. Disappointing Yeshen is what we should fear. My good opinion ..." She shrugged. Her eyes sparkled with a hint of amusement.

Fiera shivered. She turned to her father, who set the armful of scrolls down on a low table between the couches, her hassock, and the cushioned bench he preferred to perch on. His smile looked weary, a little sad, but he nodded to her and she thought he was pleased with her. Just what sort of test had she passed, in such a short time?

"Are you familiar with a minor diplomat named Barnold?" Chyrion said. He finally settled on a low chair between King Egis and the couch.

Fiera thought for a moment. "Wasn't there a footman by that name? He was assigned to Edgar? Or was that Edwyn?"

"Edgar," the king said, nodding. "He distinguished himself by reporting some unsavory activity among some diplomats maybe four years ago and worked his way up to courier work. It now appears he took advantage of the time he had access to our private quarters and took documents from the trash before they could be burned." He sighed. "Papers with signatures of everyone in the family."

"Father?" Fiera sat up straight, fighting a shiver that might twist her right off the hassock if she let it go. She could imagine all too clearly the damage that could be done if the wrong people obtained copies of signatures of the royal family. Yes, they all had to sign various documents, but those documents were handled carefully, protected, locked away so the wrong sort of people couldn't get their hands on them. And study the signatures deeply enough to copy them.

"Barnold has been in the employ of a cadre of folk from several countries that want to cause trouble for us. In this case, they have been facilitating a correspondence between you and several nobles in

Stonemount. Specifically, with King Maddix. According to those forged documents, you agree with some of his philosophies about rulers and the rights of royal blood."

"Father, I would never ..." She caught her breath, near tears with relief to know she was proven innocent before she could even protest. She took a deep breath. "Now that we know of this scheme, what do we do?"

"He and his masters don't know yet that their activities have been discovered," the stranger said. "In the story of the greedy monkey, what did the master of the house do?"

"He let the monkey keep eating until his stomach was too big to allow him to slip through a gap in the wall, and too heavy to leap up and climb over the wall. So he was captured and put to work and made to pay for all the food he stole," Fiera said, her words slow as she tried to understand why no one had introduced the stranger to her. Her father and Aireen and Chyrion wouldn't discuss such important matters of state in front of someone who couldn't be trusted with the security of Brentonwald. "Forgive me, but—"

"No, we haven't been introduced, but you knew my father, Princess Fiera. You trusted him with your dreams, and you believed him when he told you Yeshen had a task only you could fulfill." He smiled and came over to her hassock, and went down on one knee, so they were nearly eye-to-eye.

"I'm sorry, but ..." She caught her breath as memories flooded back. A man with silver streaks in his brown hair and eyes just as warm and full of life and joy. He held her hand and guided her to find the steppingstones to cross the little silver stream in the palace garden, and helped her find just the right hiding spots, when she played hide-and-seek with her brothers and sister. Fiera trembled and slid off the hassock to kneel.

"No, don't." He caught her hand to stop her.

"Steward," she whispered, and nearly yanked her hand free.

"Yes, Steward," Chyrion said. "It has been many years since we were graced with a visit from Yeshen's voice, and now we find that you were very good friends with the previous Steward."

"I didn't know. I was just a silly little girl," she protested, and turned to her father. Steward guided her back to the hassock.

"He walked among us many times, when you children were small," King Egis said, "but only the pure hearts of children with their untainted faith in Yeshen could see and hear him. It took me quite a while to learn to hear and see him clearly, and only after a great deal of pain and sorrow. I remember you bringing your friend to me." He settled on the couch beside her hassock and caught hold of her hand, holding it tight between his own. "You helped me hear Steward at a crucial time in our country's history, my dear. In many ways, you saved us."

"I didn't know," she repeated. "I didn't know he was Steward until years later, when I was studying the records and heard how Durmad tried to trick trick you and ..." She sighed and looked at these four powerful people, and trembled with suspicions she didn't dare to put into words, even in her own mind.

"And now," Aireen said, "it appears you will play an important role in perhaps saving not just Brentonwald, but this continent."

There. That was what Fiera hadn't wanted to even think.

"Stonemount must be cleansed," Steward said. "You have the potential to be a vital means of bringing about that cleansing."

"How? I know when we were children, I despised Maddix and I threatened to black his eye if he wasn't nicer to people, but ... I was an angry little child, and he was so smug and ... snotty." She shrugged and pressed her palms to her hot cheeks.

"You dreamed of being a soldier and leading our armies north through the mountains, to face down Durmad and make him confess his crimes and repent," Chyrion said.

"I was a silly—"

"No." Steward caught hold of her hand again. "Your dreams were true in their intent, if not how they are meant to be carried out. You were given your name because of visions and words of prophecy spoken when your mother carried you. If you are obedient to Yeshen's leading and pliant to his purpose, you will be the cleansing fire." He sighed. "But for a long time, you will not enjoy your duty. If you read the truth behind the great legends, most heroes suffered greatly before they triumphed. Some never saw the fruits of their labors on this side of Yeshen's Rest. Can you be strong and obedient, Princess?"

"I ... I will try." She swallowed hard to fight the shudder rising from deep inside. She couldn't determine if that was fear, trepidation, or glee, as a thousand hours of childhood daydreams of valor and adventure rose up from her memories. "In Yeshen's strength."

"Yes," her father said. "As must we all."

"What do I need to do?"

"If this ugly tapestry unrolls as we fear," Aireen said, "you will likely be required to marry Maddix." She paused, her eyes bright and intent, focused on Fiera's face.

Fiera fought down the urge to shout refusal, to leap up from the hassock and shake out her skirts, as if a disgusting, enormous rat had tried to climb up her petticoats.

"Father, I was there in the council chamber when Lord Dephlon read the report from our spies. The sketches of Maddix's most private office. The discussions our spies overheard, the documents, the arguments with that odious Lord Jaygo ... Maddix intends to marry one princess after another, breed sons on them, and kill them and use those sons to take over their fathers' or brothers' kingdoms. Bad enough I would have to let him ... use me, breed me like a mare, but to be a tool against my own brothers, against you?" She shuddered and clenched her hands tight together to fight the sensation of nausea.

"I do not see you suffering that indignity," Aireen whispered. "There is a child, yes. Then two children. You must protect them. They are not your children, and yet ... you must be a mother, or all is lost."

The very softness of her voice made it ring through the room and set off echoes in Fiera's soul. She turned to the seeress and a new shivering washed over her, to see the woman's eyes were pure silver, turning her words to a holy promise and a prophecy.

"Then how?"

"The time isn't right yet," Steward said. He settled down on the edge of the couch he shared with Aireen. "Durmad's shadows are woven all through Stonemount, making it hard to see clearly. Maddix is not an obedient, pliant servant to Durmad. That is a gift to our side, but how long can that last, before Durmad crushes him, and brings in another tool and weapon to take Maddix's place?"

"He married Bianca of Ambray, changing his plan of attack. This created a rift between him and Durmad's puppet, Jaygo," King Egis said. "As we understand, from the bits and pieces our spies have brought us, he was supposed to marry and kill Arden of Westerland first. Our people have found letters he sent to her over the years, seducing her into turning her back on everyone she loved, for him. Thank Yeshen, her eyes were opened in time. But now Bianca is dead and the signs are unclear who is Maddix's next intended bride."

"You're not going to ... offer me, are you?" Fiera said.

"Filthy, arrogant schemers like Maddix always expect everyone around them to be just as scheming and untrustworthy, and to have twice as many plans and betrayals ready to unfold," Chyrion said. "He won't want you unless he thinks he can trick you and manipulate you, and through you, Brentonwald. To be honest, we always considered you quite safe from those schemes. As you said, you have always despised him. If he deluged you with presents and poetry and sent you secret love letters, would you believe him?"

"I'd write to the nobles of his council and suggest that a fever had destroyed his brain."

That earned a grin from Steward, and a few rumbles of laughter from her father. Egis patted her shoulder. Too soon, though, his smile faded.

"Barnold and his masters' scheme appears to have been to blacken your reputation and perhaps trap you into marriage with Maddix, or risk war. Maddix already believes you are willing to think his way, see the world through his eyes. Imagine the diplomatic uproar that would result if the scheme was revealed. Maddix wouldn't hesitate to claim insult and lash out to defend his honor and dignity, painting himself as a victim. He has done that far too often in his dealings with other kingdoms. He is rather predictable, which makes him a liability for Durmad. We can only pray he stays a liability for a long time to come." He caught hold of her hand again.

"The question is if we should use the enemy's schemes and traps to trap Maddix. If he believes you can be molded into a willing puppet, perhaps we can maneuver him into a position we can use. Not just protect Brentonwald, but perhaps pierce the barriers of darkness Durmad has erected around the north. Are you willing to be a weapon that walks in stealth and silence? Are you willing to go into enemy territory, to carry Yeshen's light with you?"

"I would in essence be a spy, wouldn't I?" she said slowly, testing the words and the images behind them as they formed in her mind. "Rather than a warrior, riding into battle with swords flashing, shooting flaming arrows."

"You will not need to go to Stonemount for some time," Aireen said, and reached out to rest her hand over Fiera's free hand, resting on her knee. "If Yeshen blesses us, Maddix's arrogance and impatience will make him rebel in many small ways against Durmad's hands on the puppet strings. And consider that when you go, you don't have to marry him right away. Perhaps not at all. Torment him, dear. Make him think you are just as much a schemer as he is. Make him aware that he is not the only one to ever think of conquest through descendants. His plan to claim Brentonwald's throne for Stonemount can just as easily be turned around, so you will claim Stonemount for Brentonwald.

"Make him afraid to marry you," the seeress said, her voice softening yet becoming more powerful. "Afraid that the moment you carry his heir, he will die."

Fiera shuddered. Her dreams of heroism, of riding into battle, of enduring wounds and facing the darkest terrors … they suddenly seemed like silly, childish daydreams in comparison.

"The seeress spoke of a child," Steward said. "Maddix's son, Maxin, is an innocent. How soon until Durmad sends his servants to surround that innocent child with nurses and tutors and servants? They will spill Durmad's evil into his mind and heart and prepare him to be an even more dangerous king than his father. That could be your greatest task. Saving a child's soul from Durmad's poison."

"I'm afraid," she whispered.

"That shows great wisdom," her father said, and drew her to her feet, to enfold her in his arms. "You don't have to do this," he whispered.

Fiera clutched at his jacket and hid her face against his shoulder, and knew he was wrong. She most certainly had to do this.

~~~~~

News of the madman reached the five villages just after summer solstice. The stories that filtered through the villages from traveling merchants, or the farmers and artisans who went to the lowlands to trade varied widely. No one could agree on what the madman sought or why he seemed bent on destruction or where he had been last. The descriptions changed. Tall and red-haired. Short and heavy and bald. Thin and young, beardless and black-haired.

The only similarity between all the stories was that he killed a single woman in each village, and then went on his way. Even there, the means of murder varied. Rope, knife, arrow. Each woman seemed to die a different way, a different time of day. Taran urged the girls of the villages not to go anywhere by themselves. She had no real concern for her own safety. The villagers knew the way to her cottage through the twisted forest paths, but strangers always had to ask the headmen for help in finding the wise woman. A stranger looking for her would arouse the concerns of the villagers.

Three days before the next full moon, the stranger wolf came.

The wolves of Taran's forest all wore dark gray and silver coats and had eyes of mossy green. The stranger's coat was blacker than midnight at the new moon, and his eyes were a shocking pale blue that glowed like a flame. Magic hummed over his fur. Taran sensed him long before she caught him watching her from the edge of the trees while she did her morning chores in the cottage yard. She could almost taste the magic drifting around him, a bitterness in the air like sorrow and pain. The wolf watched her and didn't flinch away when she met his gaze.

"Well, we can sit here all day and stare at each other, or we can bid each other good day and go on our way," she said. And immediately felt ridiculous. Despite the presence of magic clinging to the wolf's fur, she knew better than to think he had been enchanted into some intelligence and could understand her words.
~~~~~

Chapter Three

The wolf bobbed his head to her and turned, flipping his tail like a man would wave in a jaunty salute, and vanished among the shadows of the forest. Taran stared for several long moments. Then she dropped down to her knees and laughed quietly.

That will teach you a thing or two about arrogance, thinking you know everything there is to know about the forest, just because the wolves hereabouts accept you.

Grinning at her silliness, she continued straightening the posts for the climbing herbs and vines and bean creepers. Every once in a while, she felt a light brushing sensation across her neck, and turned to look. She never saw those un-wolfly blue eyes, gleaming in the shadows, but she was sure the wolf watched her all the same.

~~~~~

Taran went into the forest at the full moon, to gather the healing herbs, just as her mother had always done. Eyrian had a gift for sealing magic into the herbs, using the power of the moon. Taran smelled the magic in those special herbs, a legacy from generations of wise women, mother to daughter, and she still gathered in the family tradition even if she couldn't manipulate that magic. She listened for the songs of the wolves, and they were strangely silent. Shivers raced across her skin, so she felt as if she had fur and something tried to peel it away with an icy blade. Instead of lingering in the forest after her chore was finished, she hurried home.

Kale, headman of Shallowstream, came to her the morning after the second night of the full moon to warn her that the wolves were running mad. Taran would have laughed at his assertion, except that she had sensed something did indeed disturb her friends.

"Not mad," she said. "Watchful. There is something wrong in the forest."

"The madman, perhaps, come hunting in our valley?" Kale looked so relieved to have that explanation, it startled her.

The wolves were her friends, as dear as any of the young men and women of the five villages, and it never occurred to her to be afraid of them. But Kale did fear the wolves. She could see that now.

"No," she murmured, gathering her thoughts. She remembered the stories of the madman, going from village to village, killing women. "No,
~~~~~

the wolves would not allow such evil to hunt among them." She offered Kale a crooked smile. "My mother had an understanding with the wolves. They protect our valley."

"Then what makes them behave so oddly?"

She thought of the black wolf with his blue eyes and shivered. But not in fear. The sensation that wrapped around her soul and squeezed was akin to the hunger that twisted in her belly when she saw young sweethearts slip into the shadows to kiss and whisper and laugh.

"It is something they do not understand," she murmured.

Kale had to be satisfied with that explanation. Taran realized with some bitter amusement that he was more satisfied than she was, but what other explanation was there?

Two mornings later, as she came back from harvesting the forest in the stillness before dawn, she came upon the wolf, injured, his fur almost audibly sizzling with magic. Here was her answer. Taran halted, afraid and curious, her muscles aching both to flee and to attack the strangeness lying there before her, to heal. She choked on laughter that tried to come up in her throat and clenched her fist around the metal-tipped digging stick. She had the small axe hanging from her belt and her long knife if she needed weapons.

Until this moment, she had never come upon something she didn't instantly understand. That worried, frightened, and angered her.

The wolf whimpered, his blue eyes widening with human pleading. A growl rose in Taran's throat. Anger at herself, not the wolf. Her ambivalence settled. What was she afraid of?

The wolf lay on his side in a patch of buttercups. Blood matted his muddy fur, making it glisten where it wasn't caked and dried. The broken shaft of an arrow protruded from his ribs. Taran noted the pattern on the shaft of the arrow. Someone from Shallowstream had shot the wolf.

He watched her approach, silent suffering in his eyes, his breathing a shallow, pained effort. He didn't move when she knelt a few steps away and studied him. He blinked a few times, never avoiding her regard.

"Poor beast," she whispered. "Will you let me help you?" Taran reached into her belt pouch, where she always carried an assortment of general healing herbs, and withdrew a small, waxed cloth pouch, never taking her gaze from the wolf. She sprinkled a calming powder across his muzzle. He struggled for a few seconds, barely disturbing the arrow in his side before he succumbed and slept.

Taran moved quickly. She knew the strength of her potions, but not the resistance of the wolf. She chopped down three saplings and wove their pliant upper branches together into a drag platform. She sprinkled powdered rose leaves and sage over the wound before she removed the arrowhead and shaft. More blood flowed, but that was good because she had no water to cleanse the wound. Blood would wash out any debris that would fester into illness. She used spider web, sparkling with dew, to seal the wound. The wolf never moved under her ministrations.

She slid him onto the drag and hurried to bring him to her cottage. Never before had she been so grateful that all her ancestors believed isolation was good for a wise woman's reputation and the respect from the villagers. Her solitude gave her freedom from spying eyes and gossiping tongues. The villagers had accepted the squirrels and birds, and even the fawn she had brought to her cottage to heal. But a wolf could not be ignored or forgotten.

She settled the wolf in front of the fireplace. His wound had not re-opened. Taran added kindling to the glowing coals, enough to feed them without starting a roaring fire. She tossed aromatic herbs onto the edge of the coals, so the wolf would inhale the healing vapors. Then she gently peeled away the spider web, examined the wound again, spread healing salve over it and waited until the salve dried to a soft, strong seal. Satisfied the wolf wouldn't bleed to death if she left him alone, she got up and got to work. Full day had come, after all, and she had chores to do.

A rabbit hung by its hind feet in the rafters, caught and killed the night before. Taran had planned to have it for breakfast, but the wolf needed fresh meat more. She would have to content herself with oatcakes and milk. She set the rabbit close by the wolf's head for when he awakened, stepped out of her cottage, closed the door, and settled down in the yard to work.

Kale came to see her before noon, carrying a bucket of milk and a sack of wool clippings, from Shallowstream. Usually, the headmen's children brought her the village tithes. Taran glanced over her shoulder at the cottage, fearing for the wolf, before she stood and greeted him.

"I fear you were wrong, Mistress Taran," Kale said, and set down his burdens. "The madman is near. He attacked Jurgas, out late hunting yesterday. Do not go into the forest today. Our best hunters are searching for the madman. Jurgas wounded him before he fled." Kale glanced over his shoulder at the trees surrounding her cottage.

"And wounded men are more dangerous than wounded animals?" Taran asked, repressing a smile of relief.

Likely, Jurgas was half-asleep when he saw the wolf, and mistook the beast for a man in the shadows of evening. More likely, Jurgas had used hunting as an excuse to take a skin of wine to some shady spot where he could sleep and drink the day away. He wouldn't have recognized his own father while his brain and his senses wobbled as badly as his steps.

"Perhaps. A wounded man will worm his way into your home, using pity, and then attack when he regains his strength. Animals are honest enough to fight you from the beginning."

"Of course. Thank you for the warning. But I am safe here, and well able to defend myself." She stiffened as a rustling sound came clearly from the cottage.

"Mistress?" Kale stepped toward the door.

"Do not enter. I have a wounded animal in there."

"If it is the madman, I must know."

"You doubt me?" Taran put a chill in her voice and drew herself up to her full height. She nearly lost her pose to laughter when he paled and stumbled back from her door.

"I must be sure. For your protection."

"There is no madman in my home." She didn't know whether to feel amused or angered when suspicion flashed across his face, as clear as if he had written the words in ink. "Master Kale, what man would hide in my home for *that* reason?"

"No disrespect, Mistress Taran." He blushed and stood still. "People do talk, and you are young and you haven't smiled on any of our young men."

"They don't smile at me, either." She nearly laughed when Kale shook his head, giving her a confused look, as if that detail had never occurred to him.

Could that be part of the problem? Because she was her mother's heir, people expected her to take the first step? She was supposed to invite someone to be a suitor?

"Your mother chose a traveling healer. Our parents feared she would leave us. Especially when some protested the match, and she grew angry. We don't want to anger you and drive you away."

"I am not my mother." Taran bit back hot words. She would have been angry too, if someone protested her choice of a husband. She almost blurted that to find and protect love was a very good reason to leave these people.

What if her parents had left the five villages when they married? Would her father still be alive? Would her mother? Taran remembered clearly the tears Eyrian fought not to shed, when she spoke about the sweet love she had shared with Connor, a gentle, adventurous man. The pain she felt on her mother's behalf didn't quite drive away the bitter taste of envy. At least Eyrian had known sweet love, even if death had interfered.

Kale could no longer meet her eyes. He nodded, bowing slightly, and scurried down the path through the forest. She sighed and dropped noiselessly to the ground to sit and think. Her heart pounded with the residue of her anger over Kale's insinuation that she would hide a man in her cottage. Taran had stumbled on enough trysts in the woods, the doings of lovers didn't mystify or draw her curiosity. She couldn't imagine being so lonely that she would invite a man to her bed, simply to have a child. Eyrian had held herself pure, body and heart, until Connor touched her soul. She might have grown old with him if senseless greed hadn't killed him.

A whimper and more rustling from the cottage broke through her musing. Taran stood and went to the door. She peered through a crack and found the wolf had eaten the rabbit. He looked better, less agony burning bright in his eyes, and he lay facing the door, waiting.

She took a deep breath and slowly opened the door. Her hand rested on her knife. The wolf watched her, panting shallowly. His tongue lolled out and made her think he smiled. As she approached, he lay still, rolling his eyes up in his head to follow her movements. Another whimper escaped him, a placating sound. Taran smiled.

"So, you do know who your friend is." Daring, she knelt and touched the fur of his neck, marveling at the bristly softness. The wolf held still, and she gently stroked down his back. He whined in pleasure, wriggling like the pups in the village. "I think I shall miss you when you are gone."

The wolf whined, a sad sound, and she smiled. Her mother had told her never to doubt the intelligence of the beasts of field and forest. The wolf did understand what she said.

Taran left the door open, so the wolf could watch her as she did her chores. There was water to draw from her small well, wood to chop, the new wool clippings to card and spin, her garden to weed and water. She liked the feeling of the wolf's gaze on her as she moved. His company was pleasant; quiet, yet there; depending on her, yet not demanding.

She watched him. A twitch of his ears made her stand still and stretch her senses to find what caught his attention. She saw and heard more that day because the wolf made her alert. Her senses had always been sharper than the average villager, yet compared to the wolf, she was dense and dull. Taran laughed when she thought about it.

When she talked to him, he had a look in his eyes, a way of tilting his head toward her that made her believe he understood. When he raised his head, his mouth opening slightly, it seemed to her that in another moment, words would slide from his tongue. He never did speak, but she didn't mind. His company was pleasant without speech.

When evening came, she settled down with a book to read by the fire. Every merchant in the kingdom knew Taran would pay an honest price for any book. She loved to read, to let her mind roam to places her body could not go. No matter her strength and speed, it was still no world for a woman alone to venture into.

She read to the wolf and he listened. Taran wondered if the loneliness that had grown since her mother's death was strong enough to affect her mind. Did she think of the wolf as a person now?

When he shifted his head onto her leg, she startled and nearly leaped to her feet.

"Ah, but what do I have to fear with you here?" she said, laughing at her own nerves, and set down the book to stroke his head. The wolf whined in pleasure and closed his eyes under her touch. "If only you could stay here forever. Or perhaps let me come with you when you leave? No one would touch me if I had a wolf for a traveling companion. If only my mother had borne a manchild instead of a daughter." She laughed again at the quizzical light in the beast's eyes.

"You do not know what mad creature you find yourself with. We have not been properly introduced. I am Taran, daughter of the wise woman Eyrian. I have been wise woman here since my mother died fighting the wizard Nueroch, two winters ago. My father died when I was a babe. That winter, a dreadful illness some say was a curse from Durmad swept through the villages. I nearly died. Mother never said, but I believe the battle to save my life drained me of the magic I should have."

She paused, and the wolf made an interrogative little sound, as if he asked her to continue her story. It was odd to hear her voice against the crackling of the flames. Most nights, only the songs of insects and night birds rose above the snapping of her fire and the dry whisper of turning pages. She told him of growing up lonely among the laughing, loud children of the villages. When the boys asked her agemates to dance, but not Taran, she realized she was not pretty.

"My face is too long. My chin is pointed. My eyes are the oddest green color, and my hair is coarse and curly when it should be straight and fine. I'm too strong for a woman, and though I love to sing, I have no voice for it. What man would like to spend the rest of his days with me? Age does not improve the looks of a woman like me."

She told him how her mother had trained her to be healer and wise woman. She told the wolf of the joys of learning to identify plants and all their various parts for healing, the wonder of discovering the smells, sounds, and rhythms of the forest. Taran confided to him that she would be happy to roam all her days in the forest, except she did like the company of people.

The wolf whined and tension crackled through his body. Before she could even wonder what had happened, he jumped unsteadily to his feet and limped to the door. Taran stared stupidly, until the wolf whined again. Pain and panic gleamed in those un-wolfly blue eyes. She jumped to her feet and opened the cottage door. The rising moon just barely peered over the tops of the trees, and the light sizzled over the wolf's fur. Her heart ached for him as he scurried across the cottage yard and vanished into the shadows. Her fingertips prickled at the feeling of magic ripping through the air, harsh and unrestrained.

Though she waited until the moon was high above the treetops, huge and bright and cold, with only a small bite taken out of the downward edge, the wolf didn't return. Fighting tears, Taran closed her door and went back to her fireside. The joy had fled her evening reading. She poured oats and water into a pot and set it to soak overnight by the coals, for her morning porridge. Silently chiding herself for foolishness, she propped the door open with a stick before she went to her bed.

Why did his absence make her ache inside, as she hadn't ached since her mother died? The beast was a wild animal and needed his freedom more than she needed his companionship. She decided to count herself lucky he had stayed for the day. She wiped a tear out of the corner of her eye and sat on the side of her bed before undressing. The soft scents of the forest drifted to her through the window, compelling and tempting, making her legs ache with the need to run.

The night throbbed with the songs of insects and night creatures, and the breeze danced in the branches lining the clearing around her cottage. Taran bound up her hair and took off her apron and shoes before going to the door.

She paused in the doorway and stared at the sky. The moon seemed to hang closer than ever, larger, as if in another few days she could reach up and bring it down to hold in her hands. She didn't know why the sight of it gave her such comfort. Then she ran, unable to resist the aching hunger any longer. Her feet flew, taking her to the edge of the clearing in a heartbeat. Then she was among the trees, her face and clothes streaked with moonlight and shadows. Taran ducked and ran and twisted, her feet finding the clear spaces as if they had eyes. Not a root tripped her, not a branch caught her clothes or hair or slapped at her face. She ran until her lungs were afire inside her and she felt the blood throbbing in her fingertips.

A wolf's song filled her ears, pulsing in time with her heartbeats. Taran sank to her knees by a stream, aching to join in the song. She knew the melody in her bones, in her blood, but the words escaped her. Tears trickled down her cheeks. She pressed her hands over her mouth to muffle the sobs.

Taran waited until the song finished, then dipped up water and drank deeply, before she struggled to her feet and made her meandering way home through the forest. Words she didn't know but needed to speak lay beyond her tongue and memory. Fragments of melody danced through her head, shattering into starbright dust when she tried to reach for them. The world was a dark place, even with the moon and stars shining so brightly. She had always known her loneliness, but not its depths, until the wolf came and left.

When she reached her cottage, she put the stick in the door to hold it open, then brushed her hair, washed her face and curled up on her side in her bed.

In the darkness before dawn, after the moon had set, a soft sound penetrated her sleep. Taran recognized that prickle of magic in the air. Smiling, she rolled over and looked across the cottage to the door. Two eyes as blue as moonlight gleamed in the doorway.

"I hope you wiped your feet, friend, before you came back inside. I don't want any dirty footprints tracked across my clean floor," she murmured, echoing her mother's teasing complaint, heard many times after moonlit adventures.

The wolf's teeth flashed white in a feral grin, in the soft glow coming from the coals in the fireplace. He crept across the floor and settled down on the rug next to her bed. Taran smiled into the darkness. She muffled a chuckle when she heard a soft whine. The soft, dusty, musky smell of fur floated to her nostrils. Taran smiled in her drowsiness, on the threshold of dreams, and stretched out her arm, so she could rest her hand on the wolf's back. They kept each other company through the remainder of the night, and she dreamed of racing through the forest, at the wolf's side, fast and graceful.

Chapter Four

Three days after he entered her life, the wolf no longer limped. The magic crackling through his fur had healed him. Taran still spread salve on the wound, until it vanished under his fur. Why he remained with her, she couldn't begin to guess, and she scolded herself not to question. She liked his company, and firmly turned her mind to other thoughts when he slipped out of her cottage before moonrise and returned in the darkest hours before dawn.

The wolf followed Taran as she took care of her chores, instead of sleeping in the sun. She talked to him and brushed his fur until it gleamed in the firelight. He growled warning whenever someone approached her cottage, then slipped into the shadows to hide.

When the children came to ask for help in their lessons with the village priest, or to beg the sweets their harried mothers had no time to make, the wolf peered out of the high grass to watch. His eyes sparkled with good humor as his tongue lolled out in silent laughter.

Sometimes she saw sympathy in his eyes before he rubbed his head against her leg and slipped away as a visitor approached. His warning growl turned into a crooning whimper the day a young, tearful mother came to Taran with her baby that suffered screaming fits.

In the soft crimson and gold of sunset, sometimes Taran and the wolf walked together through the forest, soft-footed, never disturbing a leaf or twig or leaving more than a smudge in the dirt. When the wolves of the forest called to each other, Taran lifted her voice to the leafy canopy of the forest and sang back to them. The first time she did that, her wolf companion jumped away from her, sideways, and stared with his mouth hanging open. Like a man would do, caught in utter shock. Taran laughed, dropping to her knees to hold her sides, until tears filled her eyes. The wolf licked her tears away and she thought she saw laughter in his eyes. The next two days, when they walked in the forest and the local wolves began to sing, he waited until she called, then joined his voice to their songs as well.

Something inside Taran ached when the sound of her wolf companion's voice made the other wolves fall silent.

The night that the moon was nearly at half, the wolf nudged her hand when he got up from his place in front of the fire. He paused halfway to her door instead of making his usual silent exit. He shuddered, and Taran leaped to her feet to go to him and rest a hand on his neck. His blue eyes looked cloudy and dark as he gazed up at her. She saw human pleading in their un-wolfly depths. His head hung low as he stepped out through the door, and his feet dragged as he crossed the clearing into the woods. Tears touched Taran's eyes when the wolf glanced back at her once more, tucked his tail between his legs, and vanished into the forest.

What was wrong with him?

A shiver lifted the hairs on her neck as an idea burst into her mind. Was this part of the magic that sizzled in his fur? If she followed and watched, would she find some answers?

Whether she did find the answers or not, Taran knew her friend was in pain, body or spirit or both. As a healer, she was pledged to help. So, she followed him. She caught up with the wolf in another clearing, on top of a little hill, its crown bare of trees and exposed to the moon.

The wolf let out a piteous howl that changed to a moan like a man's as the rays from the rising moon touched him. He snarled and snapped at some imaginary enemy and fell to the ground, writhing. Taran remembered the baby with the screaming fits. She reached into her belt pouch and found the little bag of calming powder.

The wolf let out a shriek, like a man in great pain. His limbs swelled and stretched out at unnatural angles. His fur changed colors and turned patchy. His nose flattened and sank into his face.

Taran choked back a scream. A black-haired man, clothed in dirty rags, writhing in agony, lay before her where the wolf had been.

He rolled onto his stomach and lay still a moment, panting and gasping for breath. With agonized effort, he pushed himself to his feet. Moans escaped him and he clutched his head in his hands. His footsteps wobbled as he began to walk.

Then he saw Taran. A maelstrom of emotions flickered across his face. Rage. Shame. Joy. Fear. Sorrow. Insanity lived in his heart.

A rasping sound escaped his mouth. He flung his arms wide and took tottering steps toward her. Fear moved Taran before she saw the tears in his eyes. She flung the calming powder in his face, into his open mouth and glistening eyes. Her healer's instincts told her this stranger who had taken her wolf-friend's place was no danger to her. He was in pain, but not crazed with it.

Taran knew better than to let pity cripple her, however, so she took another handful of calming powder and stepped back as she watched the stranger cough and choke and rub at his blinded eyes. He fell to his knees as he looked up at her.

"I didn't want you to see me like this." His voice was rough, rasping. "But I need your help."

"Are you man or wolf?" Taran sat down on a fallen tree trunk, ready to spring to her feet at the first hint of insanity.

"Both."

"How?" She wanted to insist that was impossible. "And why do you turn to a man now, rather than at the full moon? That is when the power is strongest to break the curse."

"If I were a man cursed to be a wolf, or a wolf cursed to be a man, yes." He cradled his head in his hands and bowed his shoulders in such obvious pain, her heart ached for him.

Taran cursed herself for a coward when she just sat there, a safe distance away, and did nothing for him. By his blue eyes, she knew this was her friend, stripped of his black fur and fangs. So why couldn't she reach out to him and offer some comfort?

"An enchanter did this to us. Man and wolf, joined together unwillingly, two bodies and souls struggling for dominance. The beast and I have made friends because we must. Our flesh however ..." He shrugged and raised his head to meet her gaze. "The strength of the full moon only makes my torment worse. The wolf half is stronger as the moon waxes in the sky. At the full moon, I am all wolf in mind and spirit, even in a man's body. At the half, there is some control. Truce," he said with a snort of what might have been bitter laughter. "At the new moon, I am trapped in the wolf's body, day and night."

"How? Why?" Taran tried to wrap her mind around the magic that could combine two bodies and souls into one creature.

Had the enchanter bungled the magic, if man and beast fought for control and were tormented with the phases of the moon? Or was that the purpose? The magic wasn't flawed, but rather done to punish the man?

Or to punish the beast?

She looked into the man's blue eyes and saw her friend. But who was her friend? The wolf whom she had helped and healed, or the man who looked out through the beast's eyes?

"This enchanter—" She paused at a dreadful suspicion. "Nueroch?" Fury made her gut twist when the man nodded. "Why did he do this to you? To punish the man, or the beast?"

"For power. For his own amusement." He straightened his back and tipped his head to look up at the moon. "It seems odd, to be sitting here in the forest, talking with you. I have not spoken with anyone other than my fellows in many turns of the moon. Years, I think."

"Years?" She pushed aside the sickening sensation of knowing he had been under this curse for years and grasped the rest of what he had said. "There are others like you?"

"And fewer every year. We die of madness or we kill ourselves, or we fail in our missions for Nueroch and he kills us. At first we had some hope that if we obeyed and pleased him, we would earn our freedom.

Nueroch never promised freedom or healing. We agreed it would be better to die making a bid for freedom than to continue in our torment. When his power failed him two winters ago, some of us managed to break free and went questing for help. Most were killed when we were seen during the madness of the transformation. He regained his strength and caught those who survived.

"We can only be grateful for Yeshen's mercy that since then, he has been unable to make more of us. The weakness returns at summer and winter solstice. Each time, we break free. Some die before he recaptures us, but we learn a little more in our quest. Whatever limits Neuroch's magic, it binds him to his mountain home. This is the first time I have managed to flee beyond his reach. So at last I could come here, seeking Eyrian."

"My mother died in the battle that weakened Nueroch. Why would you search for her?"

"He thought she had the key to controlling the magic that binds our two natures and two bodies together." He shrugged. "I should have turned around and left as soon as I learned your mother was dead, but ..." His mouth twisted, and a bit of color touched his face, rising up from his neck to his hairline. "You are intriguing, Mistress Taran."

"I?" Taran's laughter caught in her throat. "I have no magic. I certainly can't break this magic with my herbs and salves."

"I know that." He hung his head for a moment. "But I can smell magic on you. Though you don't control magic, it is woven all through your flesh and bone. It is hot and bright, concentrated in that little bit of silver you wear around your neck."

"My mother made this. To protect me and keep me whole, she said. I was deathly ill as a child. Mother wove her strongest magic to save my life, and my amulet is the lock and key." Taran rubbed her thumb over the triangle of silver and the magic prickled against her skin. Not for the first time, she wondered what would happen if she took off the amulet and broke the net of magic. Nightmares of pain, of fever that ate at her flesh, of claws that tried to separate flesh from bone and soul from body, flashed through her memory.

"I will search my mother's books," she offered. "My ancestors for many generations were wise women, healers, and had good friends among the enchanters. Maybe one of them shared a bit of knowledge that could help you. If you want to stay," she hurried to add.

"Please, yes. Here, I don't mind my curse." He smiled, and for the first time in her life, Taran felt that fluttering in her belly that she had heard other girls describe in giggling whispers to their friends.

They stayed in the clearing and talked until the moon set and he melted back into his wolf shape. His name was Bard. He had been so long a prisoner that his memories of his previous life were blurred. He had gone adventuring one spring, intending to make his fortune and come back and marry the headman's daughter. After all this time, he couldn't remember her face or name or the name of his village. Bard had become Nueroch's prisoner through mistaken identity. The enchanter thought he was someone who had wronged him. When he discovered his mistake, he shrugged it off and declared that since he had expended so much energy in combining him with the wolf, he wasn't about to let Bard go free. Others might learn what he had done and copy the spell.

"It took me years to realize that shame compelled him to keep me prisoner and force me to serve him," Bard said. He perched on the log beside her, close enough Taran felt the warmth of his body in the chill night air. "I was the first of many attempts to refine his spell. He didn't care that he made innocent souls suffer, and his pride wouldn't let the world know he had made mistakes.

"There is a cure, but Nueroch could have said it just to taunt us, because it makes no sense," he admitted. "Soon after he captured us that first time, he got drunk, and he came down to our pen in his courtyard to mock us. He said that even if Eyrian wouldn't give him the secret of making the lock, he knew the key. We would only be free when love tore us and brought us to the door of death."

"What does that mean?" Taran tried to imagine her mother weaving a spell that required a key so bloody and painful. She was sure Nueroch had twisted something easy and logical. The man was so cruel, he likely couldn't comprehend anything gentle and kind.

"Who can know?" Bard tipped his head to one side and his frown deepened as he studied her. "Please, don't be frightened, but there is another reason I decided to stay once I knew Eyrian was dead."

Taran shivered, even as his gaze seemed to warm her flesh.

"Nueroch said that even though Eyrian was dead and spread her magic to the winter winds, the secret was hidden in her child. As soon as he could find the way to take you apart, he would have the secret Eyrian refused him." Bard reached out one strong, calloused, dirt-stained hand, and gripped Taran's hand. "I stay because Nueroch is your enemy, too. He will come for you someday when he is strong enough, and I mean to protect you from him."

"I have no magic, so it will do him no good," Taran whispered.

Her mind flashed back to that moonlit night when she heard her mother's murderer talk of tearing her apart. How could the secret of joining wolf and man into one creature lie in her body? Taran pressed two fingers against her amulet. Had her mother hidden a spell, or the knowledge to create it, inside the amulet?

"Your mother loved you, yes? And you loved her? Maybe her love was so strong, she sent magic to you on her death, for safekeeping."

"If she Gifted her magic to me, I would have known before now." She shook her head and gazed down at Bard's hand, still gripping hers. She liked his touch, and nearly laughed when she wished he held her hand for some reason other than to comfort her.

"Love protects and heals, as well as torments and teases and confounds," Bard offered with a crooked grin.

"Yes . . . the loss of love can be tearing. When my mother died, I felt like my soul had been torn in pieces." Tears warmed her eyes.

This was the companionship she had longed for. She wanted to find a cure for him, even as she wished to keep the wolf with her. That wish was dangerous. The villagers might tolerate a wolf, but not one under a curse. They would destroy her friend if they ever found out. They would only see someone cursed by Nueroch, who had served him, however unwillingly, and they would want him dead to protect their families.

"I smell fear in you, friend." He caught a tear off her cheek with the tip of a long, sharp nail. "And pain."

"You will be in danger, if anyone learns you are here." She tried to smile. "And I am lonely."

"Yes, I've seen how alone you are, and that makes no sense. You are a prize worth fighting for."

"Is that the wolf speaking?" She sputtered a bit of laughter.

He stopped short, his mouth hanging open. Then he laughed, a rueful sound. "Both man and wolf, I suppose." He turned her hand over in both of his. Taran liked the warmth from the continued contact. "If you were a wolf, I would fight to win you as my mate. My man's eyes see you are strong and graceful. The children love you, the women trust you. There is only goodness in you. Why is there no sweetheart for you?"

"Because I'm … odd. I'm liked well enough, but not enough that any man would want to spend his life with me." Why did her face grow warm at his words? Ironic, that the only pretty speeches she would ever hear came from a man under a curse, who sought her out to find help she couldn't give.

When the moon sank below the edges of the trees, Bard asked her to leave him alone, so she wouldn't see his torment as the transformation came. Taran only walked far enough away that she couldn't see. The backwash of magic tingled in her fingertips, a sour note in the air. She heard his moans and the thrashing of his body.

Mother, what did you know, that Nueroch needed to know? Why did you never tell it to me, so I could help Bard and his friends now?

~~~~~

The next day, Taran napped in the hottest part of the day, curled up in the forest shadows where the breeze brought her the scent of ripening
~~~~~

berries. Bard-wolf settled down close enough to touch. He watched her, and Taran found it comforting. She had thought until then she preferred her solitude, but Bard's constant presence and regard made her feel safe and sheltered. When she slept, she dreamed of running through the forest at his side. She became a wolf whenever he turned to a man, and every time he turned back to a wolf, she became a woman again. The paradox and puzzle of it gave her a headache, and she almost regretted sleeping in the middle of the day.

When the night came and the moon rose, she let Bard go ahead of her. He returned to the clearing where they had talked the night before. She arrived as he settled down on the log, and he smiled at her through the marks of strain on his face. They talked until the moon slid down the sky toward dawn, about poems and stories and songs they had heard, the bits of news the king's messengers brought through the mountain passes, and their mutual dream of traveling the world and seeing far-off kingdoms filled with wonders.

Bard's wanderlust had brought him to Nueroch's doorstep a lifetime ago. He was originally from Ambray and had been friends with Ambrose of Stonemount when the former prince had returned to the life of a traveling healer, after the death of his wife. He was sad when Taran told him what little news she knew, that Ambrose had Gifted his magic to Princess Arden of Westerland, and King Maddix of Stonemount was so universally disliked, many suspected him of killing his wife, Bianca.

"I feel like the man who slept centuries under a curse," he complained, with a crooked grin that didn't hide the hurt in his eyes.

When the moon slid halfway behind the trees, Bard asked her to step away, so she wouldn't see him shift back to wolf. From crescent moon to half to crescent again, he had some choice and control whether he shifted between man and wolf. From crescent to full to crescent, he had no control, shifting to man when the moonlight touched him. From crescent to new moon to crescent, the wolf dominated and he stayed in wolf shape.

Taran waited for him to shift back to wolf, so they could go back to her cottage and sleep, and she wondered if Bard had been destined to come to her simply so she could provide him the comfort of company. Someone who accepted him exactly as he was, no matter what shape he wore. She wondered if Bard was somehow the answer to the half-acknowledged prayers that sometimes slipped from her aching and lonely heart.

When Taran went to the villages to tend a sickness or help deliver a baby, Bard followed her, a silent shadow. She smiled at the sensation of his gaze always resting on her. She wished he could come into the villages with her but knew better than to ask.

The moon waned in the sky. The night Bard stayed curled up by the fire and never even looked at the door, Taran fought tears.

~~~~~

A man named Borgan came to Shallowstream nearly a complete moon cycle later. He limped on a leg swathed with bandages, his scent sour with crusty blood and a wound turning bad. Kale sent his two oldest boys to fetch Taran, then settled the stranger into the cottage set aside for travelers and dosed him with sleeping powder. Bard followed her to Shallowstream, and Taran was startled to hear him growl from the shadows outside the cottage while she worked on Borgan's foul-smelling leg. When had he ever come so close while she worked in the villages? Fortunately, no one else heard.

When she left the village, Bard emerged from the shadows before the village was quite out of sight behind her. He walked close enough her skirts brushed his fur. Taran bit her lip to keep from scolding him. She looked back once, relieved that no one saw her with the wolf.

"I'm sorry," she immediately said. "I'm afraid for you. And for the wolves of these mountains. Some idiot will take it into his head that because one wolf doesn't act like a normal wolf, all of them are dangerous and should be put to death."

Bard whimpered and took the edge of her apron in his teeth for a gentle tug.

"Whatever is wrong, whatever you sense is wrong, I trust you. I promise not to invite Borgan to my cottage. Will that make you happy?" Taran bit her lip against wishing aloud that the phase of the moon was kinder. Now was not the time for Bard to be fixed into wolf shape, unable to speak with her.

If only I were a wolf, or could turn to a wolf, she mused, and her heart raced at the thought. That would solve all their problems, wouldn't it? If she could become a wolf, would Bard be more inclined to follow through on his sweet words?

The next moment, she mentally slapped herself for such selfish thinking. She owed her allegiance to the people of the five villages. Much as she longed to see the world and explore, she couldn't simply leave them unattended. And who said Bard cared for her as more than a friend? He was lonely, the only explanation for the warmth in his eyes and his protection.
~~~~~

Chapter Five

Borgan was entirely too alert for Taran's comfort when she went back the next day to check on him. He sat outside in the warm morning sunshine, chatting with several of the village elders, and carved a root burl with a two-pointed knife. Taran studied him while no one noticed her approach. Yesterday she had focused on his wound and not getting sick from the stink of rotted flesh. Now something in the air made the hairs stand up on the back of her neck. Today, she had time to use her other senses and think about more than healing.

That odd *something else* remained, and she would have called it magic. But if Borgan had magic at his disposal, why had he come to the village for help? How had his wound gone so bad? She scolded herself not to get distracted with so many questions. Distraction could be dangerous.

Bard growled from his hiding place in the shadows, very clearly upset that she was so close to the man. Only Taran had ears sharp enough to catch the sound from so far away.

Borgan was browned and muscular from an outdoors life, his hair a brown tangle of sun-bleached strands, his beard untrimmed, and overall she judged him handsome. His clothes were well-cured skins, cut with skill and care. He carried three more knives in his belt. Yesterday, she had seen his bow and double quiver full of arrows, crossbow and sword, and several coils of rope. He was a well-armed traveler or huntsman, judging by his clothes.

Elder Shambrol looked up, laughing at something Borgan said, and his gaze landed on her. "There you are, Mistress Taran. We told our guest you would be here long before noon, but he was worried." He stood and tugged on his cap in deference and offered her his seat.

Taran immediately declined. Shambrol's seat next to Borgan was the last place she wanted to perch. That *something else* lingered about Borgan, an undefined unpleasantness despite his clean clothes and hair and the sweet, tangy healing herbs that perfumed the air.

"I'm a lucky man, to stumble on a village with a pretty young wise woman to heal me," Borgan said, hearty laughter vibrating at the back of his voice. He half-rose from his bench and turned to her as he spoke.

Taran gave him credit for only pausing half a second when he got a good look at her face. The gossipy old men here might tell Borgan she was young, unmarried, Eyrian's heir, but no one would have called her pretty.

Was he simply a man who used flattery to grease his path? Was that falseness what she sensed about him?

When she asked him if he would prefer to go inside so she could tend his wound, he laughed. "Surely my friends have seen you tend far worse wounds than mine. I would rather stay out here. Fresh air and sunlight are good for healing. A magic that does not compare with your magic, of course, but those of us without such gifts must do without, yes?"

"You know so much already about healing, why did you come to me for help?" Taran put a stool in front of him. She didn't wait for him to move but grasped his ankle and put his bandaged leg into position.

"I prefer to trust my healing to those with real magic."

"Then I will make you fit to travel until you find a healer with magic. I have none. I can only heal with the help of herbs and potions, and what I learned working at my mother's side." She ignored Borgan to concentrate on his leg as she unbandaged it, washed the wound, inspected it for dead flesh and infection, and spread more salve on it.

The elders stayed, held to their chairs by Borgan's jovial words of challenge. They hurried to assure him that Taran spoke from modesty. They were proud to claim her as their wise woman and declared that magic worked on many levels.

Taran gritted her teeth in annoyance. Why did the villagers all insist that she had magic, though she had never demonstrated any and told them she had none? Was it absolutely essential for their sense of safety and pride, to have a wise woman who worked magic?

Magic did indeed work on different levels. Borgan carried some talisman that enfolded him in magic she could not decipher. She only knew that when she touched his leg, it vibrated through her fingertips, like a drumbeat. He hadn't been wearing the talisman yesterday. Why not? If her sense of magic was accurate, it had healed his leg wound enough he likely could walk by this afternoon. So why did he wait until he came to the village to use it? Why insist on using the village healer?

Taran bandaged his leg quickly, eager to get away from this man and his magic and the multiple layers of lies he told. What did he want?

She had asked the same question, over and over, when Nueroch killed her mother. This man couldn't be Neuroch. Bard would have recognized his scent. Even if he couldn't speak with her as a man, he would have stopped her from coming near Borgan. What about him made her skin prickle in warning so she wanted to leap to her feet and run?

"Stay, pretty Taran." Borgan reached for her when she stood up. She barely evaded his grip.

"I have much to do, and you have no need of my help any longer. Your leg has healed practically overnight. You will be well enough to travel by morning."

"Ah, you see?" He turned to the elders, who foolishly smiled. "She does have magic. How else could I have regained the use of my leg so quickly?"

"I think you carry some magic of your own," Taran retorted. "You did not use it before, or maybe you were too sick to think to use it before, but it works on you now."

Borgan's eyes narrowed and for a moment, sparks touched his gaze instead of humor. Then he shrugged and laughed. "You're the first wise woman I've met in all my travels who doesn't try to frighten me with words of magic and mysteries."

"You have spoken with many wise women, then?" Elder Yoran said. He rarely spoke, so his entrance into the conversation startled the others into silence. Their expressions grew thoughtful. Taran considered kissing the musty-smelling old man in thanks.

"I travel all over the known world, seeking knowledge, seeking to understand magic and healing, and the people who hold lives in their frail hands." Borgan closed his eyes as he spoke. He sounded weary, but Taran caught the bitter, hot stink of anger and pain that erupted from his flesh.

Her farewell with the elders and Borgan was polite. She had to fight not to run as she retreated into the safety of the forest. Bard appeared at her side and rubbed his head against her thigh. Taran muffled a gasp of both relief and shock and went to her knees. She dropped her healer's bag and wrapped both arms around Bard's neck so she could bury her face in his warm, musky, dusty fur.

"Who or what is he?" she whispered. "Why were you so angry with him yesterday? What does he want?"

She lifted her head from the warmth and comfort of Bard's fur. The wolf turned his head and met her gaze. She clearly saw regret in his big, blue, un-wolfly eyes. He shook his head.

~~~~~

By the next morning, Taran still had not decided what to do about Borgan, or even if she should do anything. What did he want, coming into the village with an injury so bad it could have taken his life? Why did he let it go bad? Should she warn the village headmen, and let them deal with the stranger?

Telling them she sensed magic at work in Borgan would simply reinforce their insistence that yes, she had magic, despite years of insisting she had none.

"The problem," she told Bard, as they settled outside in the cottage yard—he to sleep in the sun and she to weed her herb garden, "is that I don't know why this man wants me to have magic. It's one thing to be able to sense magic at work, to smell it clinging to people and things. It's another thing altogether to hold the reins on magic and control it, make it
~~~~~

do what you want. Or not do anything," she added, her tone pensive. She stared into nothing for several long moments as her mind gnawed on the problem of Borgan.

What did he want from her? Was he an ally of Nueroch, seeking Eyrian's magic? What did he think he could get from her?

Bard snorted and leaped to his feet, and she heard a footstep on the pebbles covering the path. His ears went flat against his skull and his lips curled back, baring his fangs.

"Please ..." Taran fought the urge to beg him to stay, as Bard melted into the shadows at the edge of the clearing.

She couldn't catch any scent with the breeze flowing crosswise through the yard, toward the newcomer. Still, she wasn't surprised to see Borgan come around the bend in the forest path. He limped, but on the wrong leg.

"You have no need of my help," Taran said, standing. She rested her hand on the knife she always kept on her belt. She wished she had her axe and digging stick, but she had left them inside her cottage. Still, Bard waited in the shadows. She thanked Yeshen for him.

"Now that is what any man needs to see with the new day." Borgan stopped a few steps away from her and looked her over. "A pretty maiden smiling in welcome."

Irritation tied a hot knot in her belly. Bard growled softly. Which part of him, wolf or man, hated Borgan more? The best way to handle this man was with the truth.

"I do not welcome you. Liars are not welcome in my home." She gestured at his leg. "You limp on the wrong leg, so it is clear you are healed."

"A liar, am I?" He laughed and took two steps closer to her. Taran dug her bare feet into the dust of her yard and vowed not to move or give him the satisfaction of frightening her. "If you have no magic, how can you look at me and say I have no need of your help?"

"What is it you want, then? I have nothing to steal."

"You value yourself so little?" he asked, his voice changing to a dangerous, low croon as he stepped closer to her.

Bard snarled, stepping out into the sunshine. His teeth flashed in the light. His eyes burned with rage. Borgan backed up several steps as Bard stalked across the cottage yard until he stood at Taran's side.

"Liar." His face lit with a kind of glee that made Taran shudder.

"How have I lied?" She rested her hand on Bard's neck. The wolf pressed hard against her side and stared balefully at the man. His growls grew louder with each passing breath.

"It takes magic to tame a beast of the forest."

"Only if kindness and friendship are magic. Go, before my friend decides you are more dangerous than foolish."

"Liars. All wise women are liars," he snarled, and reached for his sword.

Bard leaped, magic crackling blue across his fur. Borgan's snarl turned to a scream as wolf hit man. They went down, rolling across the dusty cottage yard. The sword dropped from his grip. Taran snatched it up and howled pain as flames leaped from the handle to wrap around her hand. She flung the sword away. *The echoes of incantations filled her head. For two heartbeats, she saw Borgan, his face twisted with grief and rage, standing over a fire that burned purple. He held the sword and traced designs along the blade with poisonous purple sparks of magic at his fingertips.*

Borgan shrieked, and Taran yanked free of her circling thoughts. Bard tumbled across the yard, stirring up clouds of dust. Blood filled the air, stinging and hot. Borgan scrambled to cross the yard on hands and knees. Bard leaped on him and bit hard into the back of his ankle, through the boot. Taran flinched, imagining those fangs hamstringing the man. Borgan howled, madness and pain and terror, and kicked hard. Bard yelped like a puppy and went flying.

Taran scolded herself for a fool, watching while her friend fought to protect her. She snatched up a length of firewood and leaped across the yard to club Borgan across the back of his head. He let out a choked cry and collapsed, like a puppet with its strings snipped. Fighting sobs, Taran turned to Bard. He staggered back to his feet and grinned at her, wolf-fashion, mouth wide open and tongue lolling out. She let out a gasping chuckle and dropped to her knees, to wrap her arms tight around his neck.

Borgan never stirred, while Taran fought to steady herself. She refused to cry. Anger made her legs and hands unsteady, though she admitted much of what made her dizzy was fear on Bard's behalf.

"What would I do if he had hurt you or even killed you?" she whispered, when she finally let go of the wolf. Bard whimpered, then licked her face, a wet, slobbery swipe that made her sputter laughter.

Taran tied up Borgan, hands and feet, then tied him to a sturdy tree and made sure she removed all his weapons. For good measure, she removed the talisman around his neck. It bit at her fingers and buzzed with an unpleasant residue of magic that put a sour taste in her mouth. Then she went for the village headmen and elders, and left Bard guarding the prisoner.

Kale and the others believed her. They had to, Taran realized. To doubt their wise woman would endanger all their lives eventually. They questioned her, several times, hesitantly suggesting that perhaps Borgan had thought the wolf was attacking her when he drew his weapon. She asked them to try to pick up his sword. Each man's hand burned, just as hers had, proving the sword was protected by a vicious spell. What honest man would wrap such magic around his weapon?

No one asked why Bard was there or how he had come so swiftly to protect her. Taran choked on anger when she saw them surreptitiously making warding signs against the wolf. And her, as well. He stayed at Taran's side, never making a sound. Bard didn't even open his mouth to pant until the headmen loaded Borgan onto a wheeled cart and took him away, to hold him prisoner until a messenger could be sent for the nearest judge or military outpost.

Taran wondered for the first time how much of the friendship of the five villages was true affection and how much was tempered by necessity. Had her mother or any of her predecessors doubted their place in the river valley, as she had begun to do?

"Perhaps no one has done the things I have done, or been so totally useless in terms of magic," she murmured, as she watched the cart and the headmen and elders finally vanish down the forest trail. Bard whined and rubbed his shoulder against her hip. "They fear me, now."

That night, Taran dreamed of traveling far away, seeing wonders. For the first time, guilt and a sense of responsibility didn't taint her hunger for adventure.

~~~~~

The new moon passed and the crescent returned. Taran and Bard had one night of talk under the waxing moon before the mystery of Borgan was resolved.

He was the madman of so many conflicting tales. He matched none of the descriptions because he changed his appearance with each village he entered. He was working his way west and south through Brentonwald, killing the wise women or any woman rumored to have some gift of magic, in each village he passed.

"Why?" Taran asked, after the captain of the king's garrison and the army's Gifted healer made their pronouncement before the village headmen and elders. Everyone sat still for so long, stunned by the news, her words made nearly a third of those gathered in the village square of Shallowstream jump.

"He is a prince in one of those barbarian kingdoms hiding in the Cascade Mountains," the captain said, after a few seconds of hesitation. "His wife died in childbirth and he killed the wise woman and the midwife who attended her. The wise woman, for predicting the woman would die, and the midwife for not preventing it. The word is, the loss broke something inside his mind and soul."

"So now he punishes all wise women?" Taran snorted and shook her head. "How many have died at his hand — and why did he keep insisting that I had to have magic?"

"He is collecting the magic of the women he kills, to resurrect his
~~~~~

wife," the healer said with a weary sigh. "That talisman you were wise enough to remove from him was made to steal magic as life ebbs. Whoever made it for him either follows a twisted, impure discipline of magic, or they deliberately did not tell him the truth. Perhaps because they are servants of Durmad, in those mountains, and their delight is to destroy all beneficial magic."

"What truth?" Oben, the youngest of the village headmen, asked when the healer paused.

"There is no benefit to be had, only corruption and suffering, when magic is stolen at the cost of life. Murder negates any life and healing power that remains at the moment of death. What truly frightens me—"

"Looking into his mind was enough to frighten me, thanks," the captain muttered.

"What really frightens me is that his ultimate goal is Princess Arden of Westerland."

"She has healing magic," Taran said, nodding. "Did he think he could force her to give her Gifting to him, at sword's point?"

"That doesn't matter now," Kale said, and thumped his bench for emphasis. "You stopped him, and no other women will die at his hand."

"If you could train a few dozen wolves to help my soldiers, like your wolf helped you, our job would be easier," the captain offered. "You have more than healing magic, Mistress Taran. Yeshen blesses these villages through you."

Taran wanted to cry from the sudden weight of weariness his words laid on her. The air vibrated with new tension. No child had come through the forest to her cottage since she and Bard had fought Borgan. No woman came to her without a man for escort. It did no good to ask Bard to hide during daylight hours. The people said they were grateful the wolf had been there to protect her, but their eyes and the cold, bitter scent of fear told a different story.

"As I told that madman, no magic binds the wolf to me," she said, even knowing the words would do no good. The villagers had made up their minds about her, and no amount of truth would dissuade them. "He was wounded, and I healed him, and wolves are wise enough to recognize a friend, and to show gratitude."

The captain had to believe her, but he and the healer lingered after the elders and headmen dispersed, to ask how exactly she had found and healed the wounded wolf. In return for what they both said was a tale of wonder, they shared news from outside the valley. Taran was especially concerned for Princess Arden, who had lost her husband last fall in the war everyone blamed on King Maddix of Stonemount. She wasn't surprised to hear the gossip, revealing more of Maddix's schemes and dishonorable actions, threats against the kings of smaller, less powerful kingdoms. She was grimly pleased to hear that Maddix's actions had poisoned the magic apple tree he claimed powerful wizards had given him. And laughed more to learn that all the world seemed to know now that Maddix's henchmen had stolen the tree from Princess Arden of Westerland.

Taran already knew the rest of the story, how Arden had gone in disguise to Stonemount to heal the tree and reveal Maddix's lies to all the world. The healer, Ambrose, had Gifted his healing magic to her, taking it out of Maddix's control. She was said to be in partnership with Dylan, Maddix's cousin, building a healers hall on the border of Westerland and Stonemount. And there was nothing Maddix could do to strike at them, because all the world was watching, and they knew the truth now. Few kingdoms feared Maddix, and even fewer respected him.

The sense of satisfaction fled when the captain shared his last piece of news. Princess Fiera had been sent by her father, King Egis, to investigate a diplomatic marriage with Maddix. Fiera remained in Stonemount, but there was no talk of marriage. The speculations grew more numerous every day as to what King Egis intended. Would his daughter marry Maddix? Would she help rally the nobles to give the throne to Dylan, Ambrose's grandson and the rightful heir? Or did Brentonwald have other plans to deal with Maddix's schemes?

Taran shuddered in fear for Fiera. Being doomed to marriage with Maddix was the worst possible fate the princess could face. Yet how many princesses had the freedom to choose to marry for love, or for other, more personal reasons? Taran prayed for Brentonwald's princess, that she would be safe, and could flee Stonemount soon, before Maddix turned one of his vicious schemes on her as well.

Chapter Six

Princess Fiera had few people she could trust in the palace. While she was sure many servants were sympathetic, she had no way to judge who supported her because they were good people and who simply sought to punish Maddix. How many felt trapped in their lives and roles, and how many were seeking a chance to betray someone else for a chance to step upward? She had kept a journal when she first arrived in the palace, to help her remember all the questions and bits of information to put into her regular letters home. Then she discovered that several servants had been paid to regularly read her journals and copy out the pages. Whether it was for Maddix's benefit or his enemies', or simply to be able to laugh at her, she had no way to determine.

That was when she claimed the walled garden that had once held Arden's magic apple tree as her sanctuary. The residue of magic in the ground and stagnant water and clinging to the stones of the wall, which Maddix had rebuilt out of some sense of spite, didn't bother her. She rather thought it welcomed her, though sometimes when she was feeling sorry for herself and wishing for someone to argue with, the magic seemed to sting in the air. She created a cypher for her notes and wove them into the sketches she did in the garden. She included those sketches in the courier pouches Lord Anselm sent to Brentonwald every five days. She found some amusement in knowing that Maddix's people had paid the courier to let them read everything going to Brentonwald. The courier took the payment because she told him to do so. Anything Anselm didn't want Maddix to know about, the courier hid inside a compartment in his saddle. Maddix had to be increasingly frustrated, both by Anselm's critical and honest reports on the government and people of Stonemount, and the lack of any information to use against her or Anselm or her father.

She wasn't sure how she felt about Maddix himself, beyond the disgust that had stayed consistent since they were children. Maybe a little amusement over how careful he was when dealing with her. Maddix was clearly afraid to formalize the alleged "understanding" between them, created by that entirely false correspondence. He didn't dare officially ask for her hand in marriage, and just as equally he feared to declare the entire concept a mistake and send her home.

Fiera had at first felt some sympathy for the nobles Maddix gathered around himself. They all lived in evident fear and uncertainty and searched so hard for double meanings and hidden meanings in everything she said, she was free to be entirely honest with everyone. After a month, she only felt weary. Her sympathy teetered on the edge of disdain. She wished she could simply hide in the walled garden or her suite of rooms and study and sketch until her father sent for her to come home. That wasn't possible. First, because she needed to be visible, she needed to keep her eyes and ears open, alert to the presence of Durmad's spies and messengers. After the massive mistakes Maddix had made, either Durmad would tighten the leash or he would destroy Maddix. Fiera had to put herself into a position to defend the innocent people of Stonemount.

Starting with little Prince Maxin, Maddix's son. The little boy was her most important reason for staying in Stonemount. Heir to the throne. Heir to the mess his father was making. Neglected by his father. Relegated to the sidelines by everyone but a few loyal, loving nurses. Remembered from time to time by people who hoped to use the little boy as a tool to get into his father's good graces, or even turn him into a hostage to ensure Maddix's cooperation. Fiera visited the nursery every day, and she considered her life well-spent when his hungry, cautious affection blossomed into unreserved love and delight.

To protect Maxin, to stand as his mother and have the legal right to protect him from the consequences of his father's choices, Fiera seriously considered agreeing to marry Maddix. She would simply have to find some charm, some magic, even an herbal potion to feed him secretly, so he would never take advantage of his husbandly rights, never father a child on her, never have a claim to the throne of Brentonwald.

~~~~~

Something had to be done about Princess Fiera.

King Maddix of Stonemount watched his beautiful, clever, reserved possible bride-to-be glide through the palace, and ached for something he didn't understand. She was exactly the kind of queen he wanted, regal and precise in all the social rules and patterns. She gathered up the admiration of everyone she met, and their willing obedience without threats or temper tantrums or bribes. He couldn't understand how she did it, no matter how much he watched her interact with the nobles and the ambassadors and the visiting royals.

She never claimed any authority as possible future queen of Stonemount. Most likely because that aggravating word, *possible*, presented just as high and hard a barrier to her as it did to him. He couldn't find a single clue as to her feelings on the subject. She neither confirmed nor denied the possibility when pressed by diplomats and courtiers, always managing to be gallingly truthful, never telling even the thinnest half-truth or exaggeration. How she managed to keep the admiration of everyone she met without flattery or rewards or threats, he
~~~~~

could never understand.

He had always thought that truthfulness and following the narrow path of honor and duty would be a smothering kind of prison, and yet ... how did Fiera always seem to be at peace?

The prospect of learning her secrets and having her turn that clever mind to his purposes and plans excited him. He shivered in anticipation of what she would do with her authority once she was his queen.

And shivered more at the growing suspicions that if he brought her too close, if he fully opened his mind and heart to her ... she would change him.

The few times he had ventured to bring up the subjects they had discussed, the agreements they had reached in their covert correspondence, Fiera somehow managed to convince him that he had misinterpreted what she had written. That simply displayed how clever she was, in a gallingly admirable way. Other women would claim they couldn't remember letters written months ago. Some would even claim that they hadn't written those letters at all, they had been forged. Fiera quoted large portions of their correspondence, her letters to him and his letters to her, and gave them completely different meanings. To the point Maddix had doubts about his own intentions.

He stopped referring to their correspondence and considered burning those letters. If this polite, decorous standoff continued, eventually those letters could be turned into evidence of yet another failure. A serious, embarrassing miscalculation. He needed to find his spies in the lower ranks of the court of Brentonwald, wherever they had vanished to, and get them to dig until they found his letters to Fiera, to destroy them. What had happened to those obsequious fools? They had gone silent almost from the day he received the letter notifying him Fiera was coming to Brentonwald.

Maddix missed Jaygo, and wished he knew what Clancy and Baethon had done with his clever advisor. Those two had very simple tactics for dealing with women, but slapping Fiera across the room or dragging her around by her hair would bring the wrath of Brentonwald down on the entire kingdom. Besides, Maddix didn't want to terrify Fiera into mindless subservience. He wanted her to choose to support him because she saw the wisdom of his reasons and choices, and because she willingly chose Durmad's way.

Despite the long talks they had nearly every day, despite all the subtle teaching to gradually change her perceptions and loyalties, he always had the feeling she laughed at him and silently contradicted him.

Maybe it was the fact that she said very little, and he ended up doing most of the talking during those long, private discussions they had.

Most especially, she never brought up the subject of their possible marriage. Everyone assumed they would be married, but nothing official had been said or written. King Egis had not made a declaration to the nations, announcing the match. Lord Anselm, ambassador for Brentonwald and very clearly King Egis's spy, merely smiled and commented that weddings were the province of the bride. A wise man put everything into his future wife's hands when it came to setting the date and decreeing the order of the ceremony and all the other details.

What was Fiera waiting for? The right cycle of the moon and the tides? Was she deeply involved in the oldest practices of magic? Was that how Brentonwald had become so large, so powerful? Was Brentonwald a rival for Durmad, and merely played at being loyal to Yeshen and Steward?

If that was the truth behind Brentonwald's sanctimonious devotion to Yeshen, Maddix thought he could greatly admire his future father-in-law. Maybe even turn to him for advice. Maybe even lower himself to be an ally, rather than absorb Brentonwald under the banner of Stonemount, some day far in the future.

He gnawed on the problem of Fiera every day, which stole energy and time from reworking his plans of conquest. His highest priority now was to wreak his revenge on Westerland and King Alix and that lying, sly, two-faced Princess Arden. And even more, punish his cousin, Dylan, who had stolen Arden and Ambrose's healing magic right from under Maddix's nose.

Dylan had a strong claim to the throne of Stonemount. The whispers and mutters and talk of discontent in the taverns and marketplaces were increasing, as more people remembered that unpleasant fact. According to Clancy and Baethon and their spies.

Maddix needed to send another assassin into Westerland to kill not just Dylan, but make another strike at Arden, and especially her brat, Violet. He could hurt Alix, king of Westerland, doubly hard by killing the child who was his heir until he and his new bride had their own.

The healing house Dylan and Arden had built on the border of Westerland and Stonemount drew more petitioners every day, despite all the efforts of Maddix's spies to sabotage the building and spread rumors to frighten people away.

Someone would think that enchanters were protecting Arden and Dylon and all the fools who supported and admired them.

The frustration was almost enough to take his mind off the puzzle and challenge of Fiera.

The newest report of her inexplicable activities brought Maddix close to tearing at his own hair. What kind of foolish queen spent time with the child who would be a rival to her own future child?

Fiera spent at least two hours every day with his son, Maxin. No one had thought to tell him that until now. He might never have learned what she was doing if Clancy hadn't remarked on it. Maddix actually felt a moment of terror. Maxin was his heir, his firstborn, and his only claim to the throne of Ambray. Not that Bianca's father and brothers showed any signs of sickening and dying. His spies sent into Ambray had gone silent. Either they had been caught, or they had turned traitor, like so many other couriers and spies.

He couldn't risk Maxin being endangered. Fiera was being entirely too clever. If the silly child adored her, as his nurses believed, then who would suspect her when the boy died of some idiotic accident or poison or some ridiculous childhood disease?

This was the only proof he had, in this stalemate of silence, that Fiera did intend to become his queen.

He couldn't afford that. His son was the only successful move in the long, involved game he had been playing since Jaygo brought that first letter of enlightenment and promises from Durmad. Maddix wouldn't risk Maxin's life. Not even if Fiera turned out to be the perfect bride for him, and she gladly joined him in overthrowing her father and brothers.

He had to find some way to make Fiera give up and go home to Brentonwald without giving her father any justification for declaring war. He had to force her hand, without any guilt resting on him.

He had been very good at that, what felt like a lifetime ago. Back before the poison from Arden's wretched magic apple tree had soaked into the soil and water and the very air of Stonemount, and all his careful plans began to go awry.

He wished Jaygo were still here to advise him.

Or did he?

The bottom line was that Jaygo had sabotaged him when he stole that apple tree from Arden. As much as he hated to admit it, Maddix knew Ambrose was right when he warned him that every blessing could be twisted into a curse if magic wasn't respected. Certainly, Jaygo deserved to die for that alone.

The apple tree was gone, but the poison remained. He had to get rid of that poison. Too bad it wouldn't drive Fiera away.

~~~~~

The hours of happy talking and walking with Bard under the light of the waxing moon didn't last long enough for Taran. As the moon grew, his change from wolf to man and man to wolf caused him increasing pain. The night after the moon was at half, he fled the cottage without waiting for her to put down her work and follow him into the forest.

When Taran caught up with Bard, he was a man again. Sweat soaked his rags and lines of pain bracketed his mouth and eyes. The sour smell of misery and the sweet stink of pain clouded the air so the clearing where
~~~~~

they liked to sit and talk didn't feel welcoming any longer.

"I should have found new clothes for you before this," she said, gesturing at his ragged, dirty clothes.

"Don't bother." He tried to smile. The effort seemed to sap his strength. "On the bad nights, I'd just shred them again when I change. I should be grateful, I suppose, that the state of my clothes don't affect my fur when I'm a wolf."

"Imagine the scandal if you were all patchy and had bald spots," she offered. His single snort of laughter sent a stabbing sensation through her heart.

What could she do to help him through this? Was there anything written in the journals of the wise women before her that could heal and free Bard? She turned that thought over and over in her mind until the idea was nearly threadbare. When Bard vanished into the forest to transform back to wolf as dawn neared, Taran didn't go back to her cottage, but continued to Whispering Cave. She brought home an armful of journals and scrolls. On the following nights, when Bard forbade her to go into the forest with him, she curled up by her fire and read until her eyes ached. And fought tears when she heard the howls from the throat of a man in torment.

~~~~~

Taran found no answers and that frustrated and pained her. What bothered her more, even affecting her dreams, was the growing certainty that the secret Nueroch had killed her mother over was indeed hidden in her flesh and blood and bone.

Several times, as the moon crept from full to half and Bard's torment eased, Taran considered taking off the amulet to see what would happen. It held magic. Taran had always believed the amulet was part of the healing her mother had performed on her. But what if it still performed magic on her? What if Taran should have died in that long, draining illness? If she removed the amulet, would she die?

Did her mother perhaps tie it into the magic Taran should have inherited, so there was no magic left to use for the good of others? Was the magic in the amulet so powerful, Nueroch wanted it, needed it, to heal the flaws in the magic he used on Bard and his fellows?

Could she use it to heal Bard?

"The wolf in me is … fascinated by it," Bard admitted, when she shared her theories with him the first night they could again sit and talk. "I see colors I have never seen before, when I look through the wolf's eyes." He shrugged and snorted a bit of weary laughter.

"But—"

"No. You might be right, and the amulet contains magic that affects you. If you took it off and died of it, I could never forgive myself. I would
~~~~~

rather remain torn between man and beast, and able to be with you. My freedom from the wolf has no appeal … if I lose you."

Taran caught her breath and tears scalded her eyes as she met Bard's blue, scorching gaze. Had sweet words finally come for her? She choked on something that she suspected would be sobs and laughter mixed. How ironic, that she wanted both the man and the wolf. If she found a way to separate them again, would the wolf stay or would it flee while Bard stayed?

"It's a poor friend who is happy with the sacrifice her dearest friend makes, no matter how much it makes my heart sing to have you here," she finally admitted, when the heat in Bard's eyes began to fade into uncertainty.

"I learned long ago to enjoy each moment of sweetness, and not let future torment poison it." Bard caught hold of her hand and lifted it to his lips. His beard scratched and tickled the back of her hand, but warmth expanded inside her and killed the urge to laugh.

~~~~~

The next morning, Taran went to Shady Creek to check on an expectant mother. No children ran out to meet her when she entered the village. She didn't think it odd, just assuming their lessons with the village priest were running late, until she walked through the village and saw a mother herding her four children into her cottage. The woman blanched and froze when their gazes met, and that put a knot in Taran's stomach. She turned her head away as she passed the cottage and heard the door slam.

The expectant mother, Rosamund, didn't wait outside her cottage as she usually did. Taran feared the woman was ill. When she knocked, Rue, Rosamund's mother opened the door. The woman peered over Taran's shoulder and nodded once, her mouth a flat line of determination, before she let the healer inside.

Taran shrugged aside her cold welcome and set to work checking on Rosamund's condition. Her eyes, skin, and hair were healthy and glowing, her ankles only a little swollen, and the baby kicked hard as if in greeting, when Taran cupped her hands over Rosamund's swollen belly. Both women laughed.

"He can't wait to get out, I think," Rosamund said with a chuckle. "Can you tell me, is it a boy or a girl?"

Taran sighed. Every time she tended an expectant mother, she answered the question the same way, yet everyone persisted in asking. "I have no magic to tell me such things."

Rue snorted and didn't look up from her sewing. Taran caught the flattening of the young mother's lips, the momentary spark of anger in her eyes. Something was going on here that needed settling now, rooted out
~~~~~

before it turned poisonous.

"Have I offended you, Mistress Rue?" she asked, and turned to unpack the basket of salves and parchment packages of teas to ease Rosamund through the last of her pregnancy.

"Not offended." Rue colored enough to be visible in the shadowy cottage. "But 'tis clear enough to anyone with eyes to see, you do have magic. How else do you explain the wolf that follows your heels like a duckling after its mother?"

That dropping sensation of apprehension filled Taran. Was this why the people hid their children away, why Rue was so cautious when she opened the door? Bard followed her to the edge of the forest and stayed there, vigilant as she went about her business. Obviously, some villagers had sharper eyes, and they saw him despite his skill at hiding. Or did they simply fear the wolf would appear out of nowhere at her command? Taran thought the villagers were grateful Bard had protected her against Borgan, but perhaps the danger had been gone long enough they now feared her defender?

"The only magic I employed with the black wolf was friendship. And some healing salves and calming powder," she hurried to add. "Nothing that anyone here couldn't do. I eased his pain, healed his wound, and kept him calm until he could grow used to me."

"But the beast is whole now, yes?" Rue persisted. "Then why does he stay? 'Tis not natural, so it must be magic."

Chapter Seven

Taran wanted to tell Bard's story, but she knew better. She had considered telling the elders of Bard's trouble, but she had no assurance they would pity him. More likely they would reason, since Bard was in essence Nueroch's creature, he could not be trusted. Who could know, after all, that Nueroch wouldn't punish the five villages for the hurt Eyrian had done him, even long delayed, and make Bard slaughter everyone in the five villages while they slept?

It happened in fables. Everything the villagers knew of magic came from fables, and what their wise women had showed them. Why should they trust strangers wielding magic? Look at the harm powerful wizards had done through the generations. Wise women and hedge healers and others were safe, because their magic was small, limited, and always helpful. The villagers trusted the magic they thought Taran held.

Until now.

A shiver went up her spine, a sensation as if she had fur, and an icy, wet wind ruffled it the wrong way up her back. What if the villagers decided Taran could not be trusted?

"The wolf is a stranger here, and the local wolves do not accept him," she said, begging Yeshen for the right words, the right tone, to convince this woman who was suddenly … not an enemy, but certainly not a friend. "When he is fully healed, he will leave."

And perhaps I should go with him? Taran mused, as she repacked her basket, made her farewells, and promised to check on Rosamund at the new moon.

The thought of leaving this valley and abandoning the five villages generated very little sense of guilt or regret. They were a duty, but she realized her heart was not tied to this place, these people. Taran cared more about failing her mother's trust in her than losing the only home she had ever known. Eyrian had put the five villages into her care, but the people now distrusted her because of Bard. What good could she do for them if they no longer trusted her?

The loss of the tithe of food and firewood and wool did not bother her. She could forage for all she needed in the forest. The villages needed her far more than she needed them. What if their distrust turned to enmity and even violence? If the villagers drove her out, the only thing she would mourn was the cave full of books her mother had left her.

Realizing where her thoughts led her made her pause on the journey back to her cottage, but not tremble or even weep. She marveled at the calmness that came with the admission that yes, she could leave the river valley quite easily, with no looking back.

Yet, what would her mother say, if Taran left to wander the world with Bard?

~~~~~

Two days later, Taran went to a wedding feast at Shallowstream. Thinking of the villagers' fears, she asked Bard to stay behind. He didn't whine, didn't lay his ears back and hang his head, but she saw the pain in his eyes.

"I'm sorry," she whispered, "but they're afraid of you, and the more they see us together, the more they fear me. As long as I am wise woman here, I can't let them fear me." She stroked down his back until he closed his eyes. "If I could, I would make them see you are no danger, but the greatest friend and protector they could ever have."

Bard licked her face and she sputtered and laughed. As she hurried down the forest trail toward Shallowstream, she wondered if that would be the closest she would ever come to a kiss, until Bard was fully man, alone in his body once again.

The wistful dream lingered at the back of her thoughts through the blessing ceremony, the vows, and the sharing of the cup and oatcake between the bridal couple. She laughed with the others when the groom pretended to choke on the oatcake his bride had made, but never had she felt more distant from the people here than at this moment.

Shain, the priest who tended both Shallowstream and Shady Creek, stole glances at Taran as the dancing began. She laughed at herself, wondering if he was building up the courage to ask her to dance. Maybe that uneasy look in his eyes came from someone pressuring him to talk to her about Bard. Or perhaps even court her? It made sense for the village priest to wed the wise woman. Shain was six years older than her. She remembered when he was twelve and had raided a beehive in a hollow tree. He had evaded the angry bees but not the bear who also wanted the honey. During his time laid up in bed, Shain had turned to holy studies. Many village girls thought him even more handsome with the scars down the left side of his face.

"What's so amusing?" Shain asked, startling her when he stepped up next to her.

"I'm not allowed to smile at a wedding?" She widened her eyes and pretended shock. He chuckled and shook his head and looked at the dancers twirling through the lively steps. "What worries you?" she asked, lowering her voice. No one stood close enough to overhear them.

"You." Shain looked around again, then tipped his head closer. "And
~~~~~

your friend. I noticed quite a few men watching you and having serious conversations. A good dozen have left already. Lita's mother and grandmother are the finest cooks in all five villages. Who would pass up a chance to feast when they're providing?"

"What did you hear?" She caught her breath. What were those men planning?

"Whispers and grumblings. Nothing more. The people are too eager to protect you. That would worry me, if they were so worried about my choices and my safety. But I trust your judgment. If you trust the beast, well ..." Shain shrugged. "I hope I'm wrong." He rested a hand on her shoulder. "I'd hate to steal your merrymaking for no reason at all."

"Thank you." She squeezed his hand and fought to keep the panicked thundering of her heart from showing on her face. "I think perhaps I'll wander over and see what the little ones are doing down by the well."

"Yeshen bless you and your friend," he murmured as she stepped away. "I'll bless him a dozen times over for protecting you."

Taran nodded her thanks, and hoped Bard wouldn't need the protection of the priest's blessing. She felt the villagers watching her as she wandered away from the dancing square. When she settled on the steps around the village well and handed the children some of the sweets she carried in her belt pouch, most of those watchful folk went back to their merrymaking. So, how to slip away without them seeing?

Taran sat with the littlest children, watching the others play their games in the dust. An idea came to her. In moments she started the littlest children playing Seek-Me. She played several rounds, until the watchers no longer startled when she slipped into hiding. Her heart gave a funny little twist when she slipped away from the game. She didn't like using those innocent children to distract their distrustful parents, but her anger squelched her sense of guilt.

Shain was right. The villagers didn't think she had the sense to send a wolf away if he was dangerous, so they plotted behind her back. What would she do if they tried to kill Bard? That funny little twist in her chest grew painful as her imagination painted a dozen awful possibilities in her mind.

She avoided the paths through the forest and searched for sentinels as she neared her cottage. The smells of village men sweating in fear and anger made the air thick. Did those idiots think Bard wouldn't smell them coming from a mile away? Taran paused to reconnoiter and crouched in the shadows cast by her cottage. Where was Bard?

A cold, damp spot touched the back of her neck. Taran muffled a cry of surprise and turned, leaping to her feet. Bard watched her, mouth open to pant, tongue lolling out, wolf laughter sparkling in his eyes.

"Have you been leading them on a merry chase?" she murmured.

Bard-wolf snorted. "Should I let you have some more fun, or give them the scolding they deserve?"

His look of disgust was clear enough, Taran's growing anger melted into mirth. She stroked down his neck, soothing him in silent apology. Feet scuffled through the underbrush, growing closer. Taran turned to face the sound and stepped up close to Bard, so his shoulder brushed her hip.

"Here!" Mihail shouted, leaping out and pulling back on his bowstring. He loosed the arrow before he took time to sight.

Taran stayed perfectly still as the arrow flew wide and passed between several trees before hitting her woodpile with a resounding *thwack*. The boy's yelp of terror echoed it when he finally saw her there, Bard-wolf pressed against her side.

The other hunters raced around the cottage from both sides, carrying ropes, spears, and other weapons. Two men carried a long net between them. Taran saw the leaves and twigs caught in the net and wondered how those two managed not to lose it to the forest.

"Mistress Taran." Drogo ran his big, dirty hand over the top of his balding head and gave her his usual crooked, nervous smile. "We didn't know you were back from the wedding."

"That's obvious." She met the eyes of every sweating, dirt-streaked, bruised man and boy in the group and made a silent tally. Twenty-six, of all ages. Sweaty and scratched, streaked with dirt, leaves in their hair, clothes torn. Bard had led them on a stumbling, frustrating chase through the forest. "I hope you didn't trample my herb garden or topple my drying racks or knock the lid off the well."

She muffled a snort when old Dobby flinched, meaning he was guilty of one of those offenses.

"I know why you're here, so kindly don't waste my time or strain my temper by making up excuses or telling lies," she continued.

"But—" Drogo blurted. Her glare stopped him.

"I will say this one last time, and you will tell your fathers and friends and brothers and grandfathers and sons. And I hope none of you need to have this repeated, because that will make me angry."

Several older men shuddered in their ragged boots.

Taran had heard stories of when her great-grandmother found it necessary to punish the idiots under her care. From the blanched faces and wide-eyed looks, the grandmothers of the five villages had dutifully preserved the stories to educate their sons and grandsons.

"The wolf is my friend. I trust him. More important, he is a man under a curse and he has come to me for help."

More than a third of the villagers made signs to avert evil. Taran sighed. She had probably made things worse with that revelation. Why couldn't the villagers feel sympathy instead of fear? Did they think Bard had committed some crime to deserve the curse?

"How did he tell you?" young Tobi asked. "Can you speak to animals in their own language?" His big blue eyes got bigger at the idea.

"Bard is my guest and my friend, and anyone who attacks him attacks me. Is that clear?" Taran didn't let them respond but gestured for them to go.

Their scurrying hurry to leave was almost laughable. Taran didn't feel much like laughing. She walked slowly around to the front of her cottage, Bard at her side, and stood looking around.

Strange, how everything had changed. This was no longer her home, her sanctuary. Certainly, she felt no surprise, and oddly, very little pain. How long until the people believed her when she said she had no magic, and punished her for it? Or worse, decided her magic had turned evil?

Bard whined and got up on his hind legs to rest his paws on her shoulder and nuzzle the amulet around her neck. Taran sputtered when he licked her face. She understood the message in his actions and his eyes.

She did possess magic, even if she had no way of controlling or summoning it.

"Perhaps it is time we both found answers."

~~~~~

When Bard shifted to man that night, they made their plans. He had only one true argument to keep her from going on the quest: her obligation to the people of the five villages.

"Soon, no one will come to me for help," she countered, feeling only weary. Not sad or guilty. "The children no longer come to visit me. No one comes to me alone. For years, they knew of the wolves in the forest, but trusted me and my mother to keep them safe. Now, they distrust me, and that will turn to fear, and then anger."

"I will protect you." Bard caught up both her hands in his and held them.

"Soon, someone will send to the king, to tell him that they have no wise woman, could he please find another to tend to the villages?"

"Will soldiers drive you away?"

"They will not drive me away, because I will not be here."

With Bard's help, it only took an hour to transfer her books and few other valuables to the Whispering Caves. Taran spoke the words that her ancestors had used to seal the caves in magic and protect the precious contents from damp, animals, and thieves. No one would find those caves until Taran spoke the words to unlock the magic. Or the magic woven into her blood ended because her bloodline ended.

They finished their preparations before the moon set and Bard returned to wolf shape. Taran made an enormous breakfast for them both, using all the food they couldn't take with them. Then they curled up to
~~~~~

sleep the day away.

Their plan was simple. Until they had left the mountains, they would travel at night and sleep during the day. No one would notice their passing through, no one would follow or fear them or try to stop them. Taran looked forward to spending the nights walking and talking with Bard. She fell asleep dreaming of the day when Bard would not need to fear either the full moon or the new moon.

~~~~~

"That tree is part of all the problems I've been having," Maddix told his henchmen, Clancy and Baethon, that late summer morning. "Arden's cursed magic tree. It left some poison in the ground. We need a wizard to come purify the ground, fill in that hole. Find me a strong magic wielder."

Only Fiera ever walked through the gate in the re-built wall that once shielded the magical apple tree from the public. She had claimed that sheltered spot as her private place, her sanctuary. Maddix wondered sometimes if Fiera spent so much time in there because she knew he didn't want to step through the gate.

He took some comfort from the idea that she was hiding from him. That she wasn't as strong and aloof as she appeared. The idea that she needed respite, that he was wearing her down, made it easier to bear the awful suspicion that she mocked him.

The letters from Durmad that appeared without warning on his desk said outright what he feared he saw in Fiera's eyes. Durmad called him a fool. The agreement made in his childhood, when Jaygo still guided him on leading strings, could not be broken. He owed everything he had attained to Durmad.

Maddix consoled himself that Durmad was a thousand miles away, with those wretched Cascade Mountains and several kingdoms between him and Stonemount. All Durmad could do was threaten. Maddix gathered more power every day, discovered new bits of magic, persuaded another wielder of magic to ally with him every other month. He had nothing to fear from Durmad. Soon, he might even be powerful enough to rival him, and then what good would Durmad's stern warnings and reminders do him?

Still, he needed the gardens, the palace, the entire kingdom cleansed of that puddle of magic that remained from that wretched tree.

"Wouldn't it be easier to just kidnap Arden's brat until she apologizes and fixes things?" Baethon muttered.

His black eye took a week to fade.

He and Clancy learned their lesson, however. Before the bruising on his face had faded to an ugly greenish brown, they brought a hopeful answer to Maddix.

The couple who stood before him that evening didn't impress
~~~~~

Maddix. At first. The woman had an amazing waterfall of fiery red curls, and enormous leaf-green eyes. The man looked like the sturdy outdoor sort, born to handle heavy physical work and obey orders. The kind Maddix would have conscripted into his special, elite guard to intimidate courtiers and silence protests whenever he saw something he wanted and took it.

He was ready to dismiss them on first sight as mere peasants. Possessing a handful of herb magic at best. Clancy growled something to them, and the woman raised her head and met Maddix's eyes. A mixture of fear and fury made her eyes gleam. She held out her hand. The man took it.

Blue sparks of magic swirled around their joined hands.

"All right," Maddix said. "Convince me you're what I'm looking for."

He cast his warning glare on Clancy and Baethon, making it clear that they would pay the larger penalty if these peasants didn't satisfy.

The woman extended her free hand, blue sparks of magic dripping from her fingertips to swirl through the air in a braided strand. The magic dipped down into the murky water that filled the hole where the apple tree once stood. The water bubbled and a faint steam rose from it, glowing softly in the twilight.

"You didn't actually do anything," Maddix observed. "No one does anything without asking a price, first."

"Perhaps. You don't know much of the world, do you?" the man said with a grin. He slipped an arm around the woman's shoulders and green sparks spilled from his hair, to spin around her.

Maddix nearly ordered them to leave that very moment. Arden's magic was green, and he had sworn he would never allow another holder of plantwise magic into Stonemount. But, he was a common sense man. Common sense said if plantwise magic created that wretched tree, it would deal with the poison it left. He had searched carefully in the months since Arden had so cruelly tricked and stolen from him, and he had charms aplenty to deal with plantwise magic and its bearers. He needed to defend his kingdom, so whose fault was it if they were harmed?

"It will take some time to untangle the poisoned magic," the woman said. "All we require is shelter, and silence, so no one know we are here."

Tell no one? They were in trouble, then. Hiding from someone? Maybe a more powerful wizard? Maddix let his mind spin through the possibilities of how to profit from the situation.

The fewer people who knew they were here, the better. Fewer people to smirk and mock and look down on him, for admitting he needed help dealing with the curse left behind by the apple tree. The thought of all those simple-minded, smugly righteous fools feeling even a moment of triumph over him put a bitter taste in his mouth. A bitterness that couldn't be wiped away even by anticipating how someday he and his sons and then his grandsons would rule triumphant over every kingdom south of the Cascade Mountains.

~~~~~

The couple, Alastor and Wren, had a child. A girl, five years old, named Ivy. She had been sleeping in a sling attached to the saddle of her mother's horse while her parents met with Maddix in the garden. He barely restrained himself from snapping that he didn't care, when the couple told him. The child's presence just made it harder to find a place for them to live in secrecy while they cleansed the garden of Arden's magic taint. When Baethon reported to Maddix on the failure after several hours, Maddix nearly lashed out at him with one of the many defensive charms he wore. He only restrained himself because Baethon and Clancy were still somewhat useful to him. But not for much longer, if they couldn't handle this latest simple task.

None of the usual out-of-the-way places for stashing accomplices suited the family. Wren tested every place Baethon took them to, spreading blue sparks of magic and finding some flaw, some weakness that would nullify her shielding magic. While Maddix weighed the inconvenience against his needs, Baethon remarked that the little girl was as red-haired as her mother, and she gave off blue sparks in her sleep.

"Thought that might come in handy," he added, with a diffident shrug. "Thought you wouldn't want anybody to see them and notice. Might be inconvenient later, if you know what I mean."

The bit of smugness in his tone didn't escape Maddix's notice. So the big oaf thought he was being clever, trying to win some points in his favor? Maybe.
~~~~~

Chapter Eight

This child was likely too young to be of any value, no matter how much magic her parents possessed. Yet ... could she possibly inherit magic from both parents? She would need training to be totally loyal to him. What would it cost him to keep the parents here, so he could oversee the raising of the child? His spirits rose as he imagined how powerful Stonemount would be, with a powerful enchantress vowed to serve and protect the king. How soon could he separate the child from her parents? What would it cost him?

Later. After they had dealt with the poison left by Arden's tree.

He nearly laughed aloud as memories he had ignored for years came to the fore. "I have a place to put them." The convenience, the timing, gave him an oddly grateful feeling.

Nonsense. Why should he be grateful to anyone? It was his own cleverness that came up with the solution.

"I have a sanctuary, hidden from the palace traffic. My nursemaid had a minor wizard bespell it, so no one could find it but me. She knew how much I needed my solitude."

Maddix wondered for the first time in years what had happened to Nanny Moira. He suspected Jaygo had had her sent away, along with so many other people who threatened to be a softening influence on him. No matter. The woman had done him a great service, and he meant to make use of her gift now.

It was a small courtyard and a cottage, with its own well. No one would know the family was there, with all sounds and light blocked by magic. No one but Maddix. He would have to take the family there, since he was the only one who could find the place and let them through the spells blocking the doorway.

Maddix speculated on just what kind of trouble they were in, to need a hiding place. The path they took went past the place where the servants worked, past the path leading out of the gardens to the stables. The trees in this part of the garden were overgrown and the bushes hadn't been trimmed into pleasing shapes in years. The path here was gravel and packed clay, rather than seashells or gold-painted pebbles. The wall surrounding the courtyard was nearly invisible under the ivy that clung to it. Maddix hesitated for several seconds, wondering if it was possible he had forgotten the exact place where the gap in the wall lay, hidden under the tangles of ivy. He refused to look uncertain in front of these people, however, so he struck out, reaching for the opening. He nearly swore aloud when his hand hit stone under the tangle of dead and living vines and leaves. He tried again, and his hand passed through. Snorting in triumph, he pushed aside the ivy, parting the sour-smelling, scratchy, crackling curtain.

One of the disadvantages of a secret, magic-shielded sanctuary, Maddix realized in that moment, was the lack of anyone to properly tend the place. The cobblestone-paved courtyard was carpeted with moss. Ivy formed a curtain down the walls. The thatched roof sagged in spots, gaped in others. How long had it been since he had come here? Why had he let Jaygo send away Nanny Moira? She was the only other one able to come through the doorway, and who else could maintain the place? Certainly not him.

"Well, it needs a little refurbishing, of course," Maddix said with a rusty laugh, and turned to face the family with an apologetic smile. As apologetic a smile as a king could afford to wear without damaging his dignity.

"It's perfect," Wren whispered. She traded glances with Alastor, and he nodded.

Maddix gritted his teeth and fought down a wave of unreasonable jealousy. What was it about those couples who could communicate with a glance, that bothered him so? He had no need of such unity with any person in this world.

Still ... his imagination pictured the day when Fiera chose to think like him. She was both intelligent and practical. With her by his side, he could rule the entire world. Not just the southern half of the continent.

"We'll take care of everything," Alastor said.

"Good. Let my men know what you need, and they will provide it." Maddix muffled a chuckle, imagining the reaction of Clancy and Baethon, reduced to running errands, providing supplies to repair the house. They would do it because they would understand just how vital this secrecy was to him. If they didn't understand ... maybe this was the time to ensure they stopped not understanding. Permanently.

Once these folk cleansed the poisoned magic Arden had left behind, everything would right itself in Stonemount. Maddix congratulated himself on the wisdom of his choice, and immediately set about plotting how to ensure these people entered his service and trained their daughter to serve him when she was grown.

~~~~~

Taran wondered if Bard and the wolf had been bound together so long, they melted into each other, like two candles stored in a small box in a hot garret. They were still candles, but their colors and scents merged to
~~~~~

an extent they could never be separated without damaging the other. Had that happened to Bard? Would he turn into something neither man nor wolf but both, new in the world?

"If I had some control, if I could be free of the pain, it would not be so bad," Bard said, when she shared her thoughts with him that night. "The wolf and I have made a treaty. He doesn't scratch at my mind when I am a man, and he lets me ride behind his eyes and use his senses when he hunts and explores." He snorted, rueful laughter. "He likes you very much. He sees you as a she-wolf, and very desirable."

"I was right. Much of you has melted into him," Taran said. She had to force her grin. Something inside her shuddered, and yet exulted.

Before they left the mountains, the wolves traveled with them for two days. Taran welcomed their company, and ached for Bard that he could find no real acceptance from the beasts. The wolves didn't consider him an enemy, or see him as sick or troublesome, but neither did they welcome him fully.

"They see you the same way," Bard said, when she told him. He laughed at her wide-eyed reaction. "It's true. They like you. They look up to you. They allow you to run with them, but there is something about you that makes their fur prickle."

He sighed and looked up at the moon, sliding down low toward the tops of the trees. His time as a man would soon end. He took hold of her hand, stopping her, and turned so they were face-to-face. A shiver passed through Taran when he tugged aside the collar of her shirt to reveal her amulet. A buzzing sensation washed over her when Bard touched it with the tip of his finger.

"I think this is the reason. They feel the magic here, and it makes them curious and wary and …" He shrugged. "It draws me, as well. The beasts sense the magic is part of you, and they love you too much to wish you harm."

"Can beasts wish anything?" she murmured.

"I think so. They show love and anger, fear and enjoyment. Why not have wishes and dreams?"

~~~~~

When the moon waned far enough that Bard no longer became a man at night, Taran grew as silent as the wolf. She gleaned berries and roots as she walked, eating them raw, putting some in her pack for later. This life suited her. If not for the ache she felt for Bard, his suffering, she could wish to continue this quiet traveling life forever.

After the new moon, while the wolf ran off his growing restlessness and Bard still could not emerge at night, Taran was alone. She found a quiet, deep pond and decided to bathe. The day had been hot and sticky. She hated the smell of her dirty, sweaty body and wondered how bad she
~~~~~

smelled to the wolf. He returned just after she peeled down to her thin undersmock and folded her clothes in a pile on a large rock. Taran flinched, seeing the laughter in his un-wolfly blue eyes. How much of Bard was awake and alert behind those eyes? She waited for the wolf to return to his wandering. Instead, he sat down next to her clothes and put one paw on them.

"Are you going to stand guard, then?" she asked. The words ached in her throat, after days of silence.

The wolf snorted and tipped his head to one side to watch her. Taran sighed in exasperation. The night air felt no cooler against her skin than the day had been, and she wished she could take off her smock to swim. She had never felt uneasy swimming naked in front of the wolves back home. Then again, they were only wolves. No male awareness looked out through their eyes.

"Have it your way," she muttered. Taran barely stopped from sticking her tongue out at Bard-wolf.

She took a shallow dive, nearly scraping the bottom mud with her nose before she curved back to the surface. She erupted into the air, laughing and sputtering. The wolf turned his head to follow her. Mischief sparked in her, and Taran splashed him. She got more water on her clothes than on the wolf, but her clothes did need a good rinsing. Bard-wolf did nothing but twitch his tail. She continued splashing, trying for some reaction. Still, he did nothing.

He sat perfectly still until she knelt at the edge of the pond to wring out her hair. Taran straightened and caught a flash of black coming at her. A hot, musky body bowled her over, coating her dripping body and clinging smock with dirt and leaves. When she rolled to a stop and lifted her head, a hot, slobbery tongue washed her face.

She shrieked, half in laughter, half in disgust. The wolf nosed her sides until he found her ticklish spots. Taran got up onto her knees, trying to push him away. Bard-wolf took the chain of her amulet in his mouth and tugged, trying to hold her close to the ground.

The chain snapped and he stumbled backward, his tail flopping ridiculously. Taran opened her mouth to laugh, but no sound came out.

She fell flat on her face, her limbs twisting out of her control. Something tore her to pieces from the inside. The agony stole her breath, her voice. She itched painfully, as if she had grown too large for her skin. Her body burned as fur sprouted everywhere. Her bones crackled as they changed shape, twisted by a vortex of magic pressing around her body. Sound escaped, a shriek that elongated into a howl.

Taran smelled the blood that pumped through Bard-wolf's flesh. Overpowering thirst took over her body and mind. She craved the hot taste of blood pouring down her throat. She threw herself at the wolf. He went down under her with a yelp and a whimper.

Her teeth sank into his foreleg, meeting bone, scraping loudly. She shook herself loose and fastened onto his shoulder, digging into his belly with her new claws. He growled, twisting away from her, his claws digging into her shoulder.

The pain snapped the everlasting wheel of torment to anger to torment.

Magic shivered along her body, flinging her away, making the new fur on her altered body stand up on end. She tumbled backward, magic ringing in her ears until she felt deafened. Taran-wolf whimpered and curled into a ball, waiting.

The craving left. The pain tormenting her limbs faded slowly, like a burn plunged into cold water. In the silence all around, she uncurled with shivering hesitation and rolled onto her feet. She stood still and panting, on four legs, and gazed at the wolf on his back before her. A shallow wound on his right foreleg dripped a few more drops of blood and then closed. Raw, naked patches of flesh on his chest sprouted black stubs of fur.

In the pond to her right, Taran saw two wolves. One silvery white, one black as the night. One male, one female.

The male rolled to his feet and came to her slowly, in deference and awe. Hesitant, he nuzzled her neck.

Taran could not move. It was too much of a struggle just to try to think, to understand. She wanted to accept his companionship, the partnership he offered with such a simple, all-encompassing gesture. Yet another part of her screamed against instinct and understanding. She struggled to think of her mother, of words, duties, and lessons. Of clothes, dishes, weaving, and books.

After a while, the wolf retreated, sorrow touching his eyes. Taran wished she understood her new body enough to show him the jagged tear through her desires and dreams. How could she communicate when she didn't know her own body? Or was it her body any longer?

She saw the amulet lying in the blood-spattered dust, the chain a tangled heap a few steps away. Taran lowered her head to sniff at it. A scent came from it, heady as honeyed wine, tingling like witch hazel water, buzzing in her nose like bees. That was the familiar smell of magic, but a thousand times more intense.

A howl lifted from her throat. *Mother, what have you done to me?* she begged in the wordless screaming of her thoughts.

When the moon set, the two wolves still sat in the clearing around the pond. Watching each other. Waiting. A last throb of desperation prompted her to take the amulet into her mouth, though she hated the taste, the feel of the magic filling the silver.

The magic spilled like an all-encompassing bruise through her body, itching as the fur retreated into her flesh, sharp aching as her bones changed shape. She nearly laughed through the whimpers that twisted her throat.

When she had hands again, she took the amulet from her mouth, twisted two warped links of the chain together, and hung it around her neck again. Her fingers itched as if they had touched poison ivy.

She felt the wolf's gaze on her as she quickly rinsed in the pond and put her clothes back on over her damp smock and skin. *His* gaze.

While she had been in wolf shape, she had experienced the forest as never before. She had been acutely aware of the male smell of him, the way the very air took on a new texture around his shape. Until then, she had never thought of the wolf as male, herself as female. The part of him that was Bard had been hidden enough for her to forget about such things. Now, it frightened her a little, even as she knew the fear to be ridiculous. Hadn't Bard proven he was her friend, no matter what shape he took? Hadn't the wolf proven himself to be just as good a friend?

"Oh, my friend," she whispered, sitting down in the dust. "Are you still my friend?"

Bard-wolf came to her then, his tail swinging softly. He put his head on her thigh and whimpered.

~~~~~

Taran was glad to let Bard lead, keeping her away from habitations of people when they stopped to sleep away the daylight. She did not want to see people. Perhaps never again. If the wolf was endangered because of his curse, did she face the same fate if anyone learned the truth?

What was she to do? What did that night's transformation mean? Was she under a curse, and did the amulet protect her from it? What had her mother done to her, and why?

When the moon rose the next night, a little bigger than the night before, Taran welcomed its arrival. She wanted answers. She wanted an end to the questioning, the hiding and fear and confusion. As the waning light rose above the trees, she started to pull off her clothes, then stopped to think. The magic didn't destroy Bard's clothes. She held still, frozen by the possibilities, fears, and uncertainty. She stood still, staring, until the thin promise of moon, not yet a crescent, rose fully above the tops of the trees. What was she to do?

The wolf watched her. She couldn't read his eyes, and that frightened her. Did he want her to transform? What did he truly see when he looked at her? She remembered Bard's words, saying how lovely she was in a wolf's eyes.

A sob caught in her throat, choking her. She went to her knees, shivering, unable to push past the questions to lift the amulet from around
~~~~~

her throat and allow the magic to work.

Bard-wolf whimpered and nudged her shoulder with his head. When she turned, he met her gaze, hunger and loneliness gazing from his too-human eyes.

"I wanted you to be what you were not," she whispered. "Because I was lonely. Do you ask the same from me, now?"

Taran grasped the silver amulet with both hands and felt the tingling of the power inside it. She shivered, though the night was as uncomfortably warm as the night before. The *absence* of the amulet had transformed her. The moon was the weaker power in the enchantment that enfolded her body. She and Bard were held in different patterns of magic. Nothing, however, could persuade her to take off the amulet. Not until she could think this through and understand. And find some answers.

"We are both on quests now," she murmured. "I thought I was helping you, but it seems I must help myself. Oh, Mother, did you do this to me? Is this what Nueroch killed you to learn? Or did someone curse me and you wove magic to protect me?"

Bard-wolf growled and nudged her shoulder again. The concern was clear in his eyes. With a strangled little laugh, she wrapped her arms around the wolf.

"You protect me from myself," she whispered, and hid her face in his dusty, musky fur. "I don't know what I am, or who I am." She released the wolf, sat back on her heels, and wrapped her arms around herself.

"I am not a—" She glanced at Bard, who tilted his head to one side to study her as she talked through her thoughts and fears and questions. "I am not a creature engendered through magic, but … am I like you, woven from two creatures, through magic? Maybe Nueroch did this to me. Perhaps he courted her when she was much younger. She refused him, and he matched me with a wolf, to punish her for choosing my father." Cracked laughter escaped her. "Oh, can you imagine Nueroch as a father?"

Taran slapped both hands over her mouth, closed her eyes and held perfectly still, fighting the tremors moving through her body. They were weak echoes of the tremors threatening to tear her soul and mind to pieces.

The crescent moon hung overhead before she regained her calm and could release her cramped, aching muscles and open her eyes. Bard-wolf whimpered, clearly a question, and when she smiled at him, he nuzzled her cheek.

"Whatever happened, my mother knew what to do to control that magic, so the phases of the moon did not control me and the wolf inside me did not come to the fore." Taran wrapped her fist around the amulet. "This is the secret Nueroch killed my mother to find. So he could control you and your friends. The question is, my friend ..." She swallowed hard. She was almost glad Bard was in wolf shape now. She would hate to see the hope, the hunger and questions on his man-face when she said what she thought. "If I take off the amulet forever, will I be controlled by the phases of the moon, as you are?"

Bard made no sound. He gently shoved his head between her arm and her body and pressed close, tight and warm against her. Taran laughed wearily and shifted to wrap her arms around him.

"It would not be so bad a life, would it? But how can we know that I would be a wolf when you are a wolf, and a woman when you are a man?"

Taran needed to find out exactly what her mother had done, what had brought her to be joined with a wolf, before she even considered changing her life forever.

Could she do such a thing? Would it be the right decision, or the wrong one? She could not choose just for herself and Bard. They had started out on this quest to help Bard and all his fellows who had been enslaved by Nueroch.

"Whatever we do, we cannot let Nueroch learn of this," she whispered. "If he ever captures us ... it would be better if I died, rather than give him the key to enslave thousands. Do you understand?" Taran shivered with a new chill as Bard moved out of her embrace and sat back to meet her gaze. His blue eyes were somber and cold. He nodded.

Chapter Nine

Taran pondered the question until her head ached: Who would Eyrian have gone to for help and advice in crafting such strong magic that Neuroch had killed to obtain it? Her mother would not have confided such knowledge to anyone who could not defend themselves against Nueroch. Who did that leave? Someone far stronger than Eyrian.

Taran wished she knew where to find Steward, whose devotion to Yeshen tamed the magic that controlled the foundations of the world. Surely he had the knowledge to untangle or even unravel the magic binding her and Bard.

Steward wandered the entire world, bringing wisdom and Yeshen's guidance, healing, and encouragement to everyone who would listen. Most important, he was constantly on the alert for Durmad's next attempt to break through the barriers that kept him imprisoned north of the Cascade Mountains. While common sense said if she went north, she might find Steward, Taran didn't want to do that. Nueroch served Durmad, and she didn't doubt that the twisted, broken magic that bound man and wolf together had been created to serve the destroyer. Why risk her mother's secret falling into even worse hands than Nueroch's?

Her only recourse was to pray often, asking Yeshen to guide and guard their steps.

"Sitting still is useless and foolish, and could attract the wrong attention," she told Bard-wolf, when they stopped to rest at twilight, and they shared the nuts and roots she had gleaned and the hare he had caught earlier in the day. "I need to keep searching and asking, and trust Yeshen to lead me to the right place."

She remembered how her mother used the still, moon-silvered water of their pool to communicate with her peers and friends. As easy as talking around the village well, swifter than writing letters.

A bark of laughter escaped her, and she nearly choked on the nutmeat she had only chewed twice. Taran coughed and wiped tears from her eyes. Bard-wolf's concerned look, the paw resting on her knee, made her want to laugh more.

"Kalista," she said, when she could finally speak again. "The seeress, Kalista of the Pools. We'll ask her."

Kalista of the Pools lived in Ambray. Taran had gone too far south through Brentonwald already to simply go west across the border into the neighboring kingdom. She would walk west and north, cutting across the upper eastern corner of Stonemount to reach Ambray.

"We could have our answers in less than a month," she told Bard-wolf, when she explained her plan. In answer, he licked her face, making her sputter and laugh.

With a goal now, their pace increased and they walked as long as they had moonlight, only stopping in the dark twilight of morning and evening to rest. It felt good to know where she was going, instead of simply following her nose and the sense of magic coming up through the ground and tickling her bare feet.

Three days took them to the border of Stonemount, and by then the crescent moon had grown enough that Bard could become a man at night. He asked questions and Taran felt like a teacher, guiding a pupil through his first fledgling steps learning to use magic. Bard possessed no magic, just as she possessed none. Magic possessed them. He nodded, humor sparkling in his eyes when she shared that revelation. He did not laugh, and neither did he say anything about her transformation into wolf that one night at the pond. Taran was grateful, and she felt ashamed over that, as well. What did she want to do? What could she do? When she could talk with Kalista, then she would know her choices and how to handle the transformation. Should she take off the amulet permanently and roam with Bard in wolf shape? Would that be so bad? Or should she hold onto hope that Bard could be freed from his curse and live as a man in the daylight?

Would Bard want anything to do with her, if he did become fully a man again, knowing what lurked under her skin and slept in her soul? A man cured of blindness could become disdainful of those who remained in darkness. Would Bard want her?

Taran said nothing about her thoughts, and she was grateful Bard said nothing along those lines, either. Time enough to face those questions, those possibilities of losing each other, when they had answers. And those answers could come at Kalista's pools of vision.

Several times, Taran went into the villages and smaller towns along the journey through Stonemount, to make sure of their path and to buy bread. It felt strange to talk with strangers. Her ears ached with the babble of dozens of voices, and her nose felt numb, overwhelmed with the pungent, dusty, dirty, perfumed, hot smells. She wasn't sure she liked the overload to all her senses.

"You told me you wanted to travel and explore the world," Bard told her, when she shared those thoughts with him. "You like to learn. All those sounds and smells and voices are part of another land." He laughed and scraped char off the heel of bread she had toasted over the fire, to try to melt the last bit of dried cheese on it. "I know how you feel. I liked to travel, long ago. Despite where it got me," he added with a shrug.

Bard advised her to enjoy all her new experiences, so Taran decided to do just that. She would let the questions and doubts and regrets come tomorrow, or the day after, and not let them sour the sweetness and wonder she held today.

It shamed her to admit she enjoyed hearing the gossip bantered about the village squares and the marketplaces in the towns. So much of it concerned King Maddix and his embarrassment at the hands of Princess Arden. The people of Stonemount seemed to love King Alix, Queen Caitlyn, and Princess Arden of Westerland, more than they loved their own sovereign. They certainly didn't approve of King Maddix. Taran wondered how Princess Fiera could agree to even consider marriage with him. Everything she had ever heard of the royal family of Brentonwald had been respectful. They cared about their people. Brentonwald was feared for the might of its army, but admired for its kindness when people were in need, respected and honored for the strong sense of justice that guided all actions. Messengers, traveling judges and examiners went through the land, ensuring criminals were punished for their crimes, the innocent were freed from unjust suffering, children were educated, and those needing healers and other minor magic had access to them. If a village was not large enough to have its own wise woman, then it belonged to a cluster of villages, such as Eyrian's arrangement had been with the five villages.

Taran felt it a sad state of affairs, that the people of Stonemount couldn't respect their own king. Maddix had brought it on himself.

~~~~~

Near noon on the day after they crossed the border into Ambray, Taran and Bard came on a party of villagers harvesting nuts and healing herbs in the forest. Taran first heard the sounds of people laughing and talking and singing, then a few sweet, clear notes from a stringed instrument that meant a minstrel traveled with the workers. Bard-wolf turned and vanished into the forest. Taran fought an urge to follow him, then tugged her skirts straight and tucked the loose strands of her hair back into her braids. She continued down the forest trail.

"Hullo!" one of the men shouted as she entered the clearing.

Taran smelled the sweat of the harvesters, the dull tang of nut husks rubbed hot as they were cleaned, the oil soaking into hands and sacks. The minstrel sat on a fallen tree, entertaining the littlest children and keeping them out of the way. He fell silent and one by one, the others stopped their work and stood up to look at her.

"Yeshen bless you. I am Taran, daughter of Eyrian, who was wise woman to the villages of the Aerbach Valley. I am on a quest." Taran hoped the villagers would be more curious about her quest than where
~~~~~

she had come from. As far as she knew, Brentonwald and Ambray were on friendly terms, but that did not mean these people, so far from the capital, would know that.

"Ah, then you seek Kalista?" a woman asked. She stepped to the front of the group and identified herself as Myra, their wise woman.

Taran accepted their stew and journey bread gladly, though the food tasted too spicy. She had eaten simple, plain food for too long, either whatever she could gather up and eat raw, or the occasional rabbit or squirrel or fish Bard caught for them. Taran was glad to learn Kalista, the seeress who lived in the cave of the vision pools, was less than two days' walk away. She asked questions of her hosts to keep them from probing further into her reasons for traveling.

When she joined Bard after moonrise, he was already in his man shape. He ate the bread she had saved from her dinner while she told him everything the villagers had said about Kalista. He asked few questions, such as what she hoped for when they met the seeress.

Now that she thought about it, he had been more quiet, ever since she had turned into the white wolf. Bard still hadn't asked her if she wanted to be free of her wolf shape or control it or keep it permanently. Taran didn't know if she was grateful for his reticence or if she thought he was a coward.

What did he want of her? A companion who could run on four feet with him and read the wind and the scents in the ground? Speculations got her nowhere and gave her a headache. She was almost grateful when the moon slid toward the horizon and Bard sent her away so he could shift back to wolf in privacy.

"Am I a coward, letting you protect me from your suffering?" she whispered to the night damp and shadows.

When Bard-wolf rejoined her, she stayed seated and wrapped her arms around his neck to share his warmth. They sat still until night's darkest time turned to dawn, then got to their feet and continued their journey.

They reached Kalista's cave shortly after dawn of the day after that. The woman stood in the cave mouth, facing the place in the shadows of the tall, ancient trees where they emerged into daylight. Silent, she beckoned for Taran to follow her. The wolf stayed outside.

Kalista led her from shadows into the candle-lit room of the vision pool and beckoned for Taran to look into the pool. Her face showed no emotion, no clue of what her visitor might see.

Taran looked, nearly choking on a whimper as she saw the silver-white female wolf from the pond in the forest. "What does it mean?" she whispered, to keep her voice from breaking. "Am I human or wolf?"

"Both. You have always been both," Kalista said, her voice a whisper that belied the power of her eyes, the strength in her smooth forehead and long fall of glossy white hair.

"How did I get this way?"

"The how of the past does not matter. It is the present, and how you will shape the future, that matters."

"Of course the past matters!" Taran flinched as her cracking voice bounced back at her. She struggled to her feet and stared down the woman, who was taller than her. "Nueroch killed my mother to learn the secret of how wolf and human are one. Bard needs that secret to be free."

"Does he want to be free? Sometimes, we bear our burdens so long, they become part of us and we are inconsolable, only half alive, if our torment is removed."

"Who would want to live that way?"

"The question, daughter of Eyrian, is how do you want to live? How does Bard want to live? Decide, first, before you seek what you think is a cure." Kalista gestured at the archway leading out of the pool room. A tiny smile quirked the corners of her mouth when Taran stood still, waiting, unwilling to be dismissed. "I am even older than your mother was. She was my student, for a time. Did she ever tell you that?"

"No," she whispered.

"Hmm, yes, there was so much else to teach you, and so little time. Be that as it may, I am an old woman and this room is too damp for my old bones, no matter how strong the magic of my visions. Call your friend. You two need to rest and eat and prepare for your journey."

"Another journey?" Taran snapped her mouth closed, cutting off the embarrassing wail in her voice.

"There is an ending to your quest, yes, but it is far down the road and you must grow and learn before you gain your final shape. A task awaits. You and your friend can smell magic, as most of the wiser beasts can, but you also have human minds behind those noses, so you know what to do when you find it. That is a blessing."

As she spoke, Kalista led Taran through the chain of chambers carved through the rock by water and time. They came to a wide, low-ceilinged chamber hung with tapestries against the damp of the stone, the floor thickly carpeted, with a wide fire pit in the center, full of glowing coals. The smell of stewing apples heavy with cinnamon and honey filled her head. Her mouth watered. The sweet aroma of oat bread lay under that scent, and lentil stew. All her favorite things to eat.

"Did you know—" She stopped, unsure if it was arrogance to accuse Kalista of using her powers to find out something so paltry as her guest's favorite food.

"Sit, my dear. I know your favorites because your mother told me." Kalista settled with fluid grace into a chair full of pillows, deep enough to be a bed. Taran settled on a wide, dark blue pillow on the floor, midway between Kalista and the fire pit. "Welcome, man and wolf," she said, as Bard-wolf stuck his dark nose into the golden torchlight that filled the room like water filled a deep vat.

"I don't remember you visiting us."

"No, I never had that chance. Your mother and I exchanged letters by way of the merchant caravans. The effort of speaking through the water was too great to expend it on the ordinary, everyday news of old friends. I had the sad duty of learning the fate of your father and telling Eyrian. I mourned with her. Be comforted, my dear child, that your father was a good man, more than worthy of her love, and they are reunited now in Yeshen's lands of eternal morning." Kalista's smile went crooked. "But that does not satisfy your quest, does it?"

Bard let out a soft, crooning growl as he settled down on the floor next to Taran and rested his head on her crossed ankles. He focused all his attention on Kalista, and let out a long, deep wolf sigh that earned a chuckle from the woman.

"Well, your friend trusts me. The wise creature in him knows that I am an ally. Here is the long and short of your answer: You were deathly ill as a child."

"I remember," Taran whispered, not meaning to interrupt.

"You were all that your mother loved, so she grew desperate. Eyrian was in search of rare snow-borne healing herbs, to save you. In her hunt, she found an entire pack torn to pieces to bleed to death in the snow. One white female cub remained, barely alive. Eyrian could not leave her to die and could not stop to heal her and find another wolf mother to take the orphaned cub. She took the cub with her, in her need to hurry home with the herbs to heal you. The cub fought to live, with a fierceness that gave your mother hope. Here she had a child, half-dead, and a wolf cub, half-dead, and between the two she had one strong life. She could save both, but only by joining them into one being."

Taran held still, trying to breathe, trying to reconcile the images that sometimes haunted her dreams. Like a stubborn lock finally yielding, the images slipped together with an audible *click* in her mind. Her dreams, her longing to run with the wolves of the forest, had been the wolf in her soul and flesh, trying to be free.

"I know I have taken off my amulet at other times, when the chain broke by accident or Mother gave me a longer chain," Taran said slowly. She had so many questions her tongue tangled around them, and this was the first coherent question that rose to the top of her mind. "Why didn't I change to wolf those other times?"

"Daylight and moonlight. The moon is the key. You are a woman by day, with a wolf joined to your soul. Indeed, the two of you are one being, not two separate souls fighting for dominance, as it is with your friend." Kalista nodded at Bard. "But there is a part of yourself you have never known or explored, and it will break free at the touch of the moonlight, if you remove the protection of the amulet. Your friend is held prisoner in the wolf's body, and he is able to break free when the moon is weak."

"I can never be a wolf during the day, by choice, just as Bard can never be a man during the day, by choice."

"Someone would think you were soul-sworn lovers, cursed by an enchanter who punished you for not submitting to his will." Kalista laughed, a trilling sound, when Taran's head shot up and she stared at her. "You must admit, that is how it sounds, my dear."

Her smile was so infectious, Taran couldn't resist. Soon she grinned back, finding something amusing in their rather melodramatic re-telling of the situation. The truth, however, was far crueler and less personal.

"Is there any cure? Any way to find some control over what we are, when we are?" She wrapped her arms around Bard-wolf, resting her head on top of his.

"The man can still be freed and separated into two separate beings. You, however, are one soul with two bodies. There is no dividing you without killing you." Kalista didn't look sympathetic, only somber.

Taran nodded. She marveled that she felt no surprise at the news. Maybe she had anticipated it. Bard would be free, cured, able to resume whatever life remained to him, but she would be a travesty, a freak revealed. Even if he never spoke her secret to the world, people would learn of it. Hurtful truths and strangeness always had a way of reaching daylight, no matter how deeply they were buried.

"Is there anyone who could help us? Can Steward? Will he, if I find him?"

"I think Steward can, but the question is if he will. If there is perhaps a greater purpose in the suffering forced on both of you. Yeshen grants us the gift of suffering to make us stronger, to refine us as tools for the greater purpose of his plan. To put you on the path to lead you to Steward, I give you a task suited to the skills you now possess. There was a woman raised in ignorance of the ways of magic, who found her way and learned to control her magic through trial and error. She grew up among a people who isolated themselves from the rest of the world, thinking that would give them pure souls. They mistook self-righteousness for righteousness.

"In Yeshen's grace, the young woman hid much of what she could do, sensing that she was in danger from the fears that ruled the people around her. She would be either punished for having magic in her blood, or made into a false deity. When she was old enough and strong enough, she fled, and in Yeshen's grace she found a man with plantwise magic, who taught her of Yeshen's laws. They joined their souls, but in their wandering came within Durmad's reach. He treated them well, to trick them into serving him. He foresaw that a child born of two strong streams of magic would be a powerful tool.

"The woman became pregnant, and when she and her husband realized the danger they were in, they tried to flee. Durmad's efforts to keep them within his reach caused the child to be born too soon, and sickly. In their fear and desperation, they accepted help that put them in debt to Durmad. When he claimed their child, they sought Yeshen's help. Steward helped them flee, and Durmad's servants have been seeking them ever since."

"You want us to find them and protect them? Lead them to safety?" Taran guessed.

"If you can. I fear for them. They have gone into Stonemount. Durmad has roots there, and his power blocks my vision. Two hunters such as you are, with magic in your blood and yet possessing no magic of your own, are essentially invisible to Durmad and his servants. Find the family. Bring them out of Stonemount, using the paths of the wild creatures. I see you fleeing out of the dark cloud that fills Stonemount. Be warned, child. There is blood and pain, but you will triumph. In pain and sacrifice, you will find your answers."

Kalista beckoned and lifted a brass pitcher to pour water into a silver bowl. The ripples caught the light, and in that light Taran saw a woman and a little girl, both with vibrant, curly red hair and eyes like new leaves.

Taran swallowed a bubble of bitter laughter. Of course they would have to go back there. She had hated the feel of the ground under her bare feet those few days she traveled across the corner of Stonemount.

Bard-wolf whined and struggled up to his feet. He licked her cheek and nuzzled close against her. Taran sighed and wrapped her arms around him, hiding her face in the dusty warmth of his coat. It didn't matter how much it hurt to touch Stonemount's poisoned soil. She would do it for Bard. And for the child.

"Maddix's people constantly scour the land, searching for anyone with gifts of magic. He offers rewards for those who serve him well. I fear the parents have yielded to temptation and desperation," Kalista murmured. "Start there, in the palace."

Chapter Ten

Eyrian had raised Taran on several rules of magic that applied to ordinary folk, as well as those gifted with talents and powers.

The first rule: A magic wielder always left pieces of her soul in the magic she created. The reflections and results of her magic acts replaced that bit of lost soul. Wizards who used their power to do evil or selfish things grew increasingly evil and selfish, as their souls were nibbled away and replaced with evil and selfish magic. The same happened for those who reserved their powers, vast or limited, for good actions and causes.

"Good gives good back to the one who launched the action. Evil ultimately destroys the one who sent it out," Eyrian always said.

She had taught her daughter the purpose was as important as the cure, when a very rich man with a very small affliction came to be healed. In her gazing pool, she saw he needed to suffer the slight humiliation of his affliction, which put red spots on his face and made his hands bleed. He needed solitude, isolated by his sense of embarrassment. He needed to slow down his business dealings, to stop making alliances and gathering power, until the smallness and coldness of his soul could be rectified. A man with so much power and wealth could do great and terrible things. Eyrian sent him away, telling him to live simply and quietly, until he found something more important than wealth and power. He went away scowling, grumbling, but too smart to curse Eyrian for her refusal.

Taran couldn't remember the rich man's name, but she remembered that when he came back five moons later, Eyrian smiled, embraced him, and healed him before he finished greeting her. The man went away whistling like a peasant woodcutter going to work. He gave Taran sweets and a ball with a bell inside it, and told her what a wise, good mother she had.

"The purpose is as important as the cure," Taran murmured, as she walked alongside Bard in the moonlight.

"Do you think Yeshen let this happen to us, just so we could find and rescue these people?" he asked, frowning at the forest trail ahead of them.

"I asked my mother something like that. She said it is more that Yeshen uses our afflictions and grief to make us stronger, to make us useful tools, to prepare us to help others. It is always our choice. Yeshen never makes us do anything, only offers us opportunity. If we had refused, someone else would have come to find the family."

"And we would be left in our cursed states. Punishment for being selfish?"

"I don't think I am cursed. Mother saved two lives. She gave me a gift. A puzzle and a problem to solve, yes, but ultimately a gift." Taran didn't like the hot little trickle of anger she felt, in reaction to Bard's words. Why did he have to see all this as a curse?

"That is not what I meant." He grasped her hand, intertwining their fingers and putting their palms together. The sensation tickled and a hum filled her belly. "Yes, your mother did what was necessary, and good came from her actions. But how we live now is not natural. Even if your amulet protects you from the moon's power, so you don't shift shape with the phases, it is still not natural. It is not the way Yeshen intended us to live. I want to be free. I would do far worse things than rescue prisoners to find my cure."

"Perhaps we will find a way to control what we are, what happens to us, rather than be set free and divided. Did you ever consider that?" Taran finally turned her head to look at him. Irritation melted into sadness. Bard looked so contrite over what he obviously had a hard time expressing.

"I feel as if I have been given a glimpse of a wonderful gift, an amazing way to live, if only I have the courage to embrace it and learn to use it. To learn what Yeshen intended when he allowed this to happen to me. A wolf sleeps inside me. I want to run swift and silent in the moonlight and know I have the power in my hands and feet, in my teeth and claws and strong muscles, to help and defend and guard and hunt and ..." Taran shook her head, a burst of laughter catching in her throat. Her heart raced and she found it hard to breathe.

Her legs ached to run as a wolf ran. She wanted to know the world through a wolf's keen senses. She wanted to raise her voice in a howling song to the skies and exult in the full release of all her potential.

How could she explain that to Bard without condemning him for his hopes or making him think she had begun to lose her mind?

"You cannot be divided again," he whispered, and reached with his free hand to stroke her cheek and tuck a strand of hair behind her ear. "I'm sorry. I forgot. Trying to divide you, to take away the wolf, would kill you."

She shrugged and turned her gaze back to the trail in front of them. They walked in silence for perhaps half an hour. Something pressed against her chest, a cry begging to burst free.

Why, she wanted to shout to him, *can't you simply be happy with things just the way they are?*

"Kalista took me aside, before I shifted back to wolf," Bard said, breaking the fragile semi-silence underscored by the rustling of leaves, the songs of insects and other night music of the forest. "She told me our quest offers us a chance to be changed, but first we must find peace within ourselves, or we will never be satisfied with the change. What we choose to be is ultimately more important than what we began as, or what people would make of us. No matter what faces we wear, we are first of all how we see ourselves. If we let others dictate what we are, then we become poor, stunted creatures. We must prepare for the day when the truth is revealed and we stand before Yeshen, so we are not ashamed of false masks or full of regret over time and opportunities wasted."

"Heavy thoughts to put into anyone's head, especially someone torn between two bodies and two souls," Taran murmured.

"Maybe you and I are the only ones who can fully appreciate such teaching." Bard squeezed her hand tighter.

Taran caught her breath and scolded herself not to be a fool. After all, she wasn't a silly village girl twittering over the first boy to try to kiss her. She was old enough to have children of her own.

Yes, that sharp, hungry voice inside her countered, and Taran wondered if that was the soul of the wolf. *But you have no children and Bard is the first man to smile at you and make you hunger for him. And he has not kissed you. Make sure you rectify that lack before you lose him.*

~~~~~

Bard and Taran crossed into Stonemount two nights later with a plan. It was risky to begin with. Maddix was rumored to have dozens of lower-level magic wielders serving him. The rumors said they searched the kingdom constantly for others touched with magic, to bring them into Maddix's service. Rumors also spoke of the dire fate of any who refused the "invitation" to serve their king. Though Taran and Bard had no magic of their own, they were touched with it, and that could be enough to attract the attention of Maddix's hunters.

If anyone discovered or even guessed they were there to help the family escape, then their task would become dangerous. If Maddix had found them and had them in his clutches, then they had to work quickly, before he convinced them to serve him. Despite all the truth that had been revealed about him, Maddix still had allies and admirers because he could be charming. He could tell a good story and convince people to believe him and support him.

Taran prayed every time she considered their plan, begging Yeshen that Princes Fiera was still in Stonemount. If so, she would try to get word to the princess and ask, as a citizen of Brentonwald, for her assistance.

Their plan was for Taran to settle close to the capitol and establish herself as a healer, with teaching from foreign lands. Everyone was attracted to the new and different, and that would bring people from all classes and trades to her. She would hear the gossip of the kingdom, and ask about other foreigners and magic wielders. Bard would roam at night,
~~~~~

seeking the family with his sense for magic. If Maddix had already found them, then Taran would let it be known her healing gift came from magic, and pray to be taken to the palace to be recruited by Maddix. She would search for the family. And if Yeshen blessed them, she would approach Princess Fiera and beg for her help.

~~~~~

At first, King Maddix didn't believe the first stories about the white-haired healer woman. He was sure his enemies had created the tales to taunt him, to give new life to the ridiculous rumors that he had killed Bianca, and perhaps even to make him afraid.

Every story mentioned how much she looked like Bianca. Why could no one let him forget about her, and the disappointment she had been? Yes, she had given him a son, but Bianca should have given him at least two sons. Perhaps three would have been better, in case one or even two proved disappointing.

Why did everyone dwell on how much the white-haired healer looked like Bianca? Did they think he wanted to be reminded of her? It galled him to have to keep playing at mourning her memory, to hold onto the sympathy of the doubters.

On the other hand ... how much mourning would irritate Fiera so she would take the next decisive step in the galling dance of diplomacy and innuendo between them?

Was the dratted little creature going to keep him hanging for years, leaving him guessing if breaking off the proposed marriage would irritate Brentonwald into declaring war?

How could he drive her out of the palace and make her look like the guilty party when the marriage negotiations broke off entirely?

The bigger question was what he wanted. One day he wanted to win her loyalty and admiration and support. The next day, he wanted nothing more than to frustrate her to the point she gave up and left Stonemount in a temper tantrum.

How did she leave him feeling as if the next move on the chessboard was his, without giving any hint what moves she had made? How could he move when he didn't know what traps she had laid for him?

He had three princesses all lined up, ready to throw themselves and their fathers' or brothers' kingdoms into his clutches, but he had to dispose of Fiera, first.

Why wasn't she a silly creature who believed gossip and rumors and foolish stories? Why couldn't any of the courtiers who supported him make any headway in frightening and frustrating her or even intriguing her, so she made some mistake, let slip her armor of propriety, so Maddix had some clue how to deal with her?

That thought stayed with him, as more stories came to him. His spies
~~~~~

told of the cleverness and insight of the pale healer woman, and how she seemed to see into the minds of those she healed. There was something ghostly, otherworldly about her. As if perhaps spirits spoke to her.

Maybe the ghost of Queen Bianca? That would explain why she looked so much like the late, beloved queen.

Maddix laughed for the first time in weeks, when a stray thought hit him. If only Fiera was silly enough to be frightened away by ghost stories. Specifically, stories of the ghost of Bianca, haunting the palace, determined to drive away her rival for the heart of her grieving husband.

That amusing thought stayed with him, while he sent other servants to learn more about the healer woman. He had to be certain the stories weren't all a conspiracy to make him look like a fool, after all.

It was truly aggravating how few people he could depend on. There was no knowing, from one moment to the next, which loyal servant would turn on him. No way to gauge the balance between fear and bribery to keep them loyal. Even with Jaygo's help, he had struggled for years to learn to finesse people's loyalty and devotion.

He made himself wait, just to be sure. He needed to know more about the woman before he put his plan into motion. If only it could be that simple: smuggle in Bianca's duplicate, hide her in one of the towers charmed to be invisible to nearly everyone, dress her as Bianca, and have her wander the palace gardens in the moonlight until everyone believed her ghost haunted the palace. It wouldn't matter if Fiera believed or not. The belief of everyone else would drive her away in even more disgrace than if she had been frightened herself.

~~~~~

Fiera decided Maddix wasn't just a scheming, lying, selfish brat, but he was a fool. How could he ignore his son like he did? How could he not see what a delightful, clever, adorable child Bianca had left him?

She ached for Bianca whenever she thought of her. Under her fluttery actions and sometimes inane way of speaking, Bianca had had great sensitivity and wisdom that came from a pure heart. She would have protected her son from his father's influence, no matter what it cost her. Fiera supposed she should give thanks to Yeshen every time she had evidence of Maddix's neglect of the child, rather than grinding her teeth in frustration.

Maybe she simply had some hope that the influence of the little boy would soften his heart, if he still had a heart, and make him think beyond his ambitions and ever-growing net of lies and schemes.

"Thank you, Yeshen, that he at least has good nurses to look after the boy," she whispered one afternoon as she came down the hallway to the far wing of the palace holding the nursery.

After Bianca had died, Maddix had made a great show of regret when
~~~~~

he had the nursery moved as far away from his own living quarters as possible. He pretended great sorrow over Bianca, and pain at the sight of his son. Lord Anselm's spies, and the ambassador himself, knew Maddix simply wanted to silence the boy's wailing cries for his mother.

Today, Fiera was more than an hour early for her daily visit with Maxin. Lord Anselm had been away from the palace for a fortnight, and she intended to meet him on his way to the ambassadorial wing. The silence charm they both wore, to facilitate private conversation, worked best when walking out in public, with plenty of people around them. The magic didn't create silence but generated an illusion of many voices to cover what they said. The ambassadorial quarters were heavy with all sorts of spying charms embedded in the walls and woven into the curtains and rugs. Anselm had detected their presence the very first day he arrived in Stonemount. Fiera still found a little amusement in contemplating Maddix's frustration with his spies and the minor magic wielders who produced nothing for him to use against ambassadors and other diplomats.

"Oh, Highness." The afternoon nursemaid, Fern, went pale and dropped into a deep curtsey, her hand still gripping the handle of the nursery door. "I'm sorry—"

"It's all right." Fiera smiled to smother the surge of irritation she felt more and more toward Maddix. Just more proof of what a monster he was under his charm and good looks, that servants automatically felt a flash of terror at the slightest hint they might have done something wrong. "I'm early."

"Yes, but I just put him down for his nap," the girl explained quickly.

"Then the timing is perfect. You go enjoy an extra long respite, and I'll stay with him, and tell him twice as many stories when he wakes. You've certainly earned some free time."

"Oh, thank you, Highness." Fern blinked tears away and curtsied again. She took a handful of steps backward from the door, bobbing another curtsey before turning and scurrying away.

Fiera shook her head. She wished there was some way she could take all the nurses as well as little Maxin away with her when she eventually left Stonemount. Unfortunately, the only way she could have any authority over the little boy, to protect him, was to become his step-mother, and she could think of several dozen unpleasant tasks she would prefer to being Maddix's bride.

She held her breath and slowly turned the knob. Maxin could not possibly be asleep already, although she knew the little charmer was learning some small deceits already, starting with pretending to be asleep as soon as his caretakers put him in his crib. She wanted to catch him climbing out of his crib. The little boy fascinated her. How could someone so small and chubby, who toddled around with charming clumsiness, managed to be so agile when he needed it?

The curtains had been pulled closed but rippled slightly at the touch of the warm afternoon breezes. Fiera nodded approval. She had finally won that battle. The older nurses insisted on closing up windows tight all the time, while the younger nurses advocated fresh air, as long as the little prince didn't get a chill. In the soft flashes of dim light across the shadowy nursery, she spied the crib.

Empty already.

She muffled a chuckle and stepped into the room, looking around for Maxin.

There he was, toddling toward the wall, holding his hands out.

Purple sparks danced across his fingertips for several heartbeats.

Fiera froze, losing her breath and instantly chilled by this evidence of magical potential in the child.

She reached blindly behind herself to pull the door closed, terrified that the wrong eyes would see those purple sparks and tell Maddix. The worst thing in the world for that little boy was for his father to know he had magic. If Maddix didn't warp the innocent child for his own profit, then Durmad would find out. Fiera didn't want to even contemplate the disaster that would be, if the rebel despot got his hands on the future king of a nation as powerful as Stonemount and trained him up as a willing servant.

All those thoughts froze as blue sparks spun three times around on the wall in front of Maxin and it turned transparent. A little girl with red curls sat on a little bench in front of the wall and clapped her hands. The children giggled and reached for each other's hands. Blue and purple sparks flared up from the contact.

"Sshh," the little girl said. "Mama is sleeping." She looked over her shoulder, most likely at her mother, somewhere across the cobblestones area behind her.

"Play?" Maxin said.

Fiera muffled a hurting sigh at the loneliness and pleading in the little prince's voice. She stood perfectly still, praying she vanished into the shadows, as the little girl nodded and the children clasped hands. A blue haze washed over her as she stepped through the hole in the wall. Giggling, she reached into the pocket of her dress and pulled out a muffin. The children toddled over to the corner of the nursery filled with Maxin's toys, sat down on the floor, and divided the muffin. They dropped crumbs on their clothes, just like ordinary children everywhere.

Fiera knew there was a storage room on the other side of that wall, because she had seen the nursemaids coming out of it with fresh linens for Maxin's room. So common sense said that doorway was magic. Which of the children had created it? How had they found each other? Who was the girl, and where was she? Somewhere hidden in the palace? Fiera believed Maddix had dozens of magic wielders stashed away in the palace and the many outbuildings of the palace grounds. Did his people know about the little girl? If they did, was someone watching on the other side of the doorway, ready to report at any moment that his son had magic?

How could she protect Maxin? How could she protect that little girl? It was one thing to be an adult and stand against Maddix's charm and lies and threats, but how could a child resist?

Fiera stood in the shadows and prayed for guidance, and watched the children play with Maxin's vast menagerie of cloth animals. Her legs hadn't yet begun to ache from her stiff stillness when a woman's voice came softly through the doorway. The little girl leaped to her feet.

"Mama is waking up." She giggled and pressed her two fingers to her lips. "Sshh!"

Maxin followed her to the doorway. He looked sad, but he didn't cry, didn't protest, didn't demand she stay. Fiera held her breath in a moment of fear that he would follow the little girl through that doorway.

The girl stepped through, and a heartbeat later the wall reappeared, as solid as before. Maxin settled on the floor and heaved a loud, deep sigh that brought tears to Fiera's eyes.

"Bye-bye." Purple sparks danced on two fingertips as he reached out and patted the wall.

Fiera closed her eyes, asked for guidance, then took a deep breath and moved away from the wall.

"Maxin?"

"FeeFee!" The little boy's face lit up and he leaped to his feet and ran to her, arms outstretched and giggling. "Sto-ey?"

"Oh, you always want a story. Wouldn't you rather do something else?" Fiera narrowed her eyes at him as she settled him on her hip. "How about a nap?"

"No!" He giggled and shook his head.

"Oh, all right." She let out a long sigh, earning more giggles.

Fiera settled down in the cushioned chair by the window. She wanted to ask about the little girl and the purple sparks and where that doorway led. Knowing might be vital, but she couldn't bring herself to ask him today. In a few days, after she had asked for advice from Anselm.

Chapter Eleven

"Indeed ..." Anselm's eyes narrowed and his steps slowed as they walked down the long corridor from the public chambers of the palace, heading toward the diplomatic wing.

A nearly inaudible snap, like an enormous insect slamming into a screen reinforced with magic, made Fiera flinch. Someone was employing magic to listen in on their conversation. The murmur of voices in the silence spell surged in response. She fought a flicker of a smile, knowing that whoever had sent that spell was hearing someone say particularly nasty things about him or her right that moment. Served them right, eavesdropping.

"I have complete faith in you, Highness," he said and turned his head just enough to meet her gaze.

"But?" Now she smiled.

"Oh, there is no 'but,' except perhaps to apologize yet again for putting such a heavy burden on you. Yet to protect an innocent child, to snatch him from the jaws of corruption before they snap shut on him ... there is no higher, more honorable calling."

"How?" She glanced around, fearing someone had overheard, because the ache in her throat felt as if she had shouted it. "I have no authority whatsoever."

"You have many admirers and supporters here in Maddix's court."

"Lord Anselm, you know as well as I do that means nothing. Even the fear surrounding me, first as the princess of Brentonwald, and then as the possible next queen, will not protect me. Say I were to snatch up Maxin tonight and leap into a carriage and head for the border. Even the nobles who are honorable and brave enough to stand against Maddix will not support me. He is the boy's father, and I am not his mother."

"True." He caught hold of her hand and patted it, offering comfort. And earning a few gasps from several of the people around them in the corridor. Likely astounded at either Anselm's boldness, or worried by his familiarity with the princess. "There must be another, safer option than kidnapping. We must protect the child."

Fiera swallowed hard against an odd feeling that she would laugh and weep at the same time.

"The only other option is to gain authority over the boy by ..." She sighed. "Marriage."

"I refuse to believe we must come to that dire choice. My people have nearly all the players in place, all the proof, to destroy the spies and plotters who created the false correspondence, and to place nearly all the blame on Maddix himself. The world will see it as a scheme to force you into an unwanted marriage."

"Shaming Maddix once again, and perhaps putting him in such a weak position that he succumbs to Durmad's threats and instructions completely. We have been blessed and granted more time than we thought, by Maddix's very nature. He has believed since we were children that he knew better than everyone, and his first reaction when given an order was to find another way, his way. We cannot risk driving him under Durmad's control. I will not risk Maxin's safety and his very soul."

"At what sacrifice, Highness?"

"I am afraid. I admit it freely." Her voice cracked faintly, and that made her want to laugh. She called up the memory of the children laughing together. That steadied her and gave her strength. "It is easy to say I trust Yeshen, yet what good is it if I refuse to act on that trust?"

"You were born for this, Highness. I am honored to serve you."

~~~~~

Until she settled in this town, Taran had never really thought about the freedom and safety she had enjoyed, living in the Aerbach Valley. Here in this town, she couldn't go barefoot all day, couldn't drop her chores to pursue an interesting insect or plant, couldn't sleep the hottest part of the day away and roam as long as the moon hung high in the sky. Worst of all, she lost Bard's company. He skulked in the shadows of the forest far from the edge of town and only dared come meet her in the darkest part of the night.

"I was a fool, to complain when something didn't suit me. I had no idea how blessed I was, until now," she told Bard, on that rare night when she could slip from the lodgings in the cottage of Hannah, a midwife, to meet with him. They settled in a clearing by a small pool that reminded her of the pool by her childhood home.

He whined and nuzzled her hand. The new moon had come and two days remained before the sliver in the sky would be large enough to allow him to change into a man again.

"I ask as many questions as I can, but it isn't wise to let people have any idea what I really want, on a hunt this important. And isn't that a sad way to live?" Taran snorted when Bard put his paws on her leg so he could lick her chin. Then she sighed, tipped her head back and closed her eyes. "Shall I find you some clothes to replace your rags, when the moon is large enough, so you can come into the town and perhaps eat a meal at the inn with me? There is a dance in three nights. Do you know how to dance? Do you remember how to dance? Could you teach me the dances you know?"
~~~~~

Taran chafed against the precautions Bard had insisted on. The forest was a long way away from the town market, where she offered advice and compounded medicines, teaching some of her mother's potions and powders and techniques to Daran, the apothecary, in exchange for supplies. How could Bard protect her if he was so far away?

They walked back to the town in silence and Taran muffled her sigh of regret as she put her shoes back on at the edge of the forest. Bard whined and nuzzled her hand as she stepped out into the open, and she paused to caress his head and down his neck in farewell.

She dreamed that night of *a knife made of the sickle moon. It slit her open and a silver-white wolf leaped out of her skin. Before the wolf could flee into the darkness, the moon-knife slashed again, and Taran stepped out of the wolf's skin. Then another slash, and something that was half-woman, half-wolf leaped out and pirouetted across the whitewashed meadow in the scorching moonlight, until Bard-wolf jumped down from the sky, reared back on his hind legs, tipped back the wolf's head so his man-face peered out, and sprouted hands from his paws. The two odd creatures laughed and danced across the meadow.*

~~~~~

The next day, Taran assisted Hannah with a delivery. Two men from the palace tracked her down at the house while the new baby's father poured the customary tankard of honey mead to offer a toast and blessing on the newborn's life.

"Oh, give the lass a chance to wash and rest," Hannah, the elderly midwife said when the two big, dangerous-looking courtiers told Taran to come with them. "It needs more magic than twenty healers can muster, to cure whatever ails the king now."

"Shut your mouth, old woman," the bearded one snarled. He raised his hand as if he would slap her, but the newborn's father and his brothers stepped forward, warning in their eyes. He lowered his hand and stepped back, but menace and pride burned in his eyes.

Taran didn't want any bloodshed or broken bones or arrests on her behalf, so she stepped forward and gestured for the two men to lead the way. They didn't introduce themselves to her, but Hannah whispered to her, gesturing at the men, naming them Clancy and Baethon. They were known as King Maddix's eyes and ears, and his heavy, brutal hands.

"After I stop at my room, of course, and pick up my supplies. There's not much I can do for the king with my bare hands," she said, just as smug smiles of triumph touched their cruel faces.

"Don't you have magic? You're a healer," the other one, Baethon grumbled.

"There is more to healing than magic. Yeshen filled the world with hundreds of plants and minerals that heal, and we would be poor stewards of his bounty if we did not use it to help each other." In her
~~~~~

words, Taran heard an echo of Eyrian teaching her what felt like a lifetime ago. She bit her lip against adding that King Maddix needed healing that started with a good slap across his arrogant mouth and a good thrashing across his richly attired bottom. "If the king has sent for me to perform some magic task, then it would be wise not to waste his time, and go back to the palace without me." She spread her hands. "I have no magic, command no magic."

"He's got more magic wielders than he knows what to do with," Clancy muttered. He shook his head. "No, he's not looking for magic. He's looking for ghosts." Then he chuckled and exchanged nastily amused glances with Baethon, before gesturing for Taran to lead the way.

What was that supposed to mean? Taran fought down shudders, as she realized she and Bard had not planned well enough or foreseen every eventuality. If the king didn't want magic from her, what did he want?

When she returned to her room at the midwife's house to pack her few possessions, Taran leaned out the window and whistled, soft and low, in the pattern she and Bard had agreed on. That was all she could do. Clancy and Baethon didn't look like patient men, so she doubted she even had time to wait to see if Bard responded to the signal. She made a quick prayer that he would follow her to the palace, in safety.

"Took you long enough for so little," Clancy grumbled, when Taran came out of her tiny bedroom. He stood close enough to the little door to almost get hit in the face with the frail panel. Taran wondered if he would have come in after her in another moment.

She noticed immediately that a meat pie, which was to have been dinner, had vanished from the pan set to cool on the table. Taran caught the aroma of basil, pepper and onions when Baethon exhaled. She doubted either man would do anything but laugh if she demanded they repay Hannah for the food they had stolen. However, Eyrian had showed her clever ways to handle thieves, making them punish themselves.

"Oh, good. That matter's taken care of." She picked up the pan the meat pie had baked on and set it next to the washtub full of cold, scummy water.

"Eh, what matter is that?" Clancy followed her movements with a frown.

"The constable asked Hannah to help him solve a murder. Gossip in town says the woman died because her husband poisoned some very fine ham she bought from a butcher, who had been a suitor of hers. The husband didn't like her going to the butcher's shop. Gossip says he poisoned the ham because she had a habit of nibbling while she cooked. Hannah baked a meat pie with that ham. The constable is going to offer it to the husband, and after he's eaten, mention that it was made with the ham his wife was using when she died. Depending on his reaction, we'll know if he was guilty or not."

"What if the ham was poisoned?" Baethon asked, turning pale.

"Well, we don't know if it was. But if so, then his wife will have some justice before the day is out." Taran brushed her hands off and picked up the sack with her few possessions.

"How did he know the woman was poisoned?" He stopped her with a hand on her arm when she reached to open the door.

"Oh, she suffered cramps, and the sweats, and a powerful fierce headache. Far too quickly to be an ordinary illness." She shoved the door open, stepped out, and fought not to laugh when the two men exchanged worried frowns.

Those two idiots ate the pie so quickly, they didn't notice the meat was chicken and there was more vegetables than meat to the filling. A midwife was a very respectable position in a town of this size, but Hannah certainly couldn't afford to use ham when it wasn't a holiday.

"Before nightfall, the good woman fell into a delirium and died crying about evil spirits coming from the graveyard to snatch at her. If only Hannah had been called soon enough, she could have done something." Taran sighed.

"What would she have done?" Clancy demanded.

"Oh, made the poor woman drink a bucketful of emetic. Brine and fish oil is the best, of course." She tugged her clothes straight and watched her two sweating companions from the corner of her eye.

"What does that do?" Baethon frowned. Taran hoped he hadn't started to suspect she was tweaking his nose for his thievery.

"It's to make her vomit up all the poison still in her stomach. The sooner the better. That's the easy part, of course." She muffled a gasp when both men hooked their arms through hers and doubled their pace.

"What's after that?"

"Well, eat nothing but stale bread for two days, and drink warm milk and water mixed with charcoal dust. To sop up any poison that might have gotten into the blood, you see."

"Doesn't sound too hard," Clancy muttered. He cursed and gestured at a soldier standing in the town square. The man nodded and ran to the livery stables adjoining the main inn.

"No, not really. Not compared to the charms that need to be cast. Those take time, but purging does buy some time." Taran smiled brightly and looked around when they came to an abrupt stop.

"What else?" Baethon demanded. He cursed under his breath and snatched at the reins of the first horse the soldier brought out from the stables.

"Alms to the parents of newborn children. The more, the better. Such young souls are still able to speak directly to Yeshen, and they'll ask blessings on the alms giver. And twice the alms to the midwife who delivered them." She let out a squeak when the big man grasped her waist and lifted her into the saddle. "Fortunately, Hannah heals and is a midwife, so that saves time. If someone were poisoned. But she'll be here if the constable needs her, so there's nothing to worry about. I wonder how long ago he took that pie and had the husband eat it," she mused. She pretended to be deep in thought and bit her lip against a chortle as Clancy and Baethon fell into a hurried discussion with the soldier, giving him instructions full of curses and pointing and gesturing. And, to her satisfaction, a leather purse that looked to be quite heavy with coins.

Taran wondered if she would have a chance to come back to visit Hannah and explain the mystery of the sudden largesse from the two courtiers.

She looked around as the two sweating, pale men led her away from the town at a rapid trot. Taran didn't see a dark shadow slink from the forest to follow, but she thought she felt Bard's presence. She thanked Yeshen, and prayed for wisdom in the hours ahead of her.

What did the king want from her?

~~~~~

When they reached the palace, the two men hurried to put Taran into the care of a servant and raced away, throwing promises over their shoulders that they would return shortly. From the carefully neutral expression on the boy's face, Taran guessed her two escorts were not well liked. She saw the slight twitching at the corners of his mouth, the gleam of interest in his eyes, but she knew better than to offer information. Helping the servants mock their betters might be amusing, but she could find herself in trouble, with no real friends to stand with her. No one but Bard, of course.

Could he find a way into the palace grounds without being seen? She had to find a way to escape to the gardens at night. That was the best place to meet him.

The servant boy said nothing as he led Taran from the palace gates to the gardens. No explanations, no questions. He led her to a walled garden, opened the iron gate, and gestured for her to go inside before he turned and walked away.

Taran stepped inside. She didn't like this garden. The tingling in her skin hinted at a residue of some magic still lingering in the soil. With her eyes closed, she could see something powerful and yet ill had resided once in that muddy hole in the ground. Taran settled down on a patch of shady grass, far from the depression in the ground that stank of stagnant water. What had happened here?

Taran nearly laughed aloud when the answer slipped into her mind. Of course, gardens meant Princess Arden of Westerland, with her
~~~~~

plantwise magic. Everyone in the surrounding countries had heard some version of the tale, how she had created a magic apple tree to protect Westerland, but it was stolen and ended up in Stonemount. When King Maddix lied and claimed it had been a gift from powerful enchanters, that warped the magic and began to poison the kingdom. Some believed that was why Queen Bianca had died after giving birth to a stillborn daughter. Taran had discounted the stories that said the tree had followed Arden back to Westerland, but it seemed even those were true.

So, this was the place where it had all happened. Certainly there must have been a great deal of poison in this place, for it to linger despite all Arden's healing work. Taran shivered, wondering how much more evil Maddix would commit, to cover up his lies and crimes, and how soon the poison would grow and spread across the kingdom again.

"Blessed Yeshen," Taran whispered, "let me find the child and her parents soon, and spirit them away before the poison of this place enters her soul."

~~~~~

That peasant woman looked very little like Bianca. Maddix leaned closer against the spy-hole in the wall, watching her. It would take a great deal to convince anyone that she was the ghost of Bianca. Heat rose up from his stomach and tightened around his throat, fury that Clancy and Baethon had bungled this task as well.

This woman might be a healer, but if she had any magic at her disposal, she should be reacting to the remnants of tainted magic Arden had left behind and Alastor and Wren hadn't purged yet. Those two were gallingly slow in cleansing the garden, which just showed how little strength they had. Or it revealed how strong Arden's magic had been. He didn't want to consider that, because it meant he had seriously miscalculated when he changed his plans to pursue Bianca and tossed aside Arden.

No, this woman was just another stupid peasant. At least she seemed to be cleaner than most. What was wrong with her, to just sit there with her eyes closed, head tilted back, soaking up the sunshine? Shouldn't she be curious about the little sanctuary Fiera had created? Why was she sitting on the ground, far from Fiera's table and chair?

He should just declare this attempt a total loss, walk away, and find some way to punish Clancy and Baethon. They really were becoming more liability than useful tools.

Yet he couldn't step away from the spy-hole. Something ached in him, and he knew he was a maudlin fool to let himself slip back to those foolish memories. Still, was it so wrong, to remember when he had been truly happy? Bianca had adored him, as a wife should, and when she was alive, all his plans had been coming together perfectly.
~~~~~

This woman was no Bianca. Yes, she was pale and slim and had a natural grace, but Bianca had been delicate like feathers and soap bubbles, while this woman had an underlying strength like a wild animal. Bianca would have bled if she put her bare foot on the grass, but this woman pried off her rough shoes and sank her bare feet into the grass with entirely too much delight. Clean her up, dress her hair, hang jewelry on her, put her in an elegant dress, perhaps she might superficially pass for Bianca. At a distance.

Enough to trick the fools of the Court into thinking a ghost wandered the palace?

Some of the heat in his belly cooled as he considered following through on his plan. With some adaptations. Yes, he might still have some fun, convincing people Bianca's ghost had come to haunt the palace. Certainly, this woman could never be allowed to speak. She would probably have a rough voice. She probably brayed like a donkey when she laughed, instead of sounding like tinkling bells.

But a ghost didn't need to speak.

How delicious, if he could drive Fiera away while making her look like a fool, frightened by stories of ghosts. He imagined she could be easily influenced by the fears of all those foolish servants whom she treated with far more respect and kindness than they deserved.

Yes, he decided. He would take the chance on playing an amusing trick on the court. If this peasant failed him, he could have her destroyed quickly and quietly, and no one the wiser.

Chapter Twelve

Baethon returned alone and led Taran through the evening shadows to a tower on the far side of the palace. From the sounds and smells, the moss climbing the stonework and the lack of ornamentation on this wing of the palace, she guessed this was an old section, relegated to servants. Her new quarters were in the tower, with an outside entrance. He instructed her never to step outside in the daylight. She was to spend her nights roaming the gardens of the palace, letting herself be seen, but never speak to anyone. She was to wear the clothes and jewelry waiting in her room and arrange her hair like a grand lady.

Taran wanted to laugh and ask how he thought she would know how a grand lady wore her hair, but the big man's sweat smelled of fear and anger, and emetic. When the emetic took effect, it could be painful. Especially if he drank too much. She didn't want to push him to the point of lashing out at her. She thanked him and took the three heavy keys he handed her, and nodded compliance when he told her to lock the three doors between the tower entrance and her room on the top floor. He shifted uneasily back and forth until she stepped inside and locked the first door, then he ran.

The stairs circled the wall of the tower, taking her up to the second floor where she found stores of food, a vat of water, an oven built into the wall, and enough pots and pans and dishes and utensils to serve dozens of people. What did the king expect of her, to outfit her so thoroughly? Then she climbed up to the third floor.

That floor was filled with enough dresses and shoes, veils and cloaks, scarves, gloves, and petticoats for twenty women. All in shades of pale blue, silver, cream, and ivory. Brocade and silk and gossamer and velvet. Taran shuddered and nearly dropped the keys when it struck her that the clothes were fine enough for a queen. She had heard enough stories of Queen Bianca since settling in Stonemount to know how the late queen dressed and what she looked like. People had remarked on her pale coloring and wondered how much she would look like Bianca, if dressed up "fancy-like." Several had even speculated on how King Maddix would react, if he could see her.

"Please, Yeshen …" Taran didn't even want to put into words the chilling suspicion swirling through the back of her mind.

She took a deep breath and hurried up the stairs to the fourth floor.

She found a sitting room and bedroom, comfortably furnished, including an alcove with a screen and a deep bathing tub. A tiny snort of laughter escaped her when she wondered just how much work it would take to haul enough water up from the kitchen on the second floor to have a hot bath. Someone hadn't planned this hiding place of hers very well. If she had been asked, she would have put the kitchen on the first floor, to save steps in hauling water, and rigged a bucket and rope on a pulley, to haul water up to the bathing room on the second floor, with a handy hatch for pouring water out through the wall when she was finished bathing. But no one had asked her, had they?

At least she had the keys to her prison, to lock herself inside and lock others out, apparently. How long would that freedom of movement last?

As long as she obeyed the rules Baethon had given her, apparently.

What did King Maddix want from her?

How long could she avoid giving it to him, if his request was immoral?

"Yeshen, guard me, guide me, bless my task and my search here," she whispered, and set down her sack on the table.

If she was to wander at night, could she spy and eavesdrop, and learn about the family? Perhaps this was a blessing from Yeshen?

If only she dared to seek out Princess Fiera and ask for her help. Perhaps after she had learned her way around the palace and could sneak and hide and listen and spy and become a shadow that no one noticed.

"Please, Bard, find me soon."

~~~~~

Common sense guided Taran as she prepared to follow Baethon's orders. She chose a veil that fell nearly to her waist. A veil would blur her features until she could steal glimpses of the grand ladies of the court and mimic how they arranged their hair. She chose the simplest of the lovely gowns, not because she feared soiling the rich materials and damaging the elaborate beading and embroidery, but because it fit the best. Taran's days penned up in the tower, staying silent and avoiding attention, would be spent adjusting the clothes so she could breathe when she wore them.

Finally, she was ready to go down and wander. No doubt the two brute courtiers who brought her here would be watching to see how she performed. If they realized that she had been toying with them over the meat pie, they would be in a foul mood and eager for some reason to punish her.

She sensed someone hiding in the shadows of the overgrown bushes at the foot of the tower when she stepped outside. The scent on the warm night air was heavy with musk and spices. Clancy and Baethon wore no perfumes. This was someone new. Taran stopped short, one slippered foot extended. She raised a hand to her throat and gripped her silver amulet as
~~~~~

the wolf in her soul growled softly. She tried to measure the strength of the crescent moon's silver light as it hung just above the garden wall. Was it strong enough to turn her into a wolf if she needed to defend herself?

"Bard?" she whispered, praying her friend waited in the shadows, ready to leap to her side.

"You don't sound like a ghost," a man said, repressed laughter making his voice rich. He stepped from the shadows, tall and broad-shouldered, gray-eyed and golden-haired. He wore no crown, but the sneer that curled his lip and the confidence in his stance named him.

"King Maddix." Taran nodded respectfully, though she respected the throne more than the man who currently lounged in the seat. "Am I supposed to be a ghost?" She moved out onto the grass, putting the gravel path between her and the king.

That earned her a snort, and he bowed extravagantly to her. "Didn't those two imbeciles mention that you resemble my dear, departed Bianca? In a coarse, unwashed sort of way." He walked in a wide circle around her, looking her up and down with a studying gaze that was almost a palpable touch. Taran fought the wolf's growl that filled her throat.

Her suspicions had been too right. These clothes had belonged to the dead queen, given to her create a resemblance. Why would Maddix want his dead wife's duplicate to wander the palace gardens?

"What is it you wish of me, Majesty?"

Maddix grinned, and Taran fought a warm trembling that shot through her body. Why did he have to be so handsome and so villainous at heart?

Where was Bard? She far preferred Bard's scarred, pale features, his dirt and rags and pain, to the luxury and pampered, golden good looks standing before her.

"You are a puzzle. A liar." He chuckled when she stiffened. "I respect liars. They aren't so foolish as to think that honesty and honor will grease their path through life. You call yourself a healer, yet I don't sense healing magic in you. Why do you pose as a healer?"

"It is no pose, Majesty. My mother and her mother before her were healers, and she trained me to be a healer."

"Hmm, I suppose that could be true. But I have a sense of magic, thanks to the Gifted healers in my family line." His eyes saddened for a moment, and Taran wondered who touched his memories. Then Maddix shook his head and his eyes brightened with humor. "You do have magic." He gestured at her throat.

"None that I control." She touched the amulet. The silver sizzled under her fingertips, responding to the moonlight. "My mother gave this to me when I was a child and nearly died of the fever that devastated our village. It keeps me … whole. I cannot work magic through it."

"It is foolish to tell others your weaknesses, healer." Maddix gestured out into the garden and offered his bent arm, as if she were a grand lady.

"Anyone who tries to take the amulet from me will not like what happens."

"A threat?" He shrugged when she refused to take his arm and turned to walk out under the moonlight.

Taran followed him because retreating to her tower room felt dangerous. Out in the garden, she had a chance to run and fight. She could discard her amulet and turn into a wolf.

Bard, where are you? Come to me.

Best to quiet the wolf in her and be humble and placating. Perhaps Maddix would be so amused by her, she could get information from him, discern if the family were here. She would need to be careful, though. Her mother had taught her dishonorable people expected everyone around them to scheme and cheat and lie and act with dishonor. Maddix would misread everything she said, no matter how innocent.

If he hadn't found the family yet, she couldn't give him a hint of their existence. And if they were his prisoners or his pampered guests, she couldn't let him suspect she had come to find and free them.

"Not a threat, Majesty, but a warning. I will have no control over what happens if my amulet is stolen and the defensive magic my mother created is unleashed."

"Ah, then you are being clever, pretending to be foolishly trusting. Trick your enemies into thinking you weak." He clasped his hands behind his back and smiled amiably at her as they strolled side-by-side.

Taran shuddered at the illusion of friendly companionship. The king of Stonemount wanted something from her.

"Aren't you curious why you're to dress up as Bianca and play at being a ghost?" He gestured at her clothes. "I'm having a little fun at my supposed bride's expense. She spends her time ingratiating herself with all the fools and making them admire her and whisper—" He broke off with a frown and gnawed his bottom lip for a moment. "I want the fools to whisper and believe they've seen a ghost. If people say that Bianca can't rest in peace because she's jealous, or she fears for me, and if the right people grow frightened, they could frighten even Fiera. Enough to make her run home. Quite a comedown, don't you think? From potential bride and queen to frightened little fool. And nothing her almighty father can do about it because she fled of her own choice." Maddix chuckled, his eyes brightening again.

Taran shivered, catching an odd, bitter undertone that made her wonder if that was the odor of madness.

"But none of that really matters, does it? You're here to perform a task, and I'll wager you're too clever to repeat anything you hear or see."

Maddix's eyes narrowed as he looked her up and down again, then turned and strode down the path.

Fascinated despite herself, Taran walked beside him. It was like listening to a haunted tale, knowing something horrid would happen, but unable to walk away from the storyteller. Maddix said nothing more about her apparent task of pretending to be Bianca's ghost but gave her a tour of the gardens for the next hour. He couldn't remember a single plant's name. He paid more attention to the events that took place in the garden. Where a particular lord was caught kissing a woman not his wife, or where someone was found stabbed, or where the gardener found a skeleton when a hole was dug for a new tree.

At last, he stopped by the gates into the walled garden where the apple tree had been. Maddix sighed and frowned at the closed gates. "There are so few I can trust to do their job right." His eyes narrowed. "Can I trust you?"

"Majesty," Taran ventured, "I will do my best to pretend to be a ghost, but I don't know if I can pretend to be a queen's ghost." She tried not to breathe. Madness and evil did have a smell; sweet, pungent, sickly, sour, and hot, all rolled up together, spinning inside her stomach in a hard, spiked ball.

Maddix shook his head and turned away. "This is ridiculous. I need some sleep. Lots of work to do in the morning. Arrangements to make. Idiots to send packing. But I think you'll do nicely. Meet me here at moonrise tomorrow." He walked away without waiting for a response.

"We can't leave," Bard said, his voice coming from the garden shadows behind her.

Taran shuddered as she turned to face him. Bard leaped from his hiding place and enfolded her in his arms. Just before she closed her eyes, she saw that he wore palace livery instead of his usual rags.

Bard's skin felt warm and smelled like herbs and fresh rain on tilled fields. His arms closed around her like hard, strong vines, and Taran clung to him. She hid her face in the open V where Bard's shirt hung open, and the coarse hairs of his chest tickled her nose.

"We can't leave," Bard repeated, as he rocked them back and forth slowly. "He will send people after you. You can't spend all your time in hiding or wolf shape. Not with our task incomplete."

"I'm afraid."

"I'm afraid for you."

"There is so much evil in him, but he would be shocked, I think, if someone accused him to his face. That is madness, isn't it?"

Bard laughed, the sound vibrating against her cheekbone pressed against his chest.

"Did we make a mistake, coming here? Kalista said they are here in

Stonemount. Were we wrong to think the king could have found them by now?" Taran sighed and moved back to look into his blue eyes. Something throbbed deep inside her, pleased and warmed when Bard resisted, holding her close against him.

"These gardens, the palace complex, are huge. I explored as a wolf, until the moon rose." He shrugged and tapped his nose with the side of his finger. "I envy the wolf his sharp senses, at times like these. There are many places to hide, and so much ground to search."

"And you can't go as a wolf during the day, or people would see you and call out a hunt. Wolves don't belong in this stone city."

He hooked his arm through hers and started them on a slow stroll down the garden path. Taran smiled crookedly and let him lead. She liked the vast difference between her walk with the king and walking now with Bard.

"Play along with him and his men, earn their trust—"

"What little trust they have for anyone," she interrupted, her voice so sour it changed the taste in her mouth.

"True. Earn their trust, win as much freedom as you can. I will explore as a wolf, and we will meet every night and compare what we have learned during the day. In two weeks' time, if we have found no clues, then we will leave."

"How?" she whispered. "By then, they might not let me leave."

"You will remove your amulet and give it to me. I will walk out as a man, a servant of the palace, and you will leave as a white wolf, and return to your true self when we are safely away." Bard tipped her head up, two fingers under her chin, and smiled encouragingly. Taran mirrored his smile, but she doubted the expression reached her eyes any more than it reached his.

~~~~~

Despite his pleasure in creating Bianca's ghost to frighten Fiera, Maddix seethed. The healing of the walled garden, cleansing Arden's wretched poison from the soil, was taking too long. Alastor and Wren could only work at night, of course, to prevent the court and especially the nobles who didn't fear him from finding out what he was doing. Maddix was infuriated to discover how many nobles enjoyed frolicking through the gardens until dawn. There was no predicting where they would go as they played their inane games and conducted mock hunts. He couldn't order them to stop. People would ask questions. People would spy. People would find out about Wren and Alastor and their task. Maddix knew the members of his court, and for the first time he wasn't amused by their tendency to ask more questions when they were denied answers, and to do the opposite of what they were ordered to do. Wherever the nobles didn't play on any given night, the gardeners were at work. They often
~~~~~

worked at night, to prevent inconveniencing or irritating the nobles. Last night walking with the white-haired healer had been one of the few nights the garden was empty. Far too many nights, Alastor and Wren got halfway to the walled garden and had to turn back, to keep from being seen. Maddix suspected Clancy and Baethon found some amusement in reporting these roadblocks and frustrations.

If Wren and her husband could work on the walled garden one night in every four, that was unusual progress. A week before bringing Taran to the palace to play his ghost game, Maddix took to spying on the couple whenever they did manage to reach the garden to work. He had a peephole in a sheltered niche in the wall. He had used it often since Fiera made the garden her sanctuary during the day. Every time he used it, he heard in his furious imagination all the voices mocking him. Wasn't he the king? Didn't he have the right to know everything that happened in his palace, in his kingdom, without having to hide in shadows and eavesdrop, or even ask like a weak, pathetic penitent?

He justified the peephole with the need to hear any plots Fiera might try to hatch with his formerly loyal subjects. The niche was large enough for him to stand in, so he was almost invisible in the shadows of several large trees growing close to the wall. He had nothing to fear.

More important, he had learned nothing yet. She was always alone. She sat at a little table and read, or wrote in her journal, or wrote letters. No one came to speak with her. She had a galling habit of walking around the perimeter of the empty little garden, arms wrapped around herself, a pensive expression on her face, often turned to the sky. He couldn't comprehend what she was doing.

Nor could he make sense of what Wren and Alastor were doing. Tonight, this first night since Taran took up her role of Bianca's ghost, Maddix watched them. As usual, they walked around the enclosed garden, circling the spot in the ground where the apple tree once stood, not saying much, spilling sparks of blue and green magic from their fingertips. He felt some satisfaction mixed with his irritation. This was taking far too long, and just proved how vicious Arden had been, the damage she had done to him, leaving so much poison behind herself to trouble Stonemount. What right did she have to lash back at his kingdom as she had done? He hadn't stolen her wretched little tree. It wasn't fair to penalize him, or any of his people, for what Jaygo had chosen to do. And besides, she would have brought the tree with her when she married him. She would have been more happy than a dirty little farmer princess like her deserved before he arranged for her to die giving birth to his son.

Someday, when Stonemount was larger and more powerful, and all those vicious stories about his actions had faded to whispers, he would ensure she and her idiot brother and their pathetic little excuse of a kingdom paid for their rebellion against the fate he had decreed for them.

Maddix muffled a curse, only then realizing he had heard the woman say, "Steward."

This was worse than he thought. Were they in league with that sanctimonious, sneaking spy who claimed he spoke for Yeshen?

"Can we trust him?" Alastor said.

Well, at least one of them had some common sense.

"We have to," Wren said, lowering her voice and her hands, so the sparks of blue magic swirling out of her fingertips faded away. "What is our alternative? We can't give our child to Durmad."

"We wouldn't have her without Durmad's help."

"Are you sure? If Steward is right, she was born too early because Durmad's servants attacked us. All he did was undo the damage his people caused." She pressed both hands over her abdomen, as if she felt a sudden pain.

"But we promised," her husband said.

"And what about all the things Steward says he will do with her, do to her? Can we in all good conscience allow her mind and spirit to be warped by him? If she has the great potential that Steward says —"

"Steward says," he growled. "All we have is Steward's word. It's his word against Durmad's. What has Steward done for us?"

"Offered us hope," Wren said.

"Hope is useless when there's nowhere in the world we can go that Durmad's people can't find us."

"What about Westerland?"

Maddix muffled another growl, and resolved right then and there, he wouldn't bother trying to woo them and convince them they were better off serving him. He would take their child from them and throw them in the deepest prison, and they would regret coming anywhere near Stonemount. The gall of them, thinking Westerland was a better choice.

Chapter Thirteen

Maddix seethed as he left the peephole. What would Durmad do to him if he didn't turn Wren and her husband and their child over to him immediately?

But did Durmad have to know?

That crystalized what he had considered. He would silence the parents and keep the child for his own profit and benefit. Raising her to put all her magical potential into his service was far more appealing than feigning subservience and loyalty to Durmad.

For now, though, he would let them keep working on cleansing the ground and removing Arden's curse from Stonemount.

Four nights later, Alastor and Wren were able to work again. Soon after they began, Maddix was startled when bricks a third of the way around the wall from his peephole, going north, sagged like candles in a roaring fire. A shimmering of purple and black and coppery sparks spewed from the melted spot in the wall, swirling into a thick column until they formed a tall, broad-shouldered man with tangled gray hair and beard hanging nearly to his waist.

The couple joined hands and backed away as the man approached them. Maddix blinked and shook his head, distracted for a moment to see the wall hadn't been damaged. What kind of magic was this? He nearly laughed aloud to realize he was relieved, because he certainly didn't want to have to deal with the questions that a melted brick wall would raise in the morning. This magic wielder certainly showed more consideration than others he had dealt with in his life.

Maddix shook his head, not at all amused to realize he ignored the little drama playing out in front of him.

"Did you think you could hide forever?" the man snarled. "Did you think one of us wouldn't find you and punish you?" He stalked toward them and Wren flicked her fingers, creating a wall of shimmering, transparent blue magic that stopped him short. Coppery-black sparks of magic erupted from his dark robes and battered ineffectually at the wall.

"We never agreed to what Durmad wants of us," Alastor said.

"Durmad says otherwise."

"He will destroy her," Wren began.

"He will rule the entire world through her. That was the entire reason for saving the child's life. You fools! Did you really think Durmad would care about a child who shouldn't have lived two days beyond her birth?"

"He attacked us. He made me give birth too soon!" she cried, and flung sparkling, spiky balls of blue magic at the man. He staggered back two steps, then surged forward, waves of churning blackness rolling out of him, to batter the couple backwards half a dozen steps.

"Of course he did!" He laughed, a slick sound heavy with corruption and delight that made Maddix shudder. "You were about to leave his lands. He waited centuries for one just like her to be born. She was born on his land, and that makes her his."

"No!" Alastor growled and flung up a wall of green vines of magic that surged against the blackness and pushed it back.

Their opponent staggered. Just one step. Then his magic burst forward like a dam shattering and the green magic evaporated in a puff of sparks that smelled of burned, rotten leaves.

"Your child is Durmad's tool, his property. Just like all the children you will birth, to serve him." Again, that slick, satisfied, rolling laughter that made the ground tremble under Maddix's feet.

"Never. I will give my life to protect her," Wren cried, raising her hands, and drawing a whirlwind of blue magic up from the ground.

"So be it!" He raised his hands and an answering whirlwind gathered around him, tangling his robes around his legs, whipping his long beard and hair, and spinning out to enclose the couple.

"Yeshen, hear us!" the man cried, before the wind's roar drowned out all other sounds.

The magics clashed in blinding streaks of non-light. The maelstrom of magic expanded, spinning through the garden. The three people were barely visible in the chaos of warped colors and powers. Maddix staggered back from the peephole. He smelled fire and blood, the rot of swamps, brimstone and the stinging scent of magic gone sour.

Light burst into the sky, leaping up from the chaos filling the garden. He stumbled when the ground seemed to heave and roll like the surface of the sea in a storm. He fled, heart racing, lungs struggling as if all that magic pulled the very air from the gardens. His mind was nearly blank with terror and the certainty that somehow, Durmad would know what he had seen and heard and would be furious enough to reach all the way over the Cascade Mountains and punish him.

He still had enough presence of mind, though, to vow dire punishments on anyone who saw him fleeing, sweating and shaking like a brainless peasant.

When the silence hit, it was like a wall slammed up against him and knocked him to the ground. Maddix stayed where he landed, on hands and knees, waiting for the destruction to catch up with him.

Slowly, the normal sounds of night in the palace gardens trickled over and around him. No footsteps, though. No sounds of voices. He nearly wept, then laughed at the relief he felt. That shifted to indignation, and a need to punish those who had tricked him into acting very unkinglike.

He told himself it was only common sense to go back and see what had happened. Who had won that battle of magics. At the very least, he had to exert his authority and demand someone clean up whatever mess they had made. He crept from shadow to shadow, listening for the sounds of voices and running feet. Maddix wondered what was wrong with everyone, that the palace wasn't ablaze with light and chaos, with people running around wondering what had happened.

When he reached the walled garden, the air smelled of sulfur and the stink of burned grass and charred soil and scorched rock. Yet strangely, nothing was disturbed. The hole where stagnant water had gathered was dry, but otherwise, nothing had changed. There weren't even footprints in the grass and moss to indicate anyone had ever walked there.

Fury steadied his limbs as he strode through the garden to the hidden courtyard, to confront the couple and demand an explanation from them.

~~~~~

When the storm of magic swirled up from the ground and reached to the sky like a tornado, Taran fled. She ignored the puddles of torchlight around small pavilions full of talking, singing, laughing people. Some people saw her, a white blur on the edge of their vision, sparkling with jewels, with her hair flowing out behind her like a comet, and her face pale with terror. Days later, Maddix congratulated her on the stories swirling through the palace, speaking of the evil portent of Bianca's ghost. None of those stories mentioned the black wolf at her side, which was a blessing. Full night had not fallen yet and Bard had not made the shift to man.

By the time Taran reached her tower, she had torn her dress and lost her shoes and some of her borrowed jewels, but she didn't care. The magic still buzzed and heaved in the ground under her feet and she fled into the tower. She climbed the stairs to the second floor, then the third, before the buzzing of magic stopped and the rolling of the ground no longer threatened to topple her. Then she dropped to her knees, aching, remembering the night her mother had died, the shattering of magic.

Something dreadful had happened, and she had no idea where or how or who.

She was still huddled on the floor, starting to examine the shredded condition of her clothes from the vines and rose bushes she had raced through, when Bard caught up with her. He dropped to his knees and held her, and for some time, that was more than enough for her.

Bard hadn't felt all the turmoil of magic, hadn't felt the ground heave, but he had sensed something momentous had happened. He was able to
~~~~~

think clearly before Taran, and she agreed with his plan. She would remove the shredded clothes and Bard would dispose of them, to avoid raising questions. Taran doubted Maddix had any idea of how many of dead Bianca's dresses or jewels were here.

The worst thing she could do was ask anyone what had happened. That would be admitting she had magic, enough to sense when some dreadful and powerful magic had been worked.

~~~~~

When Maddix reached the cottage in the courtyard, he found no one there but the sleeping child. He waited an hour, pacing in the little cobblestone-paved courtyard, but the parents didn't return. He went back to his quarters and tried to sleep, with no success. He returned before dawn, with a note he left on the table, demanding an explanation.

When he returned late in the afternoon, he found the child sitting in a shady corner, playing with a rag doll, still in her little nightshirt, barefoot and grubby, her face smeared with drying tears. And no sign of her parents. Maddix could only hope that if the parents were conveniently dead, Durmad's minion was also dead, and hadn't reported to his master that he had found them.

Maddix grumbled that evening at the injustice of having a child dropped into his arms when he hadn't had time to make preparations. What did he know about tending children? Who could expect a king to take care of such matters? He snarled at everyone around him, at the injustice that he couldn't assign any servants to tend the child if he wanted to keep the courtyard and cottage and child a secret. It was beneath the dignity of a king to sneak into his own palace kitchen and take food and worry about feeding the child. But he couldn't let her starve, could he? Not if this child held so much potential magic that Durmad himself had schemed to possess her. He certainly couldn't leave her to cry until someone heard and poked and prodded until they got through the guarding magic and found her, could he?

Even knowing he could now raise the child as his personal wizard, he still grumbled. He couldn't foist her off on one of his servants. They were so untrustworthy. Especially when they were terrified for their lives. Fear scrambled what few brains they had, so they made mistakes. Some were stupid enough to let their fear turn to anger, and then they turned against him. It simply wasn't right. He was the king. All his wishes should be fulfilled.

And they would be. Someday. Once his pet wizard had grown up and enforced all his commands.

No doubt the nuisance of making sure she was fed and clothed would prove to be worthwhile when she was grown up. Maddix wondered how long it took for powerful enchantresses to grow up.
~~~~~

Maybe he could convince Fiera to tend the child? After all, she certainly enjoyed spending time with his son, though he couldn't understand why. Small children were so messy and noisy and didn't know how to obey.

While Fiera was clever enough to see the profit in Stonemount having a tame wizard, he couldn't trust her not to scheme against him. She was more likely to flee and take the child to her father.

He had to find a nursemaid. Someone no one knew. Someone who had no one to depend on, so she would be totally loyal to him.

He nearly laughed aloud when he realized he had the solution right there, already hidden in the palace.

~~~~~

"You have been seen," Maddix said when Taran emerged from the tower the night after the magic storm.

"Seen, Majesty?" Taran nearly stumbled, nearly turned to call out to Bard to run. Then she saw Maddix's sharp, pleased smile, and the brightness of his eyes. She shuddered.

The man wasn't simply cruel and vicious, he was insane.

"I overheard several ninnies whispering about a ghostly, white-haired woman flying through the gardens last night. My plan is working perfectly." His expression relaxed and warmed. He bowed and beckoned for her to follow. Taran curtseyed as she had seen several court ladies do while she wandered and spied from the shadows. Maddix chuckled. She was grateful he didn't offer his elbow, as courtiers did when a lady curtseyed. She couldn't have borne having to touch him, even with layers of cloth between them.

Tonight as they wandered the garden paths, avoiding any place where there were people, he spoke of his many woes and tribulations in dealing with neighboring kingdoms, as if she were his confidant. Then he drifted into stories about Bianca.

"Sometimes I think this place would be much more pleasant with a few children running up and down the paths," Maddix mused, after he told a story about two of Bianca's nephews visiting for a month, shortly after he had married her.

He laughed when Taran just looked at him, unsure what to say. She feared turning the conversation to children, to try to gain information about the child and her parents. The most innocent question could make him suspicious. And dangerous.

"What? You don't believe me?"

"You have never spoken of your son, Majesty, so that makes me think you do not like children."

"Now, that is patently untrue." He said it with a smile and shook his head. "I am a champion when it comes to defenseless children. Come with
~~~~~

me. I'll prove it to you."

"Where, Majesty?"

"Oh, don't worry. I won't take you far." He beckoned. His face glowed, making him seem like a mischievous boy with a delightful secret.

Taran shivered, positive this was just another aspect of his madness. If she didn't placate him, he could turn against her. She needed to stay in Maddix's good graces to guarantee she could stay in the palace until she had finished searching. Bard said he had smelled magic in the garden, but neither of them could search very far when they were free to move.

Maddix laughed and caught up her hand. His hand was cold, damp and entirely too strong for Taran's taste. Her only comfort was in knowing that Bard, whether in wolf shape or man, would follow. Maddix led her through flowerbeds and crossed stretches of lawn. Everyone else stayed on the paths of painted pebbles or crushed seashells. Maddix ignored every barrier and ornamental fence. Then again, he was the king, and this was his garden.

What would have taken her an hour to walk, by following the winding, switchback paths through the garden, Taran crossed in perhaps twenty hurried minutes. She nearly opened her mouth to protest when Maddix led her to a wall of ivy. He grinned and glanced around.

"This way." He stepped three paces to the left, grabbed hold of her hand again, and walked through the ivy.

Through the wall. Taran closed her mouth tight, imagining getting a mouthful of old, rotten ivy and whatever dirt clung to the wall. A tingle of magic passed over her body. Now she understood what Bard sensed, and why he couldn't follow the path of the magic. It was a shielding magic, to hide something. Perhaps someone?

Then they were through, into a courtyard surrounded by ivy-covered walls. A little spring bubbled up to fill a basin in one corner and an arbor heavy with ruby-colored grapes filled the night air with a sweet, rich perfume. Moss carpeted the ground and a tiny, white cottage with a thatched roof sat in the middle of the courtyard, glowing in the moonlight.

"Go look inside. But don't wake her." Maddix dropped down onto a stone bench in front of the arbor and reached for a cluster of grapes.

"Her?"

"Just look. You'll see that I'm wrong. I love children. The right kind of children, of course." He snickered and popped four enormous grapes into his mouth, one after another.

Taran imagined him chewing with his mouth open, juice and pulp running down his face. She fought not to grimace and turned to go into the cottage. A tingling down her spine made her turn, with the door pushed halfway open, and glance back the way she had come. Bard emerged through the long streamers of old ivy covering the wall. He nodded to her, smiled, pressed one finger to his lips, and retreated into the shadows.

Moonlight spilled through the open windows of the cottage. A little girl with a riot of red curls huddled in the bed next to a window. Taran looked around the cottage, noting the adult clothes hanging from hooks on the wall, but no sign of the child's parents. Did she live alone? How?

She noted dirty dishes on the table, the discarded child-sized clothes on the floor, the fruit, cakes, and sweets in baskets on the table. King Maddix had provided for this little girl, but he didn't know the first thing about proper food, and obviously no servants had been in here to clean the cottage.

Taran shuddered, reliving for a few painful heartbeats that flood of scalding, broken magic. Did that explain the absence of the child's parents? Had something horrific happened to them? Had they fought other magical servants of the king?

"Who is she, Majesty?" she asked, when she stepped outside. There was another bench in the arbor, facing Maddix, so she didn't have to share the bench with him or sit on the ground. He just grinned and popped more grapes into his mouth. Taran was relieved to see he still remembered to chew with his mouth closed. "Are we still in the garden, or does the door take us far away?"

"The magic guarding this courtyard was a gift. Wise people give me gifts, because they know I'm smart enough to use them properly. We are still in the palace grounds, but no one else knows the courtyard is here."

"What about the child?"

"Oh, she's magic." He grinned and popped another grape into his mouth, chewed three times and swallowed. "I was testing you."

"I cannot use magic, Majesty."

"Perhaps." His smile just widened. What did he want from her? Why had he tested her?

"Why did you bring me here to see this child?"

"You said I didn't like children, that I didn't want children around. I love children." He sighed, and his smile wavered a little. "Especially that child. Her parents were very powerful wizards, but not powerful enough. They entrusted her to me. I'm going to take very good care of her. Maybe I will marry her to my heir. Then when she is queen, Stonemount will be the most powerful kingdom in the world, because she will be the most powerful wizard in the world."

"Who tends her? She looks as if she has been alone for some time," Taran said, trying not to let the shivering inside her touch her voice. Had she found the child Kalista sought, but too late for the parents?

"She needs a nurse. I need you more as a ghost, but ..." His mouth twisted with discontent. "I can't visit her all the time, can I? Not if I want her presence kept secret. To protect her, of course. Since you are one of my secrets, you will do nicely."

"How did she come into your care, Majesty?" Taran tried not to shudder. She wasn't sure if it came more from the loathing for him that spilled through her, or pity for the child, or relief that the hardest part of her task was done.

Taran nearly choked and missed what Maddix said next. How could she think finding the child was the hard part? They needed to escape the palace and Stonemount altogether, didn't they?

"I needed people to come in and cleanse Stonemount of a curse that wretched farmer princess flung at me. It blights everything," he said, on a gusting sigh. "A couple came to me. They claimed they could remove the magic. All they asked was that I give them a quiet corner to live for a while, and freedom to move about at night. I had this little courtyard that was my favorite retreat when I was a boy. I needed my privacy, and freedom from arrogant fools who thought they had the right to lecture me." He scowled and clenched his fists, so his knuckles turned white.

"So you hid here from unkind teachers," she offered. Taran pitied the nursemaids and tutors who cared enough to try to warn Maddix as a boy about a bad future but didn't realize that lecturing wasn't the right tactic.

Her mother had taught her that some people's souls were like wax, and others like clay. Heat melted wax and made it pliable, but hardened clay and made it brittle. Cool water made wax brittle, and slowly eroded clay into new shapes. The wrong tactics were used on Maddix as a boy. She almost pitied him.

Chapter Fourteen

"I knew this was the perfect place to hide them. It was rather fun, if you think about it, sneaking into the storerooms and kitchens and finding them whatever they needed to make that little cottage comfortable. I rather enjoyed the adventure. I only wish I could have seen the ruckus in the kitchens and elsewhere, when people discovered things missing." Maddix snorted. "Who would ever accuse the king of Stonemount of stealing from his own kitchen, eh?" His grin faded into weariness. "It's sad when even the people who were as close as my own heart can't be trusted anymore."

Maddix shook his head and got up to pace slowly. "I came down at night to watch them work. Then one night, a stranger appeared in the garden. A very powerful wizard. Turns out they were runaways, and he had come to bring them back to their master. The argument turned to magic." He shrugged. "The next thing I knew, they were all gone. Destroyed each other. The child was left with no one but me to look after her. So, you see, I don't hate children. If I did, I'd have foisted the little pup on someone else." He spread his hands in a gesture that said everything was settled.

Taran's stomach roiled in reaction to the charming smile he wore, his very visible conviction that he was a good, kind man. He only took care of the child for his own profit. What if she grew up to think and believe as Maddix did? He had poisoned Stonemount with his selfishness — imagine how much more damage this child could do once she came into her power?

Please, blessed Yeshen, I am your servant. My fate is in your hands. Move this arrogant, cruel man to put the child into my care, and show us the path of escape!

"Do you pity her?" He turned toward the ivy-hung opening into the courtyard.

"Of course, Majesty. An orphan child is to be greatly pitied."

"Good. I need my sleep, and you need to terrify the idiots and plant seeds of more ghost stories. Fiera hasn't even started to look afraid." He gestured for her to go through the opening first. Maddix chuckled, a cold sound, sending chilly prickles down her back.

Then Taran was back outside in the palace gardens. She looked around, praying for some sign of Bard.

Maddix walked with her as far as the gate of the walled garden, swept her a courtly bow, bade her sweet dreaming, and strode away through the garden. Taran shivered and stayed there in the shadows of the wall, eyes closed. She stretched all her senses until she thought she knew every scent on the wind, every beat of every sleeping heart in the palace.

Bard's warmth and the comfort of his scent wrapped around her. Taran opened her eyes and found him waiting in the shadows of the trees, with a wide, brilliant, silver stream of moonlight illuminating the ground between them. She smiled and prayed the shadows hid the tears burning her eyes.

"Come," he whispered, and held out his hands. Taran leaped through the moonlight, and it seemed to burn her flesh. As if the magic holding her to her human shape had grown weak and would shred at any moment.

Bard kept his arm around her as they walked into the deeper shadows of the garden. She trusted his sharper, wolf-trained senses to ensure they were truly alone. Then she told him all that Maddix had said.

"We have so little time," he whispered. "If Durmad's minion found the parents, then others will be able to find the child. We need to get her away from this tainted kingdom, into one that is loyal to Yeshen."

Taran swallowed hard and braced herself to move out of the warmth of his arm. She clasped the amulet with both hands. "I think I need to practice how to be a wolf."

"Taran—"

"No. Think of it. You will be a wolf by day, and I will be a wolf by night, and we will be able to guard the child no matter where we go." Taran yanked hard on the amulet before she lost her nerve and threw it to Bard.

He caught it and flinched when a bright blue spark of magic spat at his hands. He held onto the amulet.

Taran almost laughed at the shock on his face, but the sound caught in her throat, choking her, as magic surged up through her body. For half a heartbeat, it felt as if every organ in her body turned inside out and her muscles tried to leap free of her bones. A thousand pinpricks pierced her skin as silver-white fur sprouted all over her body and her elegant, borrowed dress vanished, swallowed up in magic.

This isn't half as bad as the first time, she thought, and opened her mouth to tell Bard. A howl emerged. She choked off the sound, startled to hear it come from her own throat. Taran went to all fours, then put her nose to the ground, her rump in the air, arched her tail over her back and stretched, hard, almost to the point of pain.

Something deep inside her seemed to *click* into place, like a puzzle box where the last rod was pushed in the right order and the hidden compartment slid open. Taran leaped straight up in the air and turned a somersault, head over paws, and tried to bite at the waving tip of her glowing, elegant tail.

Claws clicked on stones and then dug into the night-damp grass as she ran in ever-widening circles around Bard. He made not a sound, turning to watch her run. Taran smelled his fear for her in his sweat, heard his heart thumping in a worried staccato. Fighting the need to howl for sheer joy in living, she leaped at him and shoved him hard to the ground. He *oophed*, the air knocked out of his lungs, and she shifted to get off his chest, but kept her front paws on his shoulders.

When he blinked and shook his head and the surprise on his face turned to a frown, she licked his face, from chin to forehead. Bard let out a strangled shout, flung up his arms, and scrambled to turn over and get back to his feet. He glared at her while he wiped his face with the sleeve of his borrowed livery. Taran sat back on her haunches, her tail curled around her feet, tongue lolling out in silent wolf laughter.

They stayed still, half in shadows, half in moonlight, until Bard's glare softened. Taran twitched her ears at him and tipped her head from one side to another. She wished she could speak into his mind as her mother sometimes had spoken into hers. Perhaps when they were both in wolf shape, they could do that?

"Very funny," he murmured, and stepped forward, holding out the amulet. "Ready to go back to the way you belong?"

Taran stood up and took one step forward. Then froze at a new, intriguing, shocking thought. Did she truly belong *only* in human shape? She had lived as a human all her conscious life, but didn't the wolf half of her have just as much right to embodiment?

"Taran?" Bard went down on one knee before her, holding out the amulet on its chain. "Please, sweetheart, before someone comes and catches us."

Sweetheart? No one had ever called her sweetheart before. Did Bard truly mean it, or was it only his fear for her that spoke?

There was only one way to find out. Taran pushed her nose into the loop of the chain. Bard slid it over her ears. It was a tight fit around the fur of her throat, and Taran feared the chain would break. Then the change began. Bard cursed softly and scrambled backward, shaking his hands as if they had been stung.

"Does the magic hurt you?" she said, once her throat had returned to human.

"No. Not hurt or pleasant." He frowned, puzzled, and thought a moment. "It is simply ... strange." His frown deepened. "Does the transformation hurt you?"

"It is more strange than painful. I think as I grow used to it, I won't mind it."

"What is the difference between us?"

"Maybe that is the secret Nueroch killed my mother to find. Or maybe she told him the truth, but he wouldn't believe her …" Taran sat down, ignoring the dirt she might get on her borrowed clothes. "Think of it, Bard. My mother wove her magic to save two lives. Nueroch wove the same magic to destroy two lives, to make a slave and warrior. You resist it with everything you are. I accept what I am." She choked on a sound that she couldn't quite decide was laughter or something sad and pained.

"So the day I decide I like being this way, I'll have control and it won't hurt?" He snorted and jerked to his feet. "That is too simple. Why would anyone want to stay this way? It is wrong. Unnatural. If I had no hope of my freedom, I think I would rather die than live my life as some kind of freakish monster."

"As I am?" she whispered.

Her words might have been a shout. Bard blanched and his throat worked as if he fought to shout—or perhaps fought *not* to say something. Taran felt strangely calm, poised on the edge of euphoria. She would have laughed, but her throat felt thick with impending tears.

"No, you are no freak and no monster," he whispered, and went to his knees in front of her again. "You are Taran, and there is no one …" He closed his eyes and shook his head, and then his head drooped forward.

"No one like me in the entire world?" Taran reached out to caress Bard's cheek, but it seemed to her that the touch of his skin might burn her. She got to her feet and stepped back. "You yourself told me there are many people in this world like me, but they don't want to be."

"Taran—"

"The moon is near to setting, Bard. You should go to your hiding place before you go back to wolf." She turned around, looking for a familiar landmark in the garden with its long, moonlit shadows. A bit of laughter escaped her, bitter, muffled instantly.

"What is so amusing?"

"I wondered if your wolf side thinks I am a freak and monster."

"My wolf side only sees the female wolf who appeared before him at the pool, and he has deeply lustful thoughts for her," Bard offered with a pained grin.

"Will wonders never cease? At least someone in this world finds me tempting."

"Worth fighting for, fighting over, tearing down an entire kingdom to ensure your safety." He bowed, and stepped forward, reaching for her. "Taran, take the child tonight and let us flee and be free."

"Her parents have just died. The only person she knows is the king, apparently. He at least brought her food. Do you think any child, so recently bereft, would go willingly and quietly with complete strangers, who snatched her from her bed in the middle of the night and carried her away from the only home and the only friend she knows?"

"Thank Yeshen, you think more clearly than I do," he said, his voice and face rueful. Bard nodded and raked both hands through his hair. Sweat gleamed on his face. "Then you must make friends with her. We both must."

"Children love dogs. Perhaps you should visit her during the day, when she is alone." Taran gestured out into the darkness of the garden. "Go, Bard. We will talk about this tomorrow. Go, before you are caught changing."

"You are my sweetheart, Taran. No matter what shape you wear, your heart and soul are the same," Bard vowed, and snatched her up into his arms. He bruised her lips with a swift, clumsy kiss, releasing her before she could let out a squeak of shock.

Taran staggered back several steps, reaching blindly for something to catch her as Bard fled. She felt dizzy and realized she had forgotten to breathe. Laughing softly at herself, she inhaled, exhaled loudly, inhaled again, then hesitantly touched her tingling lips.

Her first kiss, in the moonlight, in a palace garden, from a handsome man under a curse, while she was dressed in the clothes of a queen. For such a very unremarkable person only a few moons ago, her life had definitely taken a long step into the fantastic. She wondered if people would tell the tale of her journey someday, far in the future.

~~~~

The next night, Taran waited for Maddix at the bottom of the stairs until the moon was far overhead. Somewhere in the darkness, Bard had become a man again. And still King Maddix hadn't made his appearance. She wondered if she dared hope he wouldn't appear for the evening, and started down the pathways of the garden, staying in the shadows.

"Her name is Ivy," Bard said, stepping from the shadows of the rose arbor.

"The child?" Taran nodded. She hoped the name was propitious. Ivy looked delicate, but it was tenacious. Given enough time, ivy could destroy buildings and strangle the gigantic, ancient trees, patriarchs of the forest.

"She likes me." He grinned, a white flash of teeth through his beard, and caught hold of her hands. "She is strong in magic, for one so young. She looked at the wolf and saw me hiding under his skin," he whispered.

"Will she see the wolf hiding under my—" Taran bit her lip when Bard hissed warning, released her quickly enough to make her stumble, and stepped into the shadows.
~~~~

She moved out into the moonlight and bent to pluck a stalk of lily of the valley while she waited for Maddix to approach. She straightened and stroked her cheek with the delicate little bell-shaped flowers, then turned to face him.

"I hope you will forgive me for starting without you, Majesty," she said, and dropped into a low, sweeping curtsey.

"Yes, yes, you thought I wasn't coming tonight, I suppose." Maddix nodded and looked around, frowning as he peered into the gray-on-black shadows of the trees.

"Is something wrong?"

"I could have sworn I saw someone with you. Remember, you are nothing but a ghost to everyone else. Ghosts don't speak." His mouth twisted in a vicious grin. "But wouldn't that be delicious fun if the ghost did speak? Maybe reveal some secrets to the court. Send the backstabbing fools into a panic…" He studied her for a moment, just staring into her eyes. "Later. Come. We have important work to do tonight."

Taran assumed they were going to see Ivy. She sternly reminded herself not to reveal she knew the little girl's name.

"What am I to do?" Taran asked as she reluctantly followed him back the way she had come.

"You will live with the child now."

"But Majesty —" She prayed the shadows hid her expression, because she wasn't sure she could keep from showing her relief.

"She needs a nursemaid." Maddix paused to look back over his shoulder at her. "Don't think I missed your worried expression after you had seen the child. She certainly isn't old enough to pick up after herself, and you can't expect me to do such menial chores."

Maddix couldn't be expected to help her pack, either. Taran suspected he would be heartily offended if she asked him to carry any of her bags. She packed one large bag with more sensible clothes from Bianca's wardrobe, and another bag with some food better for a growing child, and a few kitchen items. She dared to hope that Maddix had at least had the sense to remove things like knives from the cottage. The weather was warm, and she hadn't smelled any evidence of a fire in either the fireplace or the little beehive oven. Probably the child hadn't had any hot water to take a decent bath, forget about hot food.

Once she knew Ivy's true situation, she would come back tomorrow night for more food and utensils and clothes. No doubt Maddix would expect her to continue playing at being Bianca's ghost. How was she going to tend a child during the day and roam the gardens at night, without any sleep?

Please, Yeshen, help us find our escape quickly. She nearly laughed at the urgency of her silent prayer.

As she followed Maddix back down the stairs and across the gardens to the hidden courtyard, Taran thought back to what Bard had told her. Would the child, Ivy, see both souls when she looked at her? The walk was short, sparing her from working herself into a knot of nerves by the time they reached the ivy doorway in the hedge.

"Do you intend to wake the child, Majesty?" she asked.

"And have her bombard me with more of her everlasting questions?" Maddix snorted and shook his head twice. "Spare me the antics of children. No, from now on, she is your responsibility. If you want to wake her and have picnics in the middle of the night, that is your decision. All I ask is that the child is fed and clothed properly and taught to behave herself ..." His smile grew chill. "And of course, you will teach her everything you know of magic. And don't give me that tired old story about how you have no magic. Your mother was a wise woman with enough magic to create that little bauble you wear. The magic is strong enough I can feel it. I'm sure she taught you about magic, even if you inherited none of hers." Maddix nodded for emphasis and stepped through the hidden doorway.

He offered Taran his hand, just as he began to vanish. She muffled a sigh of exasperation and took as light a grip on his fingertips as she could, without dropping the bags. It wouldn't be wise to let him know that she could sense the hidden doorway, even if she couldn't see it. If he thought she couldn't find her way out and back in again, then he wouldn't be so watchful of her.

"I merely thought that it would be less frightening for the child if you were here to assure her I belonged here," Taran said, when they emerged into the moonlit courtyard.

"No one enters this courtyard without my permission. She knows that. Your presence won't frighten her. She's strangely practical, for a child." Maddix looked around the courtyard and nodded. "Do whatever you wish. Make a list of whatever you need, and tomorrow night, you can pilfer the kitchen and storehouses of the palace to your heart's content."

Without even a nod of farewell, Maddix turned and strode through the wall.

Taran dropped everything she carried and clenched her fists hard to keep from shouting her exasperation to the night sky. Then Bard slipped through the wall and hurried to wrap his arms around her. Taran wasn't sure if she should laugh or be worried. One thought came clear to her mind as she soaked up the warmth of Bard's arms.

"Did Ivy accept you so easily because she thinks only friends of Maddix's can enter here?"

Bard gave her a confused look, prompting a sputter of laughter. The tight coil in her chest unwound as Taran hurried to tell him what Maddix had done.

"He thinks he's smarter than everyone," Bard mused, and rested his chin on the top of her head. Taran rather liked the enclosed feeling. "Is that good for us, that he's so confident, or a bad sign?"

~~~~~

"Well?" Maddix muffled a chuckle when both Clancy and Baethon jumped and turned, nearly stumbling as they landed. He schooled his face into a stern mask and stepped past them, into the puddle of torchlight at the top of the steps leading into the palace from the gardens.

Really, those two had outlived their usefulness. They were like two gossipy old grannies sitting by the fire, so caught up in their muttering, they hadn't seen or heard him approaching through the garden. Maddix speculated that he could have stabbed Clancy in the ribs and garroted Baethon before either man could defend himself. That was simply pitiful. It saddened him to realize that he would have to dispose of them, when once he had relied on them to dispose of his problems.

"How has my ghost done tonight?" he prodded when neither man said anything. They just watched him, growing gradually paler as the seconds ticked by and the black of the pre-dawn sky gave way to pale gray on the horizon.

"We didn't see her at all tonight," Baethon finally said. "We went up to the tower, but she wasn't there."

Maddix muffled a chuckle. Was that what worried them? They thought the healer woman had managed to escape? He contemplated for a few moments the fun of making them race around in growing terror, trying to find her. And all the while, he knew where Taran was.

"It's a large garden. I saw her. I'm quite pleased. She is doing so well … Have you heard some of the whispers? People truly believe my Bianca has come back from the dead." He turned away, watching both men out of the corner of his eye. "Perhaps if Bianca comes back, Jaygo will as well. I have great need of his advice in these sad times." Maddix glanced over his shoulder at them, pausing long enough to meet their eyes. "I want you two to put your heads together and come up with something diabolically clever and cruel to punish whoever was stupid enough to deprive me of Jaygo's advice."

Maddix bit his lip against a chortle as he walked through the door into the palace. He imagined the anguish on the two men's faces. If he couldn't get any decent work out of those two, if they were no longer loyal or useful, at least he could get some entertainment out of them before he disposed of them.
~~~~~

Chapter Fifteen

Taran bit her thumb to hold back the tears as she watched Bard writhe in pain, transforming back to wolf in dawn's chilly, gray light. The amulet buzzed against her skin as if it contained a dozen angry bees, reacting to the splash of magic through the air. When the change ended, she crossed the courtyard to where the black wolf lay panting loudly, dropped to her knees, and wrapped her arms around him.

They were still curled up together when the light around them had turned golden warm and the child, Ivy, emerged from the little cottage. She was barefoot, dressed in her nightgown, her fiery curls a tangle hanging over her shoulders. Her leaf-green eyes widened when she saw the two sitting in the middle of the mossy courtyard.

"You have a white wolf inside you," she said, as delight lit her eyes. "The water lady said a black wolf and a white wolf will watch over me. Are you going to be my new mama and papa?"

Taran stared at the child, who showed no fear or even curiosity, just acceptance. Was this child dangerously innocent, or so secure in her powers she didn't know the meaning of fear?

Water lady? Could Kalista have managed to reach the child in her dreams, to speak words of comfort and give guidance? That would be a great blessing, and certainly make their task much easier.

Bard-wolf nudged her with his nose, the cold wet touch jolting her out of her thoughts before the silence grew too long. Taran nodded and scrambled to her feet.

"Yes, we are here to take care of you. What else did the water lady tell you?"

Ivy's smile dimmed and her little brow wrinkled in a frown of concentration. "She said Mama and Papa had to go away so the bad men can't find me. She said I have to pray and listen to Yeshen and use my magic to help people, and someday I'll see Mama and Papa again." She held out her little hand and Taran immediately clasped it. "They didn't want to go away, did they?"

"No, I'm sure they wanted to stay with you always." Taran thought she would fall into those big, green eyes. Tears filled her own eyes and she dropped to her knees again to wrap her arms around the child. She cradled Ivy close as the little girl shuddered and wept silently, soaking the shoulder of her dress.

She marveled at how easily the child accepted them. Then again, she was a creature of magic, and her parents had taught her enough that she trusted someone who spoke to her in her dreams. Taran thought of her mother's last words, how Eyrian had gone to face Nueroch, sensing this would be her last duty in protecting the five villages. At sixteen, it had been hard to lose her mother. What must it be like for Ivy, at only five years of age? Did the child fully realize what had happened?

"Was King Maddix good to you?" she asked, the first thought clear in her mind when Ivy's tears finally slowed, her shudders stopped, and she lifted her little head from Taran's shoulder.

"Is he a king? He said when I was grown up, we would play together." Ivy scrubbed her wet, swollen eyes with her fists. She stayed curled up on Taran's lap.

"Yes, he's a king. And he wants to use your magic to help him rule." Taran bit her lip against spilling all the cruel things she feared Maddix wanted Ivy to do when she was grown up.

Ivy pouted a little. "He made me stay here all alone. That's not nice."

"No, that isn't. The water lady is named Kalista. She told me there was a little girl without her mama and papa, and she asked me to find you and take care of you. I said I would, because I know how lonely you are, because my mama and papa are gone, too."

"Really?" Ivy's eyes sparkled with imminent tears.

"Really." Taran set the child on her feet, desperate to stave off another bout of tears. "Why don't we go inside and make breakfast? Are you hungry?"

"My tummy hurts. Will you make me porridge and eggs? All he gives me is milk and pie and toast."

"We'll see what we can find, all right?" Taran got to her feet and held out her hand. Ivy managed a watery smile and took her hand, and the two of them went into the cottage with Bard-wolf close on their heels.

Blessed Yeshen, thank you for this mercy. This is far easier than I thought it could be!

There were no oats to make porridge, so Taran improvised, using stale bread and currants, honey, and milk that likely would not last through the day. She shook her head at the silliness of some of Maddix's ideas of what it meant to take care of a child. Ivy nearly licked her bowl clean and chattered about the treats her captor brought her. She didn't eat many of them because her mama would not approve.

Maddix provided scented soaps and thick towels, but didn't ensure Ivy had enough water for washing. Yes, there was a spring in the courtyard, but how could Ivy handle that big, heavy bucket to bring water inside? How could she heat it? He provided plenty of desserts, but no meat and vegetables to give the child a healthy diet.

It amazed Taran that Maddix could rule his country for as long as he had without totally destroying it. He obviously had no common sense, no idea of what things truly mattered.

Taran built a fire to heat water, then neatened the cottage while Ivy splashed and laughed in the barrel half-filled with water. Then, while Taran brushed and braided the little girl's hair, Ivy used an extra brush to comb out Bard's tangled, burr-filled black fur.

Several times during that long, quiet day, Taran slipped into a vision of what the future would be like for the three of them. She saw Ivy grown up, tall and slim and graceful, wandering barefoot in a raw, untamed forest, spreading magic with every footstep and smile. She saw herself slipping easily between her wolf self and her Human self, as effortlessly as other women tied up or loosed their hair. She saw Bard freed of his curse, first carrying Ivy on his shoulders, then teaching her woodcraft, his big hands guiding her small hands with knife and plane and file. She envisioned Bard growing old and gray and stooped at her side, and the two of them watching Ivy find love and raise her own children.

Was it possible? Yes, Bard had kissed her in the moonlight, and he had spoken sweet words and told her she was beautiful. He had held her, and he grew angry when Maddix made her afraid. But when he was freed of his curse, would he still want her, knowing that a wolf slept in her soul, a wolf's claws waited at her fingertips, and fur bristled under her skin, waiting for magic to set it free?

If Bard stayed, would he want to have children with her, knowing that they would have two bodies, two natures?

Or should she content herself with only Ivy as her daughter?

To escape such painful musings, Taran concentrated on testing Ivy's understanding of magic. After a dozen basic questions, she was relieved to learn Ivy's parents had laid a strong foundation in her mind and heart, so the magic that filled her blood and bones would never be misused.

"Mama says it's just a little knife now," Ivy explained solemnly. "But even little knives can cut you bad, so I have to be careful. I can do little things now, and when I get bigger and stronger and I learn more, then I can use bigger, sharper knives, and do bigger things. But I have to always be careful, because I could hurt myself if I try to hurt other people."

"That is very wise." Taran settled down in the doorway and patted the step, gesturing for the child to sit with her. Ivy's bright little smile and the eagerness with which she obeyed tore at her heart. She could only despise Maddix for leaving the little girl alone and comfortless for two long days.

"Do you know what my mother taught me, when I was even smaller than you?" Taran smothered a chuckle when Ivy's eyes widened and she shook her head. It had only taken a few stories of Eyrian to enchant the child. "My mother said that magic changes your soul, every time you use it. Every time you do good with your magic, it makes you a kinder, wiser person. Every time you use it to help someone, it makes you stronger, and the world grows more beautiful. But, she warned me, every time you use magic to do evil, it nibbles a little bit of your soul away. It makes you dirty and cold and cruel and dark inside. You might be quite clever with your evil magic—many evil wizards are quite brilliant and rich, handsome and powerful—but you are like a rotten tree inside, full of sickness and dark, slimy things. And what is the good of holding all the power of the world, my mother used to say, if you are sick inside your heart?"

"I promise I'll never do bad with my magic." Ivy shook her head and crossed her wrists and pressed both hands over her heart, the most solemn pledge a little child could make.

Taran was hard pressed not to laugh. Had she been so adorably solemn and earnest when she was that age? She settled for wrapping her arm around the little girl and kissing her forehead.

"Do you know any bad wizards?" the child asked.

"You mean, as friends?"

Bard lifted his head from his paws, snorted and flipped his ears, making Ivy laugh. She scrambled over to sit next to him and stroke his head and back. He closed his eyes and sighed, and Taran decided there was a definite smirk on his muzzle.

"Not friends." Ivy frowned and her stroking slowed. "You said evil wizards are handsome and rich. I thought maybe you know some."

"Ah." Taran stepped back into the cottage and picked up the big, heavy brush they had set aside to be used on Bard's fur. It would take time to get all the burrs and brambles and bits of mud out of his fur, and if little Ivy enjoyed brushing him, why not take advantage of it? "No, I don't know any, to speak to them. I only know what Mother told me. She met many wizards, before she became wise woman for the river villages. But," she admitted with some reluctance, "I did see an evil wizard once." She handed the brush to Ivy and settled down on the other side of Bard.

"Let me see?"

Taran barely had time to gasp, to realize what was happening. In half a heartbeat, she felt herself flung backward in time, to that fateful moonlit night by the pool when Nueroch threatened her mother. Then she stumbled forward in time to the winter storm and Nueroch's attack on their villages, Eyrian's death, and the first time she saw Bard and realized he was a man trapped in a wolf's body.

Bard whimpered and abruptly, Taran found herself lying flat on her back, her eyes foggy, feeling Ivy patting her cheek and Bard's long, wet tongue licking her other cheek.

"I'm sorry!" Ivy babbled, over and over, tears streaming down her cheeks. "I just wanted to see. I didn't know I could do that!"

Taran struggled against a throbbing ache in the back of her head and in her temples. It twined into a twisting cord extending down into her stomach, making her dizzy and queasy. She fought to sit upright and draw the sobbing child into her lap. Surely there was someone better suited to teach her. Maybe Kalista only meant for Taran and Bard to rescue her, and then someone else would take over her teaching?

Even as she thought that, Taran wrapped her arms tight around the little girl and those tears tore at her heart. She ached at the thought of anyone else comforting Ivy, watching her sleep, brushing her hair, telling her stories. How could her heart be so intertwined with the child's, in less than a day?

Maybe this was what it meant to be a mother. Something inside her awoke the first time she saw Ivy. It didn't matter that Ivy wasn't her flesh and blood, she would do all she could to defend her. Taran was suddenly glad for the wolf under her skin. If she could learn to bring out the wolf at will, instead of depending on moonlight and the amulet, then she would feel more sure of the child's safety.

"No, it's all right," she whispered, and rocked Ivy and stroked her hair until the shuddering stopped and the tears no longer scalded her shoulder. "You made a mistake, that's all. Have you ever looked into someone's memories before?"

Ivy gulped and sat back so she could look up at Taran and shook her head. She scrubbed tears from her eyes with her fists.

"Well, now you know you can do that. I'm sure you'll be gentler next time. But consider this," Taran hurried on. She could almost hear Eyrian speaking in her head, though her mother had never needed to lecture her on certain ethics and rules of common courtesy among the higher powers of magic. "It is rather rude to go poking through someone's memories without permission. It's like going into someone's house without being invited and searching through all their clothes and toys and dishes." She frowned when Bard nudged her. By the intensity of his eyes, she knew he wanted her to add something to that rule, but what could it be? "I wish I could hear you when you are a wolf," she murmured.

"I can hear him," Ivy said. She nodded slowly, her expression going from relieved to somber. "He says sometimes I have to look without permission, like when someone is my enemy, so I can stop them from doing bad things. Or when someone is hurt so bad they can't wake up. I should look to get answers, to help other people."

"Ah. That is very wise. Bard is a very wise man. He likes being a carpenter, but he is a fine soldier, too." Taran gently stroked across his twitching ears and down his neck. "How I do wish—"

"I can hear him. Maybe I can make you hear him, too?" Ivy frowned in concentration.

Taran waited, afraid to encourage the child to do something beyond her powers or understanding, yet afraid to discourage her. Ivy's little hands cupped her ears, then shifted to Taran's forehead. A strange, airy feeling washed over her, the sensation like being let out of a tight, somewhat sour-smelling box, yet the feeling had nothing to do with smells or even anything enclosing her.

Now try, Ivy said in her head, as she repeated the process with Bard.

Taran? His voice was thick with hope.

"Oh!" Taran nearly leaped to her feet, startled at hearing Bard's voice somewhere in the middle of her head. But she couldn't leap to her feet, with Ivy still securely ensconced on her lap. Taran struggled to get control of her thoughts, swallowed hard, and nodded. She blushed at the ridiculousness of her reaction. *Yes, I hear you.*

Ivy laughed and clapped her hands, justifiably triumphant. Her laughter turned to sputters when Bard licked her face. Ivy flung her arms around him, and the next moment let out a shriek when the wolf surged to his feet, carrying her with him.

Ride, little wizard!

Taran responded to the images in his head, lifting Ivy and settling her on Bard's rough back as if he were a pony. Ivy's eyes went wide with delight and she hung on, her fists taking enormous, tight handfuls of Bard's fur. Taran stood on the stoop and watched them make three circuits of the courtyard. She heard Ivy laugh out loud and heard Bard's laughter in her head.

How she had longed to hear Bard laugh, but honestly, when had they had much chance for merriment? It amused her and startled her to realize they owed King Maddix for something.

Bard brought Ivy back to the doorway and made her dismount by simply settling his haunches on the ground, so she had to slide off. She landed with a little gasp of laughter and looked up at Taran.

"Who is he?" Ivy asked.

Taran opened her mouth to ask who the child meant, then saw Nueroch's image, floating in the air between them for a moment. "You took his face from my memories, didn't you?" She nodded, frowning at the image of the arrogant enchanter until it went fuzzy and then faded from the air. "Very neat little trick, my dear." She bent down and gently tweaked Ivy's nose, making the little girl giggle. "But that is rudeness, also. I think you didn't do it on purpose, any more than you intended to jump into my memories, earlier." She waited until the child thought for a moment, then nodded. "You and I need to learn how to keep the doors of our minds closed, and how not to pull others' doors open."

"There's an awful lot to learn, isn't there?" Ivy said with a deep sigh.

"Yes, unfortunately. And the more power you have, the more there is to learn. Especially when it comes to discipline and humility." Taran muffled a chuckle when Ivy gave her a confused little frown. "The more power you have, the easier it will be for you to start thinking you have the right to do and to take and to be whatever you want."

"That's bad thinking. Mama and Papa said so."

"And they are very right. My mama taught me Yeshen gives us our skills and special gifts to serve him, for a good purpose. He allows us to feel pain, and to be frightened, to make us strong to help others." Taran nodded. "I am glad now that I was so sick when I was a baby, so my mother joined me with the wolf cub to save my life. Now I can be your guardian."

And me, Bard said. *I am glad Nueroch enchanted me, so I can protect you.*

"What did he do to you?" Ivy settled down on the edge of the stoop so she could rest her hand on Bard's neck.

The images of Bard being captured by Nueroch and merged with the wolf flickered from Bard's mind to Ivy's and Taran's in a mere heartbeat. Taran caught her breath at the pain Bard suffered, the arrogant, unthinking cruelty of the wizard. She thought she had understood a little of what Bard went through, just from the shock of her first transformation to wolf. Now, seeing it through his eyes, reliving tiny snippets of the sensations in his memories, she understood so much more thoroughly.

"He is a very bad man," Ivy whispered. "He needs a spanking." She shook her head. "I saw a boy who stole. He was locked in the woodshed. I think he needs to be locked in the woodshed for years and years!"

The ground trembled, vibrating with magic under their feet. Blue sparks, blindingly bright indigo blots, almost solid in the air, gathered around Ivy's head, swirling like comets orbiting stars. The sparks gathered at the child's fingertips.

"No!" Taran snatched at Ivy's hands, getting hold of them despite instinct shouting to go nowhere near that magic fueled by innocent anger. The sparks instantly dissipated and she felt breathless for a moment with relief. "Remember what I said? Every time you use magic to hurt someone, it hurts you, too."

"But he needs to be punished. He did bad."

"I would rather he fight someone meaner and stronger and both of them get hurt. That is much better than you doing harm to yourself."

Is it harmful to Ivy if she just makes sure he can't hurt anyone ever again? Bard offered. *Surely if she has the power at such a young age, Yeshen meant for her to use it? Why can't she just lock him in the woodshed until he learns to behave himself?*

"You are no help at all," Taran snapped.

"He can't use his magic until he apologizes." Ivy nodded, her little frown softening. "Just like Mama makes me sit still and think until I apologize when I've been bad."

"Bottling up magic isn't ... healthy," she temporized. The idea of Nueroch frozen, helpless, unable to use his magic to threaten and get what he wanted, was a tempting, satisfying image.

"Then he can only use magic to help people," Ivy added. She nodded and stomped her bare feet twice. She snapped her arms up in the air, so blue sparks shot off her fingertips like another child would snap water droplets at a friend in teasing play.

The ground seemed to heave in a wave that rolled across the little courtyard away from them. Taran sat down quickly, although the ground didn't actually move.

What did she do? Bard demanded.

"I'm not—" Taran flinched and looked over her shoulder as bits of dirt and thatching fell down from the cottage. She held her breath until she was sure the little building wouldn't suddenly crumble and fall over on them. "I'm not really sure."

"I put his magic in the closet," Ivy said with a nod for punctuation. "He can't take it out except to help people, and he can't take it out to keep until he apologizes."

"To who?"

"To you. To all the wolf-people. Just like when I'm bad or when Papa makes Mama sad, nothing is right until we say we're sorry, and then Mama says she loves us."

Do we have to tell Nueroch we love him, to break the magic binding? Bard asked. His ears twitched and a definite, nasty wolf-grin brightened his furry face. His tongue lolled out in silent wolf laughter.

Chapter Sixteen

Taran had no time to dwell on that little revelation and to think about all the implications. She barely had Ivy settled on the bench in front of the cottage, to teach her about clear imaging to control her magic, when Maddix came barreling through the hidden doorway in the wall. Bard leaped to his feet and retreated into the shadows, hiding around the side of the cottage so that only the tip of his muzzle was visible.

"What was that?" Maddix demanded, striding up to the child and reaching out as if he would grab her shoulders. "What did you do?"

Taran choked. Maddix had felt that ripple of magic? Had it grown stronger as it traveled out from the cottage and through the palace? What would it be like when it neared Nueroch's fortress in the mountains?

Tell him the truth, Bard urged. *Tell him you punished a bad wizard for killing Taran's mother.*

"She did it without thinking, Majesty," Taran hurried to say, after the child obeyed. She rather liked the stunned look in Maddix's eyes. Unfortunately, it was replaced with a delighted, calculating expression. "It will take several years until she has the discipline she needs to control her magic and make sure she doesn't hurt people unintentionally. Imagine if there was a misunderstanding between her and a friend or guardian, and she lashed out and did irreparable damage without meaning to?"

"Hmm. Yes." Maddix stroked Ivy's hair, then stepped back, out of arm's reach.

Taran wondered how ridiculous that little precaution was. If Ivy wanted to punish him, he could be half the world away, like Nueroch, and her magic would eventually reach him.

Still, it was nice to know that he could be frightened into discretion.

"So, you have begun your lessons already." He looked Ivy over and nodded, a more natural smile relaxing his face. "You have worked wonders already. So, little one, do you like the nursemaid I have found for you? I didn't like it that you were alone so much, but I had to be careful and wait until I found just the right person."

"I like Mistress Taran very much," Ivy said, and the smile that lit her face seemed to paint the entire garden in golden tones. "And —"

No, poppet. Don't tell him about me, Bard blurted. The force of his thoughts was nearly a physical blow. *He won't understand that I'm a friend. He will only see the wolfskin I wear, and he'll capture me and take me away.*

"And she makes me good breakfast. I like hot breakfast. And she brushed my hair. And she's teaching me and tells me lots of stories," the child continued, with just the slightest hesitation.

"That's very good." Maddix nodded and wiped his hands on the seat of his long coat. Taran rather hoped they were wet with nervous sweat. "Yes, very good. Well, I will leave you to continue your lessons." He turned, heading for the hidden doorway.

"Majesty? Please, if it is no trouble, could you bring us some meat and fresh vegetables? Children need meat in their diets. Some carrots and turnips and potatoes would be lovely."

"And oats for porridge," Ivy added on a loud whisper.

Maddix's eyes widened. His mouth dropped open a little and he stared at them, visibly shocked that anyone would give the king of Stonemount a shopping list.

"If you prefer, Majesty, I could gather up all that tonight, when the kitchen staff are asleep," Taran added. "You will have to come let me out, of course."

"Yes, of course." He nodded again. "Tonight, then."

Liar, Bard said, as he came around the side of the cottage. He bared his teeth at Maddix's backside as the king vanished through the hidden doorway in the wall. *You can find the doorway just as easily as I can.*

"Yes, but if he thinks we're trapped in here, he won't be so cautious, will he?"

"What does that mean?" Ivy asked.

"That means, as soon as we can, we're going to leave this place and take you far away to a much nicer home, with people who know far more about magic than I do." Taran settled on the bench and slid an arm around Ivy's shoulders. "You need much better teachers than me."

"But he said—" She swallowed hard and shook her head emphatically. "He said that he was protecting me and lots of people want to hurt me. He said I have to stay here to be safe."

"Yes, for a little while that was true."

Ivy, we can't lie when we talk in our minds, Bard said. *I tried, to protect you from the truth about Nueroch, but it all came out anyway. This is the truth: King Maddix is a very greedy, selfish, nasty little boy deep in his heart. He was nice to you because he wants you to use your magic to help him rule other kingdoms someday.*

"Is that bad?"

"Yes, it can be," Taran said. "Sometimes people have to be forced to do the right thing, and they have to be punished because they choose to do things that break Yeshen's laws. That is what kings are for, to teach us how to obey Yeshen and live good lives. But sometimes kings are greedy and selfish. They change the laws so they win all the time, and they have fun while everybody else is sad and hungry."

"That's what he wants me to do?"

"Someday."

Believe us, little one. Yeshen sent us here to help you. Evil men who want to rule the world and break Yeshen's laws tried to take you from your parents, to use your magic for evil. King Maddix wants to use your magic to hurt anyone who doesn't do things his way.

"So we have to run away and hide?" Ivy whispered, her voice going small. Taran fought back tears as she cuddled the child close. She silently cursed Maddix, for the necessity of telling the little girl such cruel truths at such a young age.

"When it's safe, yes, we'll run away, and take you somewhere you can be a little girl and play and have lots of friends."

"But I do have a friend. Can I bring my friend when we run away?"

"What friend?"

"The little boy in the window."

What window? Show us, Bard said.

Ivy led them over to a portion of the courtyard wall opposite where they came in. She tugged aside a curtain of vines tangled with other creeping plants, to reveal a section of wall, the height and width of a doorway, where the stones looked like chunks of smoke-colored glass. The child pressed her hands against two greenish stones at her eye level. All the stones but the green ones cleared. Taran caught her breath as a room appeared before them.

Several lamps with pretty, multicolored glass shades gave enough light to make out details of the room. The walls were painted a soft shade of blue, and carpets in rich colors covered the floor. A crib sat in the center of the room. A canopy hung over the crib, and a child who looked perhaps two years old curled up among several cloth animals, sleeping. A young woman in palace livery dozed in a thickly cushioned chair next to the crib.

Taran noted the richness of the colors and materials. This was the palace nursery. How did Ivy manage to create a window into the nursery, of all places?

Then she remembered what Maddix had said about the cottage being given to him as a retreat. It made sense that whoever could weave magic to hide this little courtyard had enough strength and skill to create a window from the nursery to this place. Or perhaps not a window, but a doorway? Why make the little prince walk all that distance to get away from courtiers and people he didn't like? Ivy had said the little boy was her friend. She wouldn't consider little Prince Maxin her friend unless they could see each other, and maybe even talk, would she?

Taran opened her mouth to ask Ivy how she found this window but stopped when the little boy let out a soft whimper. The nurse didn't react.

He made another cry and turned over, reaching out one little hand. Still no response. A soft wail escaped him as his eyes opened, and he turned his head, looking around, as his face wrinkled up in preparation for what Taran feared would be a gusher.

Huh. I'd cry all the time too, if my father was Maddix, Bard said.

The door opened and light spilled in from the hallway. A woman in a deep green dress stepped into the room, and carefully closed the door behind her. Her hair was braided and wrapped around the back of her head in an ornate style. Taran shivered a little as understanding crept in. The lamp light glittered on decorations in her hair that were most likely gemstones. Lace spilled from her neckline and the cuffs of her sleeves and edged her dress. The soft smile she wore didn't go with the elaborate, rich clothes. With a cautious glance at the sleeping nurse, the young woman hurried up to the other side of the crib and picked up the little boy, stopping him before he made another sound. His unhappy little face broke into a grin that brought tears to Taran's eyes.

"There, did you think I'd forget?" the woman whispered, and swirled away to the other side of the nursery, to settle under another lamp in a chair just like the one the nurse slept in. She set the boy on her lap so they were facing each other, and brushed golden curls out of his face. "And what did you do today? I hope you had more fun than I did."

The nurse woke with a start and a tiny gasp as she turned and her gaze landed on the empty crib. She jolted up out of her chair and turned to sweep the room with her gaze. She slumped in visible relief.

"Highness. I'm sorry."

Who? Bard nudged her. *You know who that is, don't you?*

Princess Fiera. Taran blinked away more tears. The sense of rightness welling up inside her was almost overwhelming. Now, suddenly, the Brentonwald princess's continued presence in Stonemount made complete sense. She was staying here for the little prince, and not because she had fallen for King Maddix's charm, or she even feared his royal fury if she refused to marry him.

"It's all right." Fiera smiled at the nurse, then twisted her face and crossed her eyes at the little boy, earning giggles from him. "You certainly need your sleep. I wish I hadn't awakened you. Maxin and I have an agreement, don't we, my little love? I will tell you a story and you will eat your dinner and sleep the night through for your nurse and grow up to be a good and wise king."

"I must admit, Highness, I enjoy the stories too." The nurse pulled back the curtains, letting the afternoon light spill into the room. Fiera bounced the little boy on her knees, making him laugh.

Taran stepped away, guiding Ivy back with her. As soon as the child's hands left the green stones, the glass turned smoky again, and

Princess Fiera's voice didn't come to them.

What are you thinking? Bard asked as the three of them walked back to the cottage.

"We can take my friend with us when we run away, can't we?" Ivy said.

"I don't know," Taran admitted. She shuddered with the weight of that possibility, the awful suspicion perhaps Yeshen wanted them to rescue two children.

Yet wouldn't Kalista have said to look for the little prince as well as Ivy?

Princess Fiera certainly seemed to care for him. He loved her, judging by that delightful smile. And it sounded like this was a regular ritual for them. Perhaps Fiera was here to rescue the prince, just like Taran and Bard were here to rescue Ivy?

Taran went cold and a little sick, at the idea that Fiera might marry Maddix just to protect his son, to ensure he was brought up to serve Yeshen and not follow in his father's footsteps. Would Yeshen ask such a sacrifice?

Bard asked Ivy how she had found the glass doorway and how she called the prince her friend. Taran barely paid attention as the little girl told how she heard the boy crying, and she went looking. If she pressed her hands long enough against the green glass, the stones vanished and she could walk into the other room. She told how Maxin climbed out of his crib and followed her back to the courtyard, and they played in the moonlight. Bard laughed with her when she told how three times, the nurse woke up and searched all over, under all the furniture and in the wardrobe, looking for the little prince. When Maxin went back into the nursery, she never saw him until she almost stepped on him. Then she screamed.

The laughter stopped when Ivy told how the nurse picked him up and kissed him many times. She laughed through her tears and scolded him not to frighten her like that again. The hunger on her face and the break in her voice made Taran want to cry. She picked up the little girl and held her tight, aching for the loneliness and solitude the child had suffered.

"I don't know if we can," she said, when Ivy asked, again, if they could take her friend with them when they ran away from the palace. "That lady isn't his mother, but she might be if she marries his father. I think she loves him like his own mother would." She caught her breath. "As much as I love you already." Her heart clenched when Ivy's solemn little face brightened. "It might not be right to take him away from his new mother. I will try to talk to the princess and ask her what we should do, all right?"

Is that wise? Bard said. *I've heard the talk. No one agrees if your Princess Fiera wants to marry the king or if her father is forcing her for diplomatic reasons, or the king has some power over her. What if she betrays us?*

"I have to trust that Princess Fiera is as loyal to Yeshen as her father," Taran said after long, thoughtful moments, sitting on the bench in front of the cottage. "We can't leave just yet, so there might be time to find out, to watch her, maybe listen to gossip. Maybe you can sneak out during the day and hide in the shadows and listen to the servants and courtiers talking?"

There are so many stories already, and no one agrees. He sighed and settled down on the cobblestones in front of the bench. *We might be able to flee, just the three of us, and make it over the border before anyone realizes Ivy is gone. If the prince vanishes from his nursery, that can't be kept quiet for long. We could have the entire army of Stonemount hunting us down before we've left the city, forget about reaching the border.*

"We must trust Yeshen for guidance, then." Taran hugged Ivy, and wished she felt as certain and calm as she sounded.

<center>~~~~~</center>

"It tickles," Ivy said after dinner, when the three settled down on the stoop to enjoy the splash of crimson and purple in the sunset. She reached up to touch the amulet at Taran's throat. A few blue sparks of magic hissed and spat at her fingertips, and she giggled, wriggling.

"It tickles without you touching it?" Taran guessed.

She sees magic and senses it, even more acutely than you and I, Bard said. He rested his muzzle on Taran's bare feet and twitched his facial muscles so it seemed his non-existent eyebrows waggled. She laughed.

"Yes," Taran said, reaching up to stroke the amulet, "it tickles my fingers, too. But it doesn't make the skin on my neck tickle. I wonder why not?"

"Your skin is full of magic." Ivy got up on her knees and traced the area around the amulet with her index finger. It required all Taran's self-control to sit still and not leap away. She had the strangest sense that with that touch, the child could see inside her, body as well as spirit. "You don't need it anymore."

"But if I take it off in the moonlight, I'll turn into a wolf."

"No. Your magic is different from his. The moon is like ..." Ivy frowned as she thought. "Like the gears in a clock, to make it chime. You don't have chimes." She shook her head sharply. "That's not right, but I don't know how to say it."

You make me chime constantly, Bard offered.

Taran blushed and muffled a snort of laughter.

I think what she means is, if you take the amulet off now, while it's still daylight, you will turn to wolf.

"That would be ... useful," she mused. Taran's mind filled with images of running in wolf shape at Bard's side whenever she chose, and regaining her Human shape when he walked as a man. "But the amulet is my key. If I lose it while I'm in wolf shape, I'll stay in wolf shape."

"No." Ivy settled back down on the stoop and frowned, staring at the amulet. "That's not how it works. It's not the key. Maybe it's the keyhole." She stomped her little feet. "Why can't I figure out the right words?"

"You see things most students of enchanters do not see until they are three times, four times your age," Taran murmured. She wrapped an arm around the child and hugged her close against her side. "You have so much to learn, and so much power and understanding yet to grow into. The right words will come in time."

I think I understand, Bard said. He got to his feet and put both paws on the stoop next to her, framing her between him and the child. His nose nearly touched the collar of her dress. *The amulet isn't the key anymore, but a place for the key to be inserted. Or maybe ... it's like a trigger on a crossbow.*

"A trigger?" She thought about it. "Then what is the key and what moves the trigger?"

"You have to want it," Ivy said slowly. She closed her eyes, her mouth pursed into a little rosebud and her forehead wrinkled in concentration. She nodded three times, then opened her eyes. "You have to want it."

Clear as mud. Bard's tongue lolled out in silent wolf laughter. Taran wavered between laughing and scowling at him. She settled for resting her hand on his head and scratching behind his ears. *Try it,* he urged, while a low moan of wolfish pleasure escaped his throat.

Taran looked back and forth between the two. Ivy nodded, eagerness making her face bright. It occurred to Taran that the child was probably more interested in seeing her turn into a white wolf in front of her, rather than finding some kind of control over the double nature. Sighing, she stood up and stepped away from them. She tugged the chain of the necklace around until she had the clasp in front where she could see to work it.

"Catch," she murmured, as she undid the clasp, pulled the amulet off, and tossed it to Ivy.

The change began before the amulet hit the child's palms. Taran moaned at the feeling of magic writhing through her flesh, reshaping her bones, hiding her clothes in the same place where her wolf body lay waiting, and sharpening her senses. Before her heart beat three more times, she dropped to all fours, panting, her skin itching under her fur as the residue of magic faded away.

"Oh," Ivy breathed. She carefully put the amulet down and darted forward to wrap her arms around Taran's neck and press her face into the silver-white fur.

Taran could hardly breathe for the relief she felt at the child's reaction. Ivy liked her other nature, her second body. She wasn't repulsed by the change.

Try to change back, Bard urged. He caught hold of Ivy, his teeth in the collar of her dress, and tugged the child back to the stoop. *Give her room, little one.*

Ivy pouted, but she obeyed.

Change back. Taran mentally shrugged. She closed her eyes and concentrated, seeing herself as she had been just a few moments ago.

And concentrated. And took deep breaths. And willed the change to happen. Until her head ached and her teeth itched at the roots from clenching her jaw.

Why isn't it working? I don't understand this, she nearly wailed. *What am I doing wrong?*

Taran opened her eyes and found the courtyard bathed in gloom. The sun had set while she tried to regain her Human shape by the force of her will. Everything lay in twilight.

"It's the key," Ivy said. She tumbled the amulet back and forth between her hands, frowning, her eyes unfocused. Then she blinked and turned to Taran, and tears made her big green eyes glisten. "I'm sorry. I thought I understood."

Oh, don't be sad, little one. Taran nuzzled the child. *At least I know more about what I can do. It will be very helpful, being able to turn to wolf in daylight.*

Ivy held out the amulet and Taran took it between her teeth, holding it with great care so her fangs didn't puncture the thin silver. In moments, she had her human shape back. Taran held tightly to the amulet until she had the chain around her neck.

What good is a key without the keyhole? Bard mused. He lay where he had been all during Taran's attempts at shifting. *What good is a crossbow trigger if the finger that trips the trigger can't touch it?*

"It has to touch me, for the amulet to do its job, to keep me human." Taran nodded. That made sense. Still, the problem remained: how could she control the shift between wolf and human, and what to do with the amulet while she was in wolf shape? The chances of accidents happening, where the amulet could be lost, were too numerous to bear.

Chapter Seventeen

Taran put such considerations aside for later. Bard would shift to man once the moon was high enough for the light to show. Dusk now, it was time for Ivy to be put to bed, so she wouldn't witness his pain.

Taran was surprised when the child didn't resist, other than a little pout when she announced it was bedtime. She supposed Ivy was so glad to have companions again, she was unusually docile and compliant. Normal childish resistance to bedtime would return once the novelty wore off.

At least, she hoped that was true. She didn't want Ivy to be any more unusual than the heritage of immense power already made her. Taran thought of how hard her mother had worked to give her an ordinary childhood, as ordinary as the offspring of a magic wielder could be. She said a silent prayer of thanks for that blessing.

Taran felt a tingle of magic from Bard's transformation in the air, just after she got Ivy's hair brushed out and the little girl's face washed. When she had finished the bedtime story, Taran stepped outside and found Bard sitting on the stoop, dressed in Stonemount palace livery. He stood up when he saw her, bowed, and held out a hand to her. Taran laughed when he swept her into a silly, tuneless dance that spun them around the courtyard four times before she lost her breath.

"He's coming, you know," Bard murmured as they settled down on the stoop. He kept his arm around Taran and she liked that.

"Who?" She realized he meant Maddix, almost the moment the word left her lips. "Yes, he has to come let me out to play ghost, and to get food. How long do you suppose we should wait before we try to escape?"

"The question is whether he will grow complacent. I don't think it's wise to lie to him and make him think you're a docile little fool who will do whatever he wants. He strikes me as someone who doesn't trust anyone, so he expects no one to trust him."

"Except fools." Taran sighed, knowing Bard was right. "He doesn't want a fool tending Ivy. So he will know I am trying to deceive him, if I become too obedient."

"On the other hand, too many questions, too many protests, and he will grow uneasy." Bard tightened his arm around her, one brief embrace that expressed more than words how much he worried. Then he released her. Taran knew he had to hide while the king was in the courtyard, but that didn't mean she had to like it. She swallowed her protest and watched him until he had vanished into the shadows.

How long would the king make her wait until he arrived? Taran thought how long she had waited the night before. She wondered what Maddix had been doing, to arrive so much later than usual. Habits were traps, she decided. Falling into patterns made her easy prey for predators of the two-legged variety. Expecting others to stay in their patterns made her just as vulnerable.

Well, she decided, she would just make use of the time until the king deigned to arrive for their raid on the palace stores. She stepped into the cottage, brought out Ivy's dirty clothes, and set about washing them.

Somehow, she wasn't surprised when she finished the task and hung the little clothes out to dry, and the king still hadn't arrived. She went back into the cottage and sorted through the clothes Ivy's parents had left behind. They weren't fancy clothes, but still of good quality. Taran couldn't make herself try on a dress, though she knew it would be wise to make use of those clothes, when they fled Stonemount. Would Bard fit into the clothes left by Ivy's father? Would seeing him wear those clothes hurt the little girl?

That was a question to be dealt with later. Taran gathered up the clothes that needed washing and brought them out to make use of the last of the water and soap. She looked at the spot where Bard had vanished into the shadows and wondered if he sat there out of sight, watching her.

You think very loudly. A warm rumble of laughter came with the thought.

Taran shook her head, grinning at herself, and finished tipping the water out of the barrel. *I forgot about this new gift of ours.*

It is wearying. Sometimes a man likes to be alone with his thoughts.

We are people too much alone, I think. It is hard for us to be with people constantly. She sighed and turned back to the shadows. *Except for you and I together. Have you noticed that?*

That is because we belong together.

Do we? She flinched and took a step toward the dark patch, reaching out a hand to him. *I'm sorry. It's not like it sounds.*

I know what you meant. We belong together now, two of a kind. But you wonder what the future will hold for us, when we get our answers.

You will be freed of the wolf, but my wolf is integral to what I am.

You are Taran. You are yourself. You are possessed by magic, instead of possessing magic. You are a woman even when you go on all fours and wear fur, because beast and woman are so intertwined. I wouldn't want you divided. A sigh filtered through the silence that touched her soul rather than ears.

Bard. Taran hesitated to ask him to come out. *We have wasted so much moonlight,* she said instead.

"How industrious," Maddix greeted her. He beamed as he crossed from the hidden doorway and came to the edge of the spilled washing water.

He looks far too happy and satisfied with himself, Bard observed, his mind's voice woven with a wolf's snarl.

"Well, I'm delighted to see the child is so well taken care of," he continued. "Has she had any more bursts of magical talent?"

Taran nearly touched the amulet. "No, Majesty. We have talked of many things. I told her stories of my mother, to teach her about magic. She is a clever child. But still a child. She prefers playing and treats to her studies."

"Well, that will change. There is time. Not much of it, but there is time. She needs to think about her future duties." He nodded, his voice jovial, his eyes sparkling with merriment.

She wanted to slap him. Anything that could make him so happy had to be bad for her. The question was whether she dared to ask him or not.

"Shall we go look for supplies, Majesty?" She took off the makeshift apron and hung it on the line where Ivy's clean clothes swayed gently in the evening breeze. She gestured down at her damp, peasant clothes. "Or do you prefer I change clothes and be a ghost tonight?"

I will watch out for her, Bard said, before she could even think of her concern.

Maddix bowed grandly, rather than scolding her for not being dressed in her borrowed queenly clothes. She supposed that answered that concern as well. He swept aside an imaginary cloak and gestured for her to approach the wall. Taran sensed the magic vibrating in the stones, clearly marking the doorway. She pressed her hands against solid stone two steps to the right of the opening. Maddix grunted, nodded once, and stepped through the opening. She caught hold of his jacket and followed him. Tomorrow, she decided, she would find the opening and stick her hand through, and make it look like she found it by accident. After all, how many times could she pretend not to find the magic doorway when Maddix led her to the same spot every time?

Taran had more proof that Maddix was unusually pleased tonight when he held a large basket for her while she chose bread, butter, cheese, eggs and vegetables. He didn't protest more than three times when she refused the sweets he wanted to toss into the basket for Ivy. He actually laughed, muffling the sound behind his hand, when she insisted on sewing supplies, to mend some of Ivy's clothes.

Taran! Bard's voice in her mind startled her, so she almost dropped the pincushion she was about to put down on the table in the palace seamstress's workshop.

What is it? Taran glanced at Maddix, who amused himself tying knots in a large bolt of lace trim.

She's had a nightmare. Come quickly. She wants you. An image of Bard holding Ivy on his lap, his feelings of awkwardness as the sobbing child clung to him, accompanied the words.

"Majesty, please, could we go back? I don't want—" Taran took a breath. How to explain what had just happened? "The child has created a tie between us, and … she is distressed. I need to hurry back before her crying awakens the whole palace."

Maddix didn't even look at her, but waved aside her concern and went back to digging through a box of beads and bits of glittery trimmings. "A child that small could never make much noise."

"Please, Majesty, I can feel her hurt." Taran gathered up the last packet of needles and pins and headed for the door. She wanted to slap Maddix for his lack of concern. Hadn't he ever woken up with nightmares? Didn't he ever cry for his mother? How would he feel if he woke with nightmares and someone said not to worry, that he would cry himself out?

Taran wondered if that was part of what made Maddix the man he was.

"Interesting." He nodded. Taran suspected he wasn't pleased to know there was a bond between her and Ivy. Logic would say if Taran was hurt, Ivy would feel it.

She fought off a chill when it occurred to her that she might have just woven a shield for herself. Maddix would protect the child at all costs, to ensure his power in the future. He would hesitate to punish the caretaker, if harming her harmed the child. Then again, what better way to ensure Ivy's cooperation, than to threaten the welfare of someone she had come to love?

Bard, we're coming, she called, as Maddix gestured for her to pick up both baskets. A sure sign of his displeasure, she reflected, that he no longer carried one for her. Well, what did it matter? When the torment of the full moon had passed, she and Ivy and Bard would flee this place. *Ivy, sweetheart, I'm on my way back.*

~~~~~

"Mama!" Ivy flung herself from Bard's embrace into Taran's arms the moment she reached the child's bedside.

"That's all I could get from her," Bard said, and shrugged.

Taran hugged the child and rubbed her back, fighting not to smile at his obvious discomfort. Playing with her was one thing. Comforting her, driving away her tears, and fixing her problems was something else altogether.

"What about your mama?" she whispered, when Ivy's shaking calmed and the little girl's death-grip on her dress loosened.
~~~~~

"Had a dream." Ivy lifted her head from Taran's shoulder and looked at her with swollen, glistening eyes. "I dream about her all the time."

"You miss her. I know. I still dream about my mother sometimes."

"Mama teaches me. She holds me on her lap and tells me how to do things. And I can smell her and she keeps me warm and sometimes she tickles me." She gulped. "Then I wake up and she's gone again."

"Teaches you?" Bard obviously caught something that escaped Taran.

"About magic."

"Perhaps she Gifted herself to her daughter?" Taran murmured.

"Then why does she only speak in dreams?" he countered. "She would be with the child all the time. She certainly should have encouraged her not to trust the king."

"Gifting requires a touch before the point of death. My mother should have Gifted me her magic, but I was hiding the villagers while she fought Nueroch. She dissipated her magic, to ensure he didn't capture it when she died." Sighing, she settled down on the edge of the bed and adjusted Ivy so the child sat on her lap. "What did she teach you in this dream?"

"How to help you." Ivy touched the amulet with her index finger. Blue and silver sparks of magic raced along her arm and tickled when they brushed Taran's bare skin around the amulet.

"Help me?"

"I asked her. Before I went to sleep, I asked again and again how to help you so you can turn into a wolf whenever you want. And Mama showed me."

"How?" Bard whispered.

Ivy wrapped her fingers around the amulet. Then she stopped and yanked her hand away and looked up at Taran. "Do you want me to do it?"

"I don't know. I think maybe I do." Taran didn't add: *If your dream was a real visit with your mother's spirit, and not a wish-tale.* "How does it work?"

"Mama said you can't wear the amulet. It has to be part of you. Inside you. Then nobody can ever take it away from you."

"Inside me." Taran blanched at the mental image of cutting herself open, putting the amulet inside, and sewing her flesh shut. She knew that wasn't how it would happen, but she couldn't help herself. Sometimes she was too literal-minded. Was that her wolf heritage?

"Do you want me to?"

Taran stared unseeing into the child's eyes for several heartbeats, trying to imagine what it would be like to live without the amulet against her skin. It would be like cutting off all her hair. True, her hair would grow back, and she would grow used to not feeling the amulet at her throat. Wasn't it a small price to pay, to set the wolf free to live and run and howl, without fear of losing the amulet? She tightened her arms around Ivy and thought how much safer the child would be if her guardian could choose what shape to wear, to suit the moment of need.

What difference would it make in how she felt about herself? She would still be the same person, but with another gift set free to be used. How the world looked at her would change, however, once people learned what she could do. She knew better than to hope she could always keep her double nature secret. There would be fear and wonder, and even people who would try to control her, to profit from her gift. And people who would be so repulsed they would want to destroy her, without knowing anything about her heart and soul.

Taran shifted her gaze to Bard. What did she see in his face? Fear? Wonder? Envy? She couldn't tell. His words earlier that evening had been sweet, just what she needed to hear, but would giving her that control change what they had grown between them?

Did she have the right to refuse this gift offered to her?

What mattered most was protecting Ivy, and now she had a better chance of doing that. Taran would have to trust Yeshen for what would come afterward.

"Do it. Please," she added, her voice strained. If she didn't decide now, she might never decide. Of course, as her mother had often pointed out, refusing to decide was just as much a decision as saying yes or no.

Ivy scrubbed away the last tears with her fists and slid off Taran's lap to kneel on the bed. She reached up, and her fingers just barely wrapped around the amulet. Taran shuddered, a queasy, hollow sensation in her belly. There was nothing to fear, she scolded herself. Ivy would never do anything to harm her.

Blue and green sparks spun around Ivy, outlining her in a jewel-like glow. Then the sparks flowed up her arms, gathered around her fingers, then wrapped around the amulet. The magic soaked through her fingers.

A sensation like teeth of fire settled into her flesh at the dip in her collarbone, where the amulet rested. She dug her fingers into the blankets to help her hold still. She couldn't seem to close her eyes, though part of her wanted to. Bard stepped closer, around the side of the bed, to put Ivy between him and Taran. Alarm widened his eyes and he looked grim, but he kept silent. Taran was grateful. Who knew how a single word or an unguarded touch could disrupt Ivy's magic at the wrong moment?

"There!" Ivy blurted, and stepped back, yanking on the chain.

Taran flinched, her voice catching in her throat so she choked on her cry of shock. The burning flared up from the spot on her collarbone to enfold her body, just for a heartbeat. She blinked away the hot tears and saw Ivy only held the chain. The amulet had vanished.

And Taran remained in Human form.

"Did it work?" she rasped.

"I think so." Bard frowned and reached out to press one finger against Taran's collarbone. A spark leaped from her flesh to his fingertip, making him flinch.

"What do you see?" Taran didn't wait for him to respond, but leaped from the bed, her legs slightly wobbly, and darted over to the tiny mirror she had found among Ivy's mother's possessions. She turned it into the light from the oil lamp so she could see.

A triangular black patch covered her skin, just the size of her vanished amulet, right below the dip in her collarbone. Bemused, Taran let go of the mirror with one hand and touched the mark with her fingertip. Blue and silver sparks spun around her finger for a heartbeat, then vanished back into her skin.

"Do it," Ivy urged her. She smiled hesitantly, as if she couldn't decide if she deserved a hug or a spanking.

That broke Taran from her daze. She put down the mirror and stepped back from the bed so she stood in the largest clear spot of floor. Then she looked at Bard and Ivy and hesitated.

Silly featherhead, she scolded herself. *You know what will happen. You won't hurt anyone.*

Gritting her teeth, Taran closed her eyes and directed all the strength of her will to the mark of the amulet. It occurred to her that it looked like something had been burned into her skin, like a brand, marking forever the change in her.

Faster than thought, the sensations of shifting shape flowed over her. It tickled and scorched, but the pain she expected in her bones was instead a stretching sensation. Or perhaps more like being kneaded, like bread. Taran dropped down onto all fours and turned in a circle three times, trying to see herself, trying to determine that everything had changed properly.

That was almost too easy!

"Did it hurt?" Bard asked.

"Not at all," Taran said when she was only halfway through shifting back. It made her throat ache and her words started as a growl. Laughing, she picked up Ivy and settled the girl astride her hip. Ivy squealed laughter as the two spun around the room.

Bard joined them after the first circuit, one hand resting on Taran's shoulder and the other at Ivy's waist. The three laughed and twirled until Taran hit the stool with her hip. Ivy shrieked, giggling, as she and Taran broke away and tumbled down onto the bed again.

He helped them sit up. Taran clearly saw the envy that darkened his eyes, and she ached for him. They had set off on this quest to find *his* answers and cure, hadn't they?

"We will find your cure," Taran vowed. "No matter how long it takes, no matter where we have to go, you will be set free."

"That isn't—we can't—there are larger duties now," Bard said, shaking his head. His smile grew wistful. "We are parents to a powerful young enchantress now. That is far more important than my problems."

"No," Ivy declared, her expression far too earnest and mature for a child so small. Taran could believe that her mother had Gifted herself to her child in some way at the moment of death, and guided her. Ivy raised her hand, palm up, making her words a solemn vow. "I promise I'll help you, too. Just like for Taran."

"The three of us together." Taran took hold of Ivy's hand, and Bard caught hold of the child's other hand and offered his free hand to Taran. "I do swear this," she whispered, moved by the same instincts that had guided her all her life. Perhaps that had been the wolf in her. "I do swear, we are bound together for all time, each caring for the other, taking each other's burdens and sorrows, joys and triumphs as our own. Down through the ages and generations, this vow shall stand."

She shifted her hands in their grips so they were palm-to-palm, fingers interlaced. Bard and Ivy did the same, and a blue spark as big as Ivy's fist traveled around the ring they made, sizzling in their blood, before a burst of light erupted from the center of the circle, blinding them all for a moment.

"Witnessed and sealed," Bard murmured.

Chapter Eighteen

Two days of relative peace weren't enough to lull Taran into a sense of security. They certainly weren't enough time to rest and gather her thoughts. Every waking moment was spent answering Ivy's questions, teaching her with stories about the magic Eyrian had performed or the things her mother had taught her. And when Ivy slept or Bard played with her so Taran could rest, plans for their escape swirled through her mind.

Maddix had been entirely too clever, putting first the child and then her in the hidden courtyard. No matter what route they took to escape the palace, they would not be able to avoid lighted areas and guards.

"Can we use your likeness to the dead queen to help us?" Bard mused, when she shared her fears with him.

"And how do I explain Ivy?"

"We'll find a way. Ivy prays for answers. How can Yeshen refuse a child like her?" He caressed her cheek with the backs of his fingers. His hand shook.

"When the moon is kinder to you, then we will leave."

"The danger increases for all of us, the longer we stay here." Bard tangled his fingers in her hair and gently tipped her face closer to his. She kept her eyes open, refusing to lose a single moment of seeing him as a man. His kiss was as light as thistledown, but it shook Taran to the depths of her heart and soul.

Tears blurred her vision, but she refused to blink as he walked away, to endure the transformation in the shadows, where she couldn't see him suffer.

~~~~

"My son is two years old," Maddix said, forcing a chuckle, when a hot spark deep in his belly threatened to turn his innards into a raging fire. He offered a puzzled little smile to the man who had introduced himself as a scholar named Karait, but whom Maddix doubted was anything of the sort. "I am honored that Durmad is so concerned, but … even in the most gifted family lines, a child's potential does not appear so soon. It is too soon to put a tutor over him, most especially a tutor in magic."

"True." The old man's voice was as dusty and frail as his appearance, but a chill swirled through Maddix's office and threatened an icy blast if he did not tread carefully with this visitor. "Yet our master has sent me to observe and prepare for the day that magic does begin to bloom in the
~~~~

child. Magic does run in your family line, after all. It would be a great tragedy if yet another gift should slip through your hands, would it not?"

His lips twitched, threatening a smile. Maddix thought he saw pointed teeth behind those thin, pale lips.

Another coal landed on the fire inside him. Rage at this slap of innuendo. Was Durmad blaming him because Ambrose chose to Gift his healing magic to Arden? What did he think Maddix could have done differently, to control Ambrose and force his hand when he passed on his magic to another?

Maddix sat still, his eyes narrowed in what he hoped was a thoughtful expression. He would have prayed if he had anyone to pray to, begging for the certainty that this magic wielder sitting in his office, this tutor in magic sent by Durmad, couldn't read his thoughts. What if this magic potential Durmad sensed in Stonemount wasn't in Maxin? What if he felt the power of the child, Ivy?

He had to move her to a more secure, magically shielded place. Maddix refused to take the risk that one of Durmad's spies would find the girl and steal her away, send her north. And worse, tattle, claiming Maddix had betrayed him by keeping the child's presence a secret.

Yet ... what if those spies were sensitive enough to sense magical potential in Maxin, even this young?

The thought of one of Durmad's servants slithering in here, poised to influence Maddix's son and heir, to train his loyalty away from his father, and even worse, steal away the magic talent that by all rights should be devoted to serving Stonemount ... that infuriated Maddix enough to drive away all his fear.

Who had betrayed him? Who had noticed the seeds of magic in his son and chose not to tell him?

"Of course, you are correct. We must protect my son in every possible way. Guard and guide his future," Maddix said slowly, offering a thin smile, making his tone gentle and reasonable. "When do you wish to start working with him?"

"Oh, not me." The man's dry little smile twisted slightly in distaste. "I will settle into quarters in the city and the servants you will hire over the next several months will report to me. They will be my eyes and ears, watching the boy, waiting for the first blossom of power. They will gradually replace anyone I deem either unreliable or potentially dangerous, a barrier to our master's plans."

Maddix needed all his self-control not to twitch when this vile creature used the word "master," referring to Durmad. No one was master over the king of Stonemount. Ivy, properly trained, would slap him with that unpleasant truth, hard enough to keep him in the far north, and teach him not to set his greedy eyes on the kingdoms that Maddix intended to rule someday.

Karait kept the meeting short, leaving the impression that he found something distasteful in Maddix's office, perhaps in the entire palace. He left a thick envelope of instructions for the new regimen for Maxin's education and had the audacity to tell Maddix to read all of it thoroughly before he began implementing it. Who did this arrogant buffoon think he was talking to? Kings had far more important things to do than deal with nursemaids and training schedules and altering what food the boy ate and magically examining the servants who dealt with the boy.

Holding onto his most pleasant and reasonable mask and tone of voice, Maddix agreed to everything. It took all his self-control not to fling the entire envelope across the room, into the fireplace, the moment Karait stepped out of his office. Likely the man had spells wrapped around it to make sure his instructions were carried out. Maddix shivered at the certainty that some of those spells were curses, punishments to be inflicted on him if he didn't obey.

Very well, he would read them—after he had some of his pet magic wielders check for traps and tricks and curses, and maybe even poison on the paper. Maddix wouldn't put it past Durmad's people to think it more expedient to kill him and take over the entire kingdom, to get their hands on Maxin. If the boy had that magic potential they sensed.

Maddix left the envelope sitting on his worktable in his office and went for a long walk in the gardens, while he thought and planned. The first step in protecting his son and whatever magic the boy might possess was to put new nursemaids in charge. Starting with women who had enough magic in their blood to sense when it stirred in others. What he needed was someone who could throw a shield around Maxin, so no one would sense any more flickers of magic stirring in him. He needed women who could stand against the nasty tricks and threats that Karait and others like him would employ to push them aside, so they could slip their own spies and conspirators in, to influence Maxin.

"No," he growled when he had walked without paying attention to his steps, until he found himself in the rarely traveled back sections of the massive gardens. "The first step is to put the girl into hiding. She has magic, not just the potential. They'll come after her first, and Durmad will accuse me of plotting against him, because I didn't turn her over the minute that idiot of his killed her parents." He snorted, a grin twisting his face for the first time since Karait presented the glowing black stone that proved he spoke with Durmad's power. "Because of course, yes I was. But where to put her? Why can't that courtyard be secure enough?" He flinched, thinking he heard a footstep. Were Karait's spies already following him?

Maybe putting Ivy into the courtyard had indeed shielded her from

Durmad's seeking magic? Was all this a ploy to make him panic, make him take foolish steps, make mistakes and bring the girl out where she could be sensed and snatched right out of his hands?

Maddix nearly threw himself to the ground to kick and roar like he had as a child, when he felt as if his father's loyal servants and Durmad's emissaries were tearing him in two different directions. Why couldn't they all leave him alone to do things his way? He was king of Stonemount. He was more than capable of destroying everyone who opposed him. Why should he share his power and glory with anyone? Least of all a scheming brute who let himself get locked away behind a pitiful wall of mountains and had to depend on others to set him free.

No, he wouldn't move Ivy. Not until he had conferred with his strongest magic wielders and determined just how far and how much Karait and his people could see, how strong they were, how far they had penetrated into the palace. And just what he could do to destroy as many of them as he possibly could without Durmad realizing that his followers hadn't fallen to the attacks from Steward and other magic wielders who resisted him.

Still, he kept walking down the neglected, magic-shielded pathways of the gardens, to the courtyard and cottage. He needed to check on Ivy just the same.

Laughter met his ears when he stomped through the hidden doorway in the wall. He paused in the shadows with strands of ivy falling over his shoulders. Maddix froze, not even rubbing his eyes to clear them, and stared.

Ivy laughed, holding on with both hands and gripping tight with her knees, as a black wolf carried her around the mossy courtyard on his back. Taran sat on the bench next to the cottage door, mending Ivy's clothes. She glanced up at the wolf and child, smiling, and bent back over her work. Other than the laughter and the soft padding of the wolf's paws in the thick moss and the rustling of a light breeze through the leaves, there wasn't a sound to be heard.

The whole scene made Maddix shudder. The child should have been screaming, not laughing. The wolf should have been snarling, baring its fangs, not gamboling like a freakish, furry pony. Taran should have been waving a cudgel at the wolf, to separate beast and child, not calmly going about her household chores. At the very least, she should have been screaming for help.

Oddly, Maddix sensed a conversation took place, but he couldn't hear it.

The laughter, the smiles, the whispering of the wind in the ivy and the trees stopped, as if even the wind held its breath. The wolf went still as a stone. The child slid off his back and wrapped her arms around his neck. Taran stood. She watched Maddix and held out her hand to the child. Ivy scampered to Taran's side, and the wolf followed her, leaping ahead in a few steps to put himself between the little girl and the king.

"Majesty?" Taran rested one hand on the wolf's head, and the other hand on the child's shoulder.

"All this time." Maddix staggered forward two steps, and suddenly the laughter erupted. It burned in his throat, like the residue of drunkenness. "I've been wracking my brains, trying to find an answer, a tactic, and … It's here, with you."

"Was there something you wanted?"

'Wanted?" More laughter lodged in his throat, choking him.

Ivy whimpered, a soft sound, muffled when she pressed her face into Taran's skirts, but loud enough to chill him and still the churning in his head and stomach.

"Why is that thing here?" Somehow, Maddix kept from shouting. He pointed at the wolf, as if Taran might not know what he meant. "How is it here? How are you both still alive? What magic is this? You do have magic, despite what you've said."

"Bard is my new Papa, just like Taran is my new Mama," Ivy said.

"Your new—" Maddix swallowed laughter that threatened to shatter his sanity. "How do you command it?"

"I do not command him at all." The faintest smile caught up Taran's mouth.

"No wonder you have no fear, with that beast to protect you."

"Bard isn't a beast," Ivy said.

"Of course not, he's a very well-trained, tamed creature. The most loyal guardian you could ever hope to have." A stream of plans flashed anew through his mind, the advantages he could gain from an army of wolves loyal to him. "Why does he follow you?"

"He loves her." Ivy frowned, her mouth pursed in a tight rosebud of anger when Maddix snorted. "He does!" She stomped her little foot. Then again. Then a third time before she fled into the cottage in the face of Maddix's amused disbelief.

"How can a beast love?"

Taran turned her head to the wolf, and again Maddix had the sensation of a silent conversation. Perhaps he was going mad? No, he refused to accept that.

"The truth, Majesty, is that Bard is a man under a curse, and I am trying to find the magic to free him."

"A man?" His grin flattened. He took a breath to shout, to ask her if she thought he was a fool. Then it struck him: Taran had no reason to lie. "Who enchanted him?"

"For the good of Stonemount, Majesty, do not seek out this enchanter.

141

He will not aid you unless it will profit him. He will destroy you. Or worse, he will destroy everything and everyone precious to you, simply for amusement."

"It sounds to me as if you have very ... intimate experience with this enchanter."

"He killed my mother. He savaged the five villages she tended, just to force her out to face him. He bonds men and beast into one creature and does not care that his magic is faulty, unfinished, and those he takes as his slaves suffer for his carelessness."

"Suffer? How?" he snapped.

The wolf woofed low and deep in his throat and took a step forward. Maddix fought not to move and yield ground. Not to an idiot who didn't have the sense to avoid antagonizing a powerful enchanter.

If Taran were telling the truth, and not trying to mock him, or drive him mad.

"Bard says I should tell you. He says if you are foolish enough to beard Nueroch in his den, to try to buy his services, you will deserve everything he does to you."

"Bard says?"

"He speaks into my mind. And Ivy's."

"Interesting. Well, Bard, will you speak to me?" Maddix summoned up a friendly smile.

"Majesty ..." Taran's smile looked weary. "You would not like what Bard would say to you."

"This Nueroch. Where is he?"

"In the Swordtop Mountains of Brentonwald." Her lips twitched, a barely concealed smile, when Maddix flinched.

"Why does this Bard think you can help him break his curse?"

"Because Nueroch killed my mother to find a magical secret he could not discover for himself. What my mother could learn with her vision pool and do with potions and the gathered magic of our ancestors, I must do by going on quest." She sighed, weariness visibly pushing her down to sit on the bench. The wolf sat down at her feet, lying so he faced Maddix, keeping himself between the woman and the king.

"Well, Bard, what will it take to persuade you to stay, to forsake a cure and take service with me?"

"Come tonight under the light of the full moon and see what Bard suffers, and then make your offer. If you can." Taran met his eyes, and Maddix didn't like the weariness and anger he saw in her gaze. He didn't like the feeling that Taran judged him and found him lacking.

"Fair enough." He nodded regally and turned to leave. He nearly missed the opening in the wall. That infuriated him.

~~~~~
~~~~~

"We need to leave as soon as possible," Taran said. She hated to put that somber look in Ivy's eyes. Then again, the child had lost her sparkle when Maddix interrupted their play in the courtyard.

"The king doesn't want Bard here?" The little girl looked at her dinner of bread and milk and slowly pushed the bowl away.

"On the contrary." She sighed and picked up the child, settling her on her lap. "The king wants Bard to stay. I think he wants to find a way to put more men under the curse."

"Curses are bad."

"The full moon hurts Bard when he changes from wolf to man. When the moon rises tonight, I want you to stay in your bed and hide under the blankets and plug your ears. He doesn't want you to hear his pain." Taran stroked curls off the child's forehead, trying to soothe away what she couldn't erase from her own heart. "The king will come to see what happens at the full moon. Then ... we will leave. Hopefully, he won't expect us to flee."

"Will we take Mama and Papa's horses?"

"Horses?"

"Papa taught me how to talk to them," Ivy whispered, just a glimmer of childlike delight coming back to her eyes.

"Can you talk to them now, without seeing them?" Taran held her breath, praying for a good answer. Horses would help them enormously. She and Bard could run as wolves, but they would need food and clothes and money to make a journey far enough to escape Maddix's reach. Ivy couldn't carry everything they would need.

"They don't like it when people ride them, so the people who take care of the stables don't treat them nice. They leave them outside."

"Will they be ready, when we need to run away?" Taran kissed Ivy's forehead when the girl nodded. "I think they'll be happy to see you again. Now." She settled Ivy back down on the stool. "Eat your dinner, then we should start packing."

~~~~~

Maddix spent the remainder of the day in a bouncing state of anticipation. It took all his concentration to focus on the council of lords meeting, and he resented the necessity of re-establishing his domination over the nobles. They were especially irritating when they argued for what they considered the good of the common people.

That galling defeat and humiliation at Arden's hands — with the help of his great-uncle and cousin, to make matters worse — had set him back months in his plan to establish total control over Stonemount. The ugly truth was that the lords no longer feared him. What was even more bitter to admit was that his father had been right. Fear and respect were not the same thing, and respect was more valuable than fear.
~~~~~

Then, to add to his frustration and impatience for nightfall, when he could see the wolf turn into a man, he returned to his office, anticipating a solitary dinner, and found Fiera waiting for him. He nearly spewed a stream of profanity, demanding to know what she was doing there. The chess board set up next to his desk answered that question. His face burned when he remembered. In an attempt to charm her and keep her from suspecting that he was behind the stories of Bianca's ghost haunting the palace, he had invited her to play chess every afternoon at this hour. Fiera had taken him up on his invitation twice so far.

The most aggravating part of finding her here was the realization that any other day, he might have enjoyed this. A chance to talk, to catch her in unguarded moments, and implant thoughts in her mind, to make her doubt her principles and beliefs. His throat burned with the furious words he held back. For a few moments, Fiera didn't know he was there. Her head was bent over a book, and her lovely face wore a gentle smile.

The only thing more irritating to him than a woman who read was a woman who enjoyed what she read. A woman who read had an ugly tendency to think for herself. His mother had been that way, and several wives of troublesome nobles. Jaygo had needed to eliminate them so he could intimidate and influence their husbands without interference. If he couldn't frighten her away, Maddix couldn't afford to let Fiera think for herself. He had to train her to think like him.

Chapter Nineteen

Swallowing down his vexation and stifling a demand that Fiera never bring a book into his presence again, Maddix schooled his expression into delight, and held out his hand to her. He tried to ignore the quiet voice in the back of his mind that commented that he never needed to scold Bianca like that. Sometimes he missed Bianca. He cursed her once again for betraying his plans by dying before he needed her to do so.

"My darling Fiera. How lovely you look today. Your presence in the midst of my dreary schedule gives me great delight."

Fiera's smile still made his heart skip a beat, even though he told himself a dozen times a day that she bestowed that warm, beautiful expression on everyone, whether they deserved her kind regard or not. Somehow, he could never find the right words to convince her of the need to be more discriminating with her kindness. She either laughed, apparently thinking he was being humorous, or she gave him a look that was both confused and a touch offended.

"Could I ask a great favor of you?" She closed her book on her lap. Just like Maddix feared, it was some dreary discussion of Yeshen's teachings and prophetic visions in history. Why did Fiera insist on cluttering her mind with such things? Why couldn't she be like other charming women and focus on fluttery, sugary poetry or setting new fashion trends? "It's about Maxin."

He blinked, and fought back several other responses, most of them angry. Were his suspicions about Brentonwald's true nature correct? Was she in league with Karait? "Something about my son concerns you?"

"Indeed. Why did you change his afternoon nurse? He adores Fern. She can get him to eat his dinner and take his bath without any fuss. He was quite distraught when this new woman came to take care of him. He cried himself to sleep, and she was so upset with him I feared she might spank him."

"Fern?" Maddix blinked and shook his head, half-hoping he would wake himself up from a confusing dream. "Why are you concerned with my son's caretakers? How did you even know what happened?"

Fiera gave him a look that was half frown, and half amusement. "Clearly, your spies have fallen down on the job. Or maybe they didn't think it worthwhile to tell you I visit the nursery every afternoon?"

"Still?" His voice cracked.

Fiera chuckled. Her cheeks pinked in an utterly charming way. "Maxin is quite my favorite person in the entire palace, and the hour I spend with him is the most pleasant of every day. It gives me the strength to endure the company of most of your court, quite frankly."

"I thought you started those visits to impress me, to trick me into thinking ..." Maddix sighed and finally settled into his chair opposite her.

"Thinking what?" She fluttered her eyelashes.

He chuckled, and pushed back the brief, hungry ache for some deeper understanding between them. To have her smile at him like ... like Arden had smiled at that soldier husband of hers on their wedding day.

"Why does it matter to you? Maxin is a baby—"

"He's nearly three years old, clever, and chattering away quite delightfully."

"He is?" Maddix blinked. How had that much time passed? He tried to recall the last time he had looked in on his son. He shook away that question. "Again, why does any of that matter? Even if you were his mother, certainly you have more important things to do than fuss over how many nurses he has or if he likes any of them."

"You truly have no idea what matters in this world, do you?"

"On the contrary." His heart raced hot as all his amusement fell away. "Leave the welfare of my country to me, Princess Fiera. Indulge all you wish in your womanly concerns, with my blessing."

"Is that a bargain?" She tipped her head to one side, her expression turning serious. Somehow, that frightened him, just as strong as the irritating suspicion that her smiles mocked him. "If I leave your statecraft to you, will you give me authority over Maxin?"

"Gladly!"

"Will you put it in writing?" She flushed darker pink, and for a moment he thought he saw something like alarm in her eyes.

Had he finally pushed Fiera far enough to make her lose her aggravating balance and calm and confidence? How could he use this against her?

The plot to frighten her away with the ghost of Bianca wasn't working. Could he perhaps use this, twist this agreement, into an accusation against her? Bring in false witnesses to tell stories of how she was threatening his son? Trying to turn him against his father and his kingdom? Could he shame Fiera into leaving Stonemount, at long last?

"Gladly," he snapped again, and had to fight to keep from baring his teeth. He refused to give her any hint that she had given him a weapon to use against her, at long last.

He called in his secretary to write up the simple agreement, then called in several of the nobles who were always waiting to speak with him, to act as witnesses. They signed the multiple copies of the agreement, sealed with wax and their signet rings. Maddix didn't like the way each noble seemed to pause in reading the document, almost at the same place, before signing each copy. Why did they need to read so carefully? What did it matter that he was making Fiera his son's guardian? As soon as he could weave together the plot to discredit and shame her, she would flee Stonemount and he could annul the agreement and he could finally return to his plans of conquest.

His thoughts turned to tonight's revelation before Fiera walked out of his office with two copies of the agreement. He waved away the last few words of the nobles as they made their farewells. Maddix's imagination swirled through multiple possibilities for how to use an army of man-wolves, where to deploy them best in his plans. Soon, Durmad would regret scolding and lecturing him, and telling him how best to take over the world.

~~~~~

Maddix found some small pleasure in feigning a foul mood and declaring he would not waste his time on the entertainment offered to the court that night. He called for several decanters of the best wine, slammed the doors on the heels of the departing servants, and chuckled at the growing fear on their faces. No one would dare to bother him tonight. If anyone thought they glimpsed their king scurrying through the twilight shadows of the garden, they would turn away quickly, in fear that he would vent his current rage on them. Maddix had done just that often enough to have a pattern. Most courtiers would be gathered in their conspiratorial clumps, discussing how to regain their king's favor and ease his temper, and trying to determine just who had enraged him now.

He chuckled as he considered revealing the truth behind tonight's adventure. Or maybe he would never reveal the source of the magic that would give him an army of man-wolves. He changed his clothes to simple garb, dark enough to allow him to blend into the shadows between the buildings and among the trees, and hid his hair under a cap.

Just to be careful, he took two knives with poisoned blades and fastened them to his belt. He had learned, through bitter experience, never to expect anything to work out exactly as he had planned it. If the black wolf Taran had named Bard attacked him, or went after the child, Maddix intended to kill it. He could afford to lose an army of man-wolves, and he could threaten a dozen women with no families into raising Ivy for him, but he couldn't replace a magically gifted child who would grow up completely loyal to him and no one else.

He opened the secret doorway that would take him from his apartments, down a hidden flight of stairs, and out a door directly under his balcony, into the gardens. He snarled at himself when he saw how deep the twilight had grown. He was running late, and this time there was
~~~~~

no one he could blame but himself, which irritated him to no end. He wanted to be in the hidden courtyard before the moon rose. If only that passageway that led directly from his nursery to the courtyard hadn't vanished when Jaygo got rid of his nurse who gave him the courtyard. He wouldn't be surprised if that was the reason, and not any failing on the part of Nurse Willow. At least she had loved him without any reservations. He hoped Clancy and Baethon had made Jaygo suffer for a while before they killed him. The man had ruined far too many of his plans.

Just a sliver of moon showed on the horizon, visible over the low garden wall behind him, as Maddix reached the hidden doorway. No one was to be seen when he stepped into the dark courtyard. He fought down a totally ridiculous surge of panic and stomped one foot into the soft moss. The spicy, fresh smell of the crushed moss sickened him. He looked around and took a deep breath to call out, then hesitated. Asking where everyone was would make him sound like a frightened child. He wasn't afraid. Taran couldn't find her way out of the courtyard without his help.

But Ivy can, that treacherous voice inside his mind whispered. *Ivy is full of magic. Even though the door is hidden by spells, she has much more magic.* Maddix wondered if he had been a fool. He hated it whenever that unpleasant sensation washed over him.

A shadow separated itself from the thick shadows to the right of the cottage. He held his breath, and the thudding of his heart seemed painfully loud. Then Maddix saw the gleam of those odd blue eyes of the wolf, the glistening of those large, white fangs in the twilight. The wolf came closer, mouth hanging open, eyes bright, and Maddix had the sickening, infuriating sensation that the beast laughed at him.

Maddix nodded to it. The wolf nodded back, stretching out one paw and making a somewhat elegant bow, head down and nearly touching the moss paving the courtyard.

"Can the woman hear you? Where is she?"

"I am here, Majesty," Taran said, and stepped through the doorway of the cottage. She raked her fingers through her hair and bound it back with a bit of ribbon. Her eyes were enormous and her hair seemed to gleam like moonlight in the shadows.

Moonlight filtered softly into the courtyard, making the shadows slowly grow darker, deeper, and contrast against each other. The wolf slid like a flow of oil through the shadows to her side. It rubbed its head against her arm. Taran stroked the beast's head in a tender caress that made Maddix uneasy, watching it.

The wolf walked over to the far corner of the courtyard and lay down on the moss. Taran crossed to stand by Maddix near the wall. She flicked her gaze toward him once but watched the wolf.

"Bard doesn't want me to be here. He doesn't like it when I see his suffering," she said, and wrapped her arms around herself.

"Maybe we can find a wizard who can ease the suffering," Maddix offered. After all, he reasoned, feigning concern and sympathy often worked wonders in persuading people to do what he wanted. He had played with different plans of action; bribing Bard, threatening him, cajoling, offering huge sums of money, land, a noble title, to convince the man-wolf to swear fealty and bring the gift of transformation to others who would be loyal to him.

Moonlight stretched a thin beam over the wall behind Maddix. It angled down just enough to be noticeable and hit the wall above the wolf's head. The seconds ticked by and the beam of moonlight angled lower as it crept down the wall, until it touched Bard.

The wolf sat up. Moonlight flicked over his ears, making the black tips look silver. A low moan escaped his closed jaws and Maddix flinched. That sounded too much like a man. He glanced at Taran. She stared at the black beast, eyes gleaming with tears. Maddix swallowed hard, not certain what he felt, and positive he didn't like it. Could she actually care for the wolf? He thought about what Ivy in her childish silliness had said, about Bard loving Taran. Could there possibly be a tie between the woman and the wolf?

How, Maddix wondered, could he use that to his advantage?

The wolf curled up on himself, shuddering so the movement was visible in the shadows. Maddix flinched and barely kept from crying out when the fur changed color, going from black to a mottling of black and red and gold in a liquid flow, like a wave washing across a beach. A long, agonized howl escaped the wolf, turning into the desperate, strangled cry of a man in mortal pain before it broke off with a sob.

"What in—" Maddix took two steps forward before he caught himself. Was he hallucinating, or did that wolf wear his livery?

The wolf unfolded, limbs stretching out at odd angles, the head melting like candle wax. Then, in what seemed only the blink of an eye, a man in royal Stonemount livery lay on the ground. His groans barely penetrated the thudding of Maddix's racing heart. Taran darted across the courtyard. She lifted the man's sweaty, black-haired head into her lap and stroked his forehead. Maddix stayed where he was until the man turned, rolling onto his back, his limbs straight and no longer trembling.

"Fascinating," he said. "Yes, I can see how you would want to end that suffering. But think of the advantage of being able to shift shape."

"There is no control, Majesty. The moon dictates what shape he wears." Taran didn't look at Maddix as she spoke but concentrated on the man.

"Then I will find a wizard who can repair the spell and grant control.

I am in contact with dozens of wizards around the world. They will help if I ask. If I pay handsomely enough," he added slowly. Maddix repressed a smirk when Taran finally looked up and met his gaze.

"There is not enough money in the world," she began.

"For you, perhaps." He waved his hand to brush aside foolish protests. "Come, you and the wolf—Bard, you said his name was?—the two of you will be quite comfortable, well-paid. You won't regret a moment of living in Stonemount's service. And in return for your service, I will help you."

"The moon is my master," the man said. He opened his eyes. It disconcerted Maddix a little to see those blue eyes hadn't changed. "Its strength dictates how easy or hard the transformation will be."

"What's the use of magic if you're helpless and sick from it?" Maddix didn't care that his words ended on a whine.

"There are other nights when he is a man, Majesty, when the shift is not painful and when he can hunt and think unimpeded," Taran said. "This is the worst. Tomorrow night will be easier, and the night after that."

"Very well, then. I will come back in two nights when you are more comfortable, and we will make our bargain." Maddix rubbed his hands. "Yes, indeed. You will not regret a moment of it." His mind spun with ideas as he found the opening in the wall and stepped through.

~~~~~

"No, we won't regret it for a moment," Taran murmured, as soon as Maddix's backside vanished through the invisible doorway. "Because we won't do it."

Bard slowly got to his feet. "You do have quite a talent for lying."

"Maddix wouldn't know the truth if it bit his nose off," she snapped, but she matched his smile. "How do you feel?"

"By the time we have Ivy awake and ready to go, I'll be fully myself." He tugged on the black and red coat. "I'll be glad when I can get rid of these colors. Does he think just because I took his livery out of necessity that he can order me?"

"He thinks Yeshen made the world to be his plaything, and it is his right to punish anyone who won't let him win." She shook her head and turned to go into the cottage. "You can't wear that livery when we escape, you will be too visible. Take some of Ivy's father's clothes now."

~~~~~

Maddix muffled a curse and skidded to a stop on the gold-painted seashells paving the path that led straight to his hidden doorway. Just one more puddle of shadow between his hiding place and that sheltered alcove in the garden. Who were those imbeciles strolling through the garden when he wanted it empty? He caught his breath when the two figures stepped into the spill of moonlight and he recognized Lord

Anselm, King Egis's watchdog, and Princess Fiera.

Did he imagine her pallor, the somberness in her expression, or was it just the moonlight washing out her usual vibrant coloring? And when had Anselm ever shown such warmth and concern in his expression?

Maddix's heart skipped a beat at a sudden burst of inspiration. How could he use this against them? Accuse Anselm of being Fiera's secret lover? No, a far more humiliating accusation: start rumors that Anselm cared so deeply for her because he was her father. That would humiliate King Egis and Brentonwald, and free him of the pressure to marry Fiera, because then her royal blood would be called into question.

Brilliant.

When Taran made her midnight trip through the gardens tomorrow night, he would tell her to not only let herself be seen, but whisper hints of those accusations. The people loved Bianca, and if they believed her ghost had been roused, then they would never doubt her words.

Anselm bowed to Fiera and backed away. She took a few steps further into the strengthening moonlight, settled on a bench, and bowed her head, to rest it in her hands. She looked tired. A little sad.

Maddix wondered if she didn't want to be here any more than he wanted her here. Maybe she was trapped just as much as he felt trapped.

The idea that they had something in common gave him a strange feeling. He was surprised just as much as Fiera when he stepped out of the shadows and approached her. She didn't raise her head until his steps crunched on an especially large piece of shell and it broke with a loud crack. Maddix admired her when she didn't flinch, but sat straight and watched him, her face unreadable and more pale than Bianca's in the moonlight.

"How … pleasant to find you out here. And how unusual to find you alone," he added. "Are you feeling well, Princess?"

"I could say the same for you. Have your spirits improved?" She actually sounded solicitous, rather than being arch or mocking him.

Maddix waved away the question. "Some nights, it is a drudgery more than I care to endure, to deal with the court. I often find solitude refreshing. It gives me time to think. Time for questions to come to the fore." He considered settling on the bench next to her. Such closeness usually flustered younger court ladies. Fiera didn't fluster easily. He chose to stay standing, putting himself five steps back from her. "Perhaps you can help me with a puzzle."

"With what matter?"

"The wizard, Nueroch."

"What do you wish to know of him?"

Maddix went on the alert, close enough to catch a slight flinch in the corner of her mouth, a tightening of her eyes, at mention of the wizard's name. "You do know him? He is from Brentonwald?"

"I never saw him. But I know of him." She shook her head and pursed her lips. "Father would have nothing to do with him, and *nothing* ever frightens my father. He never invited Nueroch to the palace with the other enchanters and magic wielders in the kingdom, never asked him for advice or flattered him, never sent him gifts to celebrate important events."

"That sort of behavior usually leads to trouble. All the old stories say so."

"Hmm, ordinarily." Her eyes narrowed as she studied him for a few heartbeats, likely trying to determine what he wanted. "Nueroch wants to be left alone. My grandfather sent gifts to Nueroch, invited him to the palace. It's only sensible, after all, to treat powerful people with great respect, and to treat possible enemies even more delicately than your good friends. Have you seen the great precipice on the south side of the palace?"

"No, but I've heard about it." Maddix wondered how she would react if she knew he had the floor plan of her father's palace in great detail and had paid quite handsomely for maps of the secret passageways that riddled the palace and the rocky promontory where it sat, overlooking the Sagrad River. He had spent a few pleasant hours trying to puzzle out how the side of the cliff face had been sheered off so cleanly, the rock melted like glass in a furnace.

Chapter Twenty

"Grandfather persisted in making overtures of friendship to Nueroch, until one day the wizard sent back all the gifts and the entire envoy party, enclosed in a fireball. That precipice is where it hit."

"Ah." He nodded. "No wonder your father doesn't invite him into the palace. His manners are atrocious. A man who can't control his temper … well … that detracts from his power, don't you think?"

Fiera's lips twitched, fighting a smile. He gritted his teeth and swallowed down a snarl. As if he could hear her thoughts, he knew she was thinking the same about him. There was a difference, as Jaygo had lectured him far too often, between letting his fury control him, and using his rage to keep the incompetents and rebels around him in their places.

"Nueroch is so powerful, what does it matter how much power he loses?" Maddix shook his head and forced a smile, as if the subject didn't matter to him. He wondered just how powerful the wizard was, that Bard had escaped him.

Did that mean Nueroch was losing his power, or he had lost control of his creations? Just how useful an ally would he be? Perhaps it would be wiser to turn to some other wizard to help him learn the secret of the spell that bound Bard with the wolf.

The problem was finding a wizard of the proper temperament who wasn't already a vassal of Durmad, with foolish notions of loyalty. This particular bit of magic was his weapon alone to claim and use.

~~~~

Fiera felt too restless to go to her rooms and try to sleep. Not until she knew Anselm was safely out of the palace and on his way to Brentonwald with the second copy of the paper, proclaiming her Maxin's guardian. How soon until Maddix realized what a foolish mistake he had made? He was too proud to publicly rescind the grant of authority because that would be admitting he had made a mistake. He would search for the copies, to destroy all evidence, and likely intimidate or even brutalize the nobles who had witnessed the document.

She still felt a little dazed at how the whole situation had turned out. She certainly hadn't planned to ask for guardianship of the little prince when she went to complain about the change in nurses. The new night nurse had nearly wept in gratitude, when Fiera relieved her of her post and reinstated Auntie Pearl, a grandmotherly little woman who reminded
~~~~

her of her own favorite nursemaid. The nurse who had replaced Fern, however, was a different story. She was angry enough to proclaim that "no Brentonwald bully with pretensions of being royal," and then stopped herself before she said anything more. Why the woman wanted to be Maxin's nurse, Fiera couldn't understand. She clearly disliked the little boy, perhaps disliked children in general. Maxin feared her. He had wept on Fiera's shoulder for a good ten minutes after she sent the nasty woman away and cried more when Fern returned.

Remembering how that woman had muttered incoherent threats as she stormed away, Fiera decided she needed to check on Maxin before she went to her rooms. Perhaps it would be wise to bring him and Auntie Pearl to her rooms for the night, just in case that woman came back. She had to have some ulterior reason for becoming Maxin's nurse. Most likely political. But based on what Fiera knew of the rumored alliance between Durmad and Maddix, she could believe Durmad had sent one of his minions to influence the boy from the cradle.

Moonlight spilled into the nursery when Fiera opened the door. She paused in the doorway, confused, because the curtains were closed. Instantly alert, she crept into the room and followed the long streak of moonlight to the far wall, where there was no window.

That little red-haired girl sat in the doorway that shouldn't have been in that wall. Maxin knelt facing her, and the children held hands. Beyond the doorway, Fiera saw cobblestones, and a brick wall and a thatched roof. The girl looked up and let out a cry as her gaze met Fiera's.

"It's all right," she whispered, and went to her knees in front of the children. She glanced over her shoulder at the big, comfortable chair where Auntie Pearl was fast asleep. That wouldn't last much longer.

"Ivy?" The woman's voice came from beyond the cottage. "What's wrong?"

A pale-haired woman stepped into the frame of the doorway. She stared at Fiera for maybe two heartbeats, then dropped into a curtsy. "Highness." She trembled, just for a moment, then visibly braced herself. "Please, Highness, don't say anything? Don't tell them?"

"Tell them what?" Fiera wrapped an arm around Maxin. The little boy looked at her, his eyes big, and clutched at the front of her dress.

"We have to go away," the little girl said. "It's not safe here. I have magic and the king—"

"Ivy." The woman stopped her with a touch on her shoulder. "Highness, I beg you, as a citizen of Brentonwald, let us slip away. Kalista of the Pools sent me to find this child and rescue her."

"Did Maddix put her here?" Fiera shuddered as suspicions swirled through her mind, telling her a story she didn't like. The woman nodded. "Then go, with my blessings and my prayers."

"Can we take Maxin?" Ivy whispered. "He's my friend."

"I'm sorry. No, this is his home and ..." She sighed and tightened her arm around the little boy and stood. "I promise you, I will take care of him as if I were his own mother. He will be safe."

"Thank you, Highness." The woman tugged gently on the child's shoulder. "Ivy, we need to go. Say your goodbyes."

She made another curtsey, then stepped away, hurrying back to the cottage. Ivy blinked away tears and said goodbye to Maxin and waved up to him. He reached out to her, so Fiera went down to one knee to put him back on his feet. She blinked away tears as the children hugged. The moment the little girl stepped out of the doorway, it turned into chunks of glass, then became a solid wall again.

Fiera cuddled Maxin as he sniffled and whimpered Ivy's name a few times. He looked up at her, solemn and big-eyed, then put his head on her shoulder and closed his eyes. Fiera breathed a prayer of thanks and settled in the other big, comfortable nursery chair. Soon, he went limp. She watched him sleep and thought about what she had learned, what she had guessed, and prayed for the safety of the pale-haired woman and Ivy.

~~~~~

"Are your horses ready?" Bard finished tying the two rucksacks of clothes together, so they could hang over his shoulder, front and back.

"All ready." Ivy nodded. Her face gleamed with eagerness in the moonlight. "They missed me. Nobody takes them out to run or brushes their coats like Papa used to do."

"Well, we're going to take very good care of them from now on." Taran brought out the last basket of food. She wondered if perhaps it was too much, or even if they would need it.

Yesterday, she had been sure it wasn't enough to last them until they were safely out of Stonemount. Then again, yesterday the plan had been to go through the forests to Ambray and avoid all contact with people. Thanks to Ivy's contact with her parents' horses, the trio's options had grown. They would ride directly to Westerland's border. No need to hide in shadows. There was more than enough food for the much shorter journey. Whenever he was about to transform to wolf, Bard would go ahead of them, so he wouldn't frighten the horses, and wait until they caught up with him. Whenever he was a man, she would take wolf shape to serve as sentinel and guard.

By nightfall tomorrow, they would be in friendly territory. She even toyed with the idea of seeking sanctuary and help with Princess Arden. After all, a Gifted healer such as the princess of Westerland might have knowledge of something that could cure Bard.

Or maybe just give him control over the transformation?

Taran put that thought away as soon as it came clear in her mind.
~~~~~

Bard wanted to be free of the wolf, and the wolf wanted to be free of him. She couldn't ask them to stay bound together, just so she would not feel like a monstrosity, painfully unique in the world.

"Are you ready?" Bard murmured. He half-raised his hand, as if he would again stroke her cheek with the backs of his fingers. That gesture had become a habit. Taran wondered how much longer those touches would last, once he was cured.

"Ready." She mustered up a brave smile and nodded. She handed him the larger basket of supplies and handed the smaller basket to Ivy. "Remember, no matter what you see or hear or what people tell you to do, you listen to Bard and you get to the stables and your horses. Nothing else matters. Understand?"

Ivy nodded. Sober understanding of their situation warred with excitement on her face. Taran quite understood the little girl's feelings. She couldn't wait to be out in the forests and under the open sky again.

She checked the livery Bard had found for her, as a disguise, then closed her eyes and concentrated. She half-feared that the magic Ivy worked had only been alive once. Shaking off that crippling thought, she willed her wolf side to come forward. A faint prickling of magic stung her fingertips and toes, danced along her skin and shot sparks from the ends of her hair. Then Taran was on all fours and the night came alive with scents that threatened to drown her with their potency. Snorting, she turned around three times, leaped and turned a somersault, just to test her new body. Ivy clapped her hands, her face bright with delight.

With a flick of her tail in salute, she strode to the opening in the wall. With wolf-sight, she saw the silvery-blue haze of magic behind the ivy, obscuring the opening in the wall with illusion. A single spark shot out to perch on the end of her tail as she slid through and out into the gardens.

The plan was for Taran to gain the attention of whatever guards might be stationed around the courtyard. Just because she pretended not to be able to find the hidden doorway didn't mean Maddix believed her. His cleverness, she suspected, came from his inability to believe what anyone said. He had contingency plans for contingency plans.

She wondered what contingency plans he had to ensure Bard cooperated with his desire for an army of man-wolves. The thought of the cruelties Maddix might attempt made her fur stand up stiff. A snarl escaped her, just as she caught a whiff of man-scent.

Two men, with a preference for strong spirits and leather. And multiple scents of cheap perfume. Taran shook her head at the conflicting messages brought on the wind. These men were closest to her, so she crept through the shadows of the garden until she caught up with them.

~~~~~

Clancy and Baethon meandered through the garden, grumbling in
~~~~~

between gulps from two large bottles of wine.

"Idiotic," Baethon muttered. Clancy grunted agreement. "Somebody needs to knock some courtesy into him. Who does he think he is, blaming us for—"

He paused as a white, gleaming vision stepped from the bushes to his right, about twenty steps ahead, and waited for them to come down the path toward it. Baethon rubbed his eyes with his fist and looked again. The vision stayed there.

"For everything, when it's his own stupidity and stiff neck that messes up all our plans," Clancy grumped, filling in the silence. He tilted back his bottle and spilled one mouthful down his throat and another down the front of his jacket.

Baethon kicked a few pebbles from the path, aiming toward the gleaming vision ahead of them. "Did he say anything about sending a white wolf to wander around with that stupid girl?" He gestured at the vision, now only four steps away on the path.

"White wolf?" Clancy turned his head to stare at the moonlit creature standing in the path. He didn't stop so much as he managed to take a step backward without tangling his legs.

The white wolf shook her head and spun three times, chasing her tail. Then she flicked her tail at the two staring men, hard enough it brushed their hands. Two bottles slipped and shattered on the pebbles as the wolf darted between them, so her fur brushed against their thighs.

Baethon and Clancy turned as one man, nearly running into each other. They grappled for their swords, usually used to intimidate the innkeepers who provided their wine. They nearly slashed each other now. Letting out warbling war cries, they raced down the path after the wolf.

~~~~~

Taran ran, grateful for the long walks Maddix had led her on. She knew where each path led, what turns took her back to the main path through the gardens and which ones would take her in circles. She flicked her tail at the two men and laughed silently, wolf-fashion, when her insolent gesture earned curses. Their cries brought a handful of palace guards running from three different directions. Taran howled delight. Several men paused, stunned, while the others shouted louder and ran faster.

Her paws skimmed as light as mist over the garden pathways. Taran counted the men. More than she and Bard had estimated would be on duty this late at night. Was that a good sign? Had their plan succeeded and drawn everybody away who might see Bard and Ivy and stop them before they reached the stables?

How are you doing? she called to Bard. *I think everyone is chasing me.*

There are a few lights in windows. I think you have an audience, but that
~~~~~

should be helpful, he responded after a moment. *We're nearly to the last gate out of the gardens. Down to the river, and up again to the stables, and we'll be free.*

Someone is talking about getting a net, she informed him a few minutes later. Taran slowed enough to look back over her shoulder and give her pursuers a chance to catch up. She didn't want to lose them. The plan was to draw everyone away from the stables and the gate out of the palace grounds, so Bard and Ivy could find her parents' horses and get out of there without anyone seeing them and raising the alarm.

You're doing too good a job.

Frustrating them? Good. Taran glanced over her shoulder again. She couldn't let anyone break away from the pursuit to fetch reinforcements or other weapons.

We're here. No one in sight. Bard sent her an image through his eyes, of three silvery-gray horses approaching the fence in the stable yard, nickering softly. Ivy dropped her basket and darted across the cobblestones to climb the crossbars of the fence and cling to the smallest of the three horses.

That answers that question, Taran quipped. *I'll be there soon.*

Be careful!

She darted through an archway into a shadowy courtyard with a fountain that chuckled and splashed in the moonlight. The courtyard was dotted with rose arbors, the warm air heavy with perfume. Most important of all, it had a wide door decorated with brass scrollwork. The ladies of the court came to this fountain courtyard on pleasant days to sew in the shade. Or they came out here in the twilight for trysts with their admirers. Taran shifted back to human, opened the door into the palace, stepped back, and shrieked at the top of her lungs.

When the pursuers tumbled into the courtyard, they found Taran huddled on a bench in the rose arbor furthest from the doorway. She shuddered, skirts wrapped tightly around her ankles, cap pulled down to her eyebrows, and shrieked again when someone touched her arm.

"Did you see it?" Clancy demanded, his face red and dripping with sour wine-scented sweat. "The white wolf? Did you see it?" Taran barely raised her head from the protective circle of her arms. She gestured toward the open door of the palace. "What did you do, idiot girl?"

"I was coming out. My lady wanted a note left for — it jumped at me when I opened the door. I tried to run away, and it —" Taran forced a few ragged sobs. "It's in the palace!"

As one body, all the guards and night gardeners, led by Clancy and Baethon, poured through the doorway. Taran waited until the last one had vanished into the darkness of the hallway, then she slid off the bench and ran. Once she reached the cool shadows of the garden again, she shifted back to wolf.

Bard was just lifting Ivy into the saddle of the smallest of the three horses when Taran raced into the stable yard. No horse made a sound or even flicked an ear at the appearance of a wolf. She shifted back to human, only a few steps away from them, and only the largest one, a gelding, nickered at her.

Helpful, having beasts that are used to magic, Bard thought to her as he finished adjusting the stirrups to Ivy's legs.

Very, she agreed, and walked over to the mare, whom she assumed Bard wanted her to ride. The horse flicked her ears and snuffled at the hand Taran held out to her.

They like you, Ivy said. All three horses bobbed their heads.

Bard helped her up into the saddle of the mare, then he ran ahead and opened the gate out of the palace. Taran took the reins of his horse and led the way out into the street. After he closed the gate, he ran to catch up with them, then mounted and took the lead. After all, he had been exploring the streets of the city as man and wolf.

Are we safe? Ivy asked, after they had ridden for nearly twenty minutes in silence. The palace still loomed over them, though half a dozen streets and turnings lay between them and it.

Almost. Taran wondered how much of the child's caution was innate wisdom, and how much was the result of pain, loss, and fear that had come too early in her life. *When we reach Westerland, you can be like any other little girl. You'll have toys and puppies and time to play and lots of little girls and boys to play with,* she promised.

I want a little sister. Mama said she wanted to give me a little sister when we were safe. Can you give me a sister?

Give it time, little one, Bard responded, when Taran scrambled to think of a response. *Taran and I aren't even married yet. We have to be married before we can start making babies.*

Taran noticed Bard didn't smile or even look over his shoulder at her as he responded to the child's innocently dangerous question. She feared he only said it to placate Ivy so she wouldn't ask more difficult questions.

~~~~~

Maddix groaned at the muffled sound of fists pounding on the outer door of his apartments. Who would dare interrupt him at this time of the night? He had awakened maybe half an hour ago, from a dream that something had gone terribly wrong, but he couldn't remember enough details to know what, exactly. He had turned to the second decanter of wine to put him to sleep like the first had. His last mouthful of wine was still strong in his mouth, and the pounding had shattered that lovely, drifting and falling sensation. Maddix kept his eyes closed, determined to fall asleep again.
~~~~~

Wakefulness slammed down on him, pulsing in time with the fists on the door. From the sharpness of the thuds, Maddix guessed whoever had been at the hall doorway had come inside and now banged on the door from the antechamber into his sitting room. Muffling a curse, he slid out of bed and reached for his robe.

"You two are dead men." Icicles filled his voice as he glared at Clancy and Baethon standing in the doorway.

"You said we were to watch for a black wolf after the moon set," Baethon blurted. He paused long enough to wipe sweat and grime and blood from several scratches off his face. "What about a white wolf while the moon is still up?"

"White?" Maddix took a step back. He shuddered, and his mind seemed to freeze up as he grappled with an idea he sensed he didn't want to consider.

Fury had him turning and slamming his fist into the wall, denting the plaster and brocade covering it. Of course—the girl was a wolf just like the man, but she apparently had far more control than he did. Why else would the black wolf follow the woman?

The girl dared to lie to him. She had the power already. That was why the man wanted her help in breaking the curse. She had the power, the control. And she had escaped the courtyard without his help. Maddix could almost laugh at himself, that he had assumed she was trapped there. He had suspected, he had feared, but he hadn't listened to his sense of impending trouble.

Chapter Twenty-One

Maddix snarled at himself. He should have listened to his first furiously panicked instincts and moved the girl and the child to the subterranean chambers of the palace. Asking his magic wielders to assess the situation had been a dangerous waste of time.

"Well, what are you two buffoons standing there for? We have a witch to capture!"

"I don't—" Clancy glanced at Baethon, who just shrugged and shook his head.

Snarling, Maddix ordered them to the stables to check for the horses that had given the hostler so much trouble. What other horses would they take, after all, but the horses that dratted child's parents had been riding?

Refusing to listen to the fear sending hot spears and icy daggers through him, he went first to the courtyard. He snarled at himself for being foolish enough to hope the girl was only playing, enjoying a night of freedom, to run through the gardens.

But no, the cottage was empty. The silence seemed to jeer at him.

He was halfway to the stables when Clancy and Baethon met him, accompanied by a handful of guards and gardeners who all looked rather worse for wear. All but the two henchmen quailed under Maddix's furious glare. They showed more resentment than fear, and he promised himself he would deal with them later and enjoy every moment of it.

"Gone?" he asked, very sure he knew the answer already.

Clancy pointed at a barefoot, half-dressed boy who shivered and didn't resist when two guards dragged him to the front of the group.

"A man and a lady—" The boy's voice broke and he glanced up once at Maddix. "A white lady like poor dead Queen Bianca."

Maddix nearly struck out at the boy when half the other men murmured and made various signs to ward off evil. "Just those two?" he said instead. "What about a child?"

"A little girl. Yes, sir. My lord. Majesty." The boy tried to bow, but it was difficult with two burly men holding him upright. "They had a little girl with them. I think she was a wizard. She made the horses come to her without saying nothin'. No sugar or bread or apples or nothin', and those were the meanest horses in the entire palace."

Maddix gritted his teeth and swallowed his fury. He refused to show any weakness before underlings. He had hesitated to have the horses put down, fearing Ivy's parents had protected them with some magic. Now he wished he had taken the chance.

"A gift for controlling beasts isn't much magic at all," Baethon muttered.

"No, sir," the boy said, nodding and then shaking his head. "But she held out her hand, the little girl did, and the locks on the gates popped open and the horses came out high-stepping like they were on parade and they stood still and they even showed the man where the right saddles were to fit them."

"Where were you while this was happening?" Maddix said.

"I was trapped up in the loft, sir. Majesty." The boy hadn't learned from his first attempt and tried again to bow. "I was scared near to dyin'. As soon as they left, I came down and went for the guards. They stole from the king's stables. Couldn't let them get away with it." The boy tried to look indignant, but the stern expression just emphasized the dirt ground into his skin.

Maddix supposed from the boy's half-dressed state that he had actually told the truth. He would still have to be punished for not stopping the three thieves, but there simply wasn't time.

"How long ago did they leave?" he asked.

Finally, after nearly half an hour, Maddix, Clancy and Baethon were mounted and heading down the road that Bard, Taran and Ivy had taken. He couldn't include the palace guards on the hunt. The fewer people who knew about Ivy and the man-wolf magic, the better for everyone.

Maddix followed a hunch and took the western gate out of the city. Less than a mile down the road leading to the Westerland border, they met up with the old man who collected the toll when people passed out of the valley. He claimed the ghost of Queen Bianca had come flying through, mounted on a ghostly gray horse. A fire spirit on a second gray horse laughed and shot blue and green sparks at him when he asked for the toll.

"Did she pay it?" Maddix snapped, when the old man shook his head, a bemused smile parting his long, tangled gray beard.

"Yes, Mi'Lord. The serving man with her paid me. He asked me not to tell anyone they were going to Ambray."

"You believed him?" Baethon let out a bark of laughter.

"Why wouldn't I? The poor dead lady was just going home, wasn't she?"

Maddix didn't have time to order Clancy to have the man horsewhipped. Tonight, everyone in his kingdom was incompetent, and he was clearly the only one who could catch the fugitives.

The real question was if Bard was telling the truth about going to Ambray, and foolish enough to trust the toll-man not to tell anyone, or if he thought he was clever and trying to confuse anyone who followed them.

"Bet he was lying," Clancy said, as they rode away from the toll gate. "Should have taken the Potters Gate if they were going to Ambray. This is the shortest route to Westerland."

Maddix growled and focused on the road ahead. He would rather die—no, change that, he would rather Clancy died, than admit the bumbler had figured out the conundrum first.

The three settled their horses into the ground-eating trot they could maintain all night. And all the next day, if they had to. Maddix wagered with himself that none of the three fugitives was used to traveling by horse. The child was too frail to handle the grueling pace for long. Taran and Bard were both just filthy peasants, used to going on foot rather than saddle.

On foot, indeed! Maddix cursed. Taran had the power to become a wolf, and never told him. How dare she? He had given her the honor of living in his secret courtyard, entrusted the care of an orphaned child into her keeping, and this was how she repaid her king? By keeping secrets, and then kidnapping that child from under his nose?

She would pay. He would capture her and torture her until she begged to give him the magic, the secret of merging men with wolves. Then she would beg him to let her die.

~~~~~

The moon had dropped halfway below the horizon when Bard led their small party deep into the trees, out of sight of the road, then called a halt to rest. The clouds of approaching pain in his eyes told Taran the transformation was almost on him. She nodded, squeezed his hand, and reached up to help Ivy slide out of the saddle. The little girl fell asleep almost before Taran finished settling her in a nest of blankets, in the shadows of a clump of bushes. She tended to the horses next, murmuring to them, marveling at the softness of their skin, the spicy-sweet scent of their breath. The horses were dirty, their coats needed a good brushing, and their manes and tails were tangled, but they were beautiful, intelligent creatures. The horses nuzzled her hands and delicately lipped bread and pieces of apple out of her hands. Then when she stepped away, they ranged themselves around the bush where Ivy slept, setting themselves up as guards.

"Thank you," she murmured. Taran suspected the horses were thirsty, simply because she was thirsty. She could drink from the water skin tied to her saddle, but that wouldn't serve for the horses. She had nothing to dig with, to create a trough for them, even if she dared give up all the water and the weak wine they had brought in the four skins among their supplies.
~~~~~

What could she do? She thought while she stacked the saddles and sorted through their few sacks and baskets. Taran nearly laughed aloud when she remembered her newest talent.

The mare she had been riding only flicked her ears twice when Taran shifted to wolf. She pointed her nose into the wind and began hunting for water.

Taran found the water less than ten paces away from the road, a thin stream meandering slowly between two wide banks. Judging by the shallow slope of the banks and the wide strip of water-worn pebbles on either side, this had been a much wider stream at one time. All that mattered to her was that the water was moving and fresh, so the horses would drink it.

Bard met her, a wolf again, on the way back to their impromptu camp. Taran told him what she had found.

Do you think maybe we can talk to the horses the same way we do now? It would make leading them away from Ivy a little easier, he added.

Taran tried to talk to the horses. They looked at her and flicked their ears, then turned all their attention back to Ivy.

Maybe you can't use words with them, Bard offered. He stepped up to the big gelding he had been riding and touched the horse's nose with his own. The gelding snorted, then went still and stared into Bard's eyes.

The smallest horse whickered and bobbed her head, and walked away, heading in the direction of the stream. Taran moved up to take its place and Bard followed the horse. He reported less than a minute later that the horse had gone to the water to drink.

When the smallest horse returned, the mare went to the water and Taran kept watch in her place. When the mare returned, the gelding took his turn. The mare nudged Taran toward the blanket she had spread on the ground earlier, when all three horses had resumed their post over the child. Taran had a momentary, blurry image of herself lying on the blankets, asleep.

Thank you, she said, though she wasn't sure the mare understood. Without shifting back to human, she curled up, tucked her nose under her tail, and was instantly asleep.

"It's quite comfortable for sleeping," she told Bard, when he nudged her awake an hour later. Taran stretched and paused for a moment to look at the sun sitting on the horizon. "I didn't get nearly as much rest as I would have liked, but now isn't the time for sleeping, is it?"

Bard shook his head, then walked over to Ivy's nest. The horses stepped back, allowing him access to the sleeping child. The smallest horse walked away, heading toward the water.

"Good idea," Taran murmured. "Ivy, sweetheart, wake up. We have to wash our faces before we ride again."

When Ivy didn't move immediately, Bard licked her face. She squealed and sputtered and sat up. Taran was grateful when the little girl burst into giggles.

Bard kept watch over the camp while Taran took Ivy to the stream to wash their faces and refill the water skins. As the horses returned from drinking their fill, Taran saddled them, then gave them another piece of bread and apple. They had food to spare. Not much, but the horses had earned it.

The day passed quickly, hot and dry and bright, good traveling weather, according to the people who joined them on the highway. Taran welcomed the company, because that made them harder for their enemies to spot than if they were riding by themselves. Still, she resented the groups on the road, passing them either heading toward the border or taking the road to cross Stonemount to the lower portion of Brentonwald. Every time someone approached them or slowed down to match their pace for the sake of company, Bard had to leave the road and travel through the forest on either side of the road. He kept in contact with her, and sometimes made her laugh with his witty comments about their temporary traveling companions. Still, she missed his company. She resented the fact that he had to hide. Some people were so citified, had so little contact with wild animals, they might have mistaken Bard for a guard dog rather than a wolf, but Taran couldn't take that chance.

Besides, when King Maddix sent out soldiers to hunt them down and bring them back, he would tell his men to look for a black wolf in the company of a white-haired woman and a red-haired girl.

The sun climbed higher and seemed to hang forever at noon zenith. Ivy fell asleep in the heat and slumped in her saddle, until Taran lifted the child over to ride in front of her. She liked the way Ivy snuggled up against her without opening her eyes. Perhaps the little girl dreamed her mother held her. Taran hoped that was so, and the child got some comfort out of the dream.

A band of merchants joined up with them two hours from sunset. The woman riding at the head of the long train of ten wagons and thirty mounted guards urged her horse over to ride with them. With a glance, she asked permission from Taran, and brought a handful of paper-wrapped candies from the pouch at her waist. Ivy's eyes got big when she saw the treats, and Taran couldn't have said no, even if she wanted to. The horses liked the woman, letting her ride alongside them without any reaction. Taran had already learned to trust the horses' judgment.

"You and your little one heading to Westerland?" the woman said, laughing when Ivy snatched a bright red sweet. She winked at Ivy and unwrapped a dark purple one to pop into her mouth.

"Our first trip there," Taran said, nodding.

"Another hour, and we'll be over the border. I travel this road every other month, and I'll be stopping at the new healer hall to trade with the princess and her folk."

"We're that close?" She stood up in the stirrups, trying to see a little further down the road, which seemed to have reached the bottom of the dip in the landscape. All she could see was the packed dirt and gravel of the road, moss and grass and scraggly trees on either side of it.

"Close enough to smell the difference in the air," the merchant woman, Maeve, said with a grin.

Can you? Taran asked Bard.

I don't think so. We're still too far away, but I would think a healer hall with all those herbs would be very easy to smell.

I can feel something nice ahead of us, Ivy said. *It's tickly. And … it's a feeling, but it's a taste and a smell and music, all wrapped up together. I don't understand.*

Why don't you save your questions for Princess Arden when we see her, all right? Taran offered. She had a sudden vision of Ivy switching the conversation to audible, and alarming Maeve with the oddness of her questions. This close to safety, they couldn't afford a mistake.

But why is everything all mixed up? I can smell colors, and taste voices.

It's magic, Taran hurried to say, hating the panic in Ivy's mental voice. *Strong magic. Your ability to sense magic is changing as it grows.*

This is what it was like for Taran and for me, when we first started using our wolf bodies, Bard offered. *Don't worry, little one. We won't let anyone hurt you.*

Taran echoed him, and then turned her awareness outward again. The border of Westerland and the strong, Gifted magic of Princess Arden and her healer hall were less than an hour of riding away now. She concentrated on that blessing. Soon, they would be safe.

This is the place where, in all the really nasty tales of wizards and dragons and evil kings, our enemy would catch up with us, Bard said.

Taran turned to look for him in the shadows alongside the road. She wished she had something to throw at him. Fortunately, Ivy hadn't heard, being busy laughing at a curious little wooden puppet Maeve had brought from her saddlebags. It was worked with rods she held in one hand and seemed to dance on the edge of her saddle.

Tell your new friend you want to go faster, to be beyond the border before sunset, Bard urged.

Taran didn't even have to think why. Sunset was a dangerous time, even without the threat of King Maddix and an army of black and red-clad soldiers thundering down on them.

"Wise," Maeve said, when Taran asked if she minded traveling a little faster. "The crush for lodging is usually at sunset. If we get there beforehand, we have a better chance at the best rooms." She laughed at the puzzled look on Taran's face. "I forget, this is your first time. A whole town has sprung up around the healer hall. Housing for the healers who come to learn there, and for those who come for healing. A market and taverns to serve the families while they wait, and for the students when they're not busy brewing potions and studying the ill. And it's safe. The kings of all the neighboring countries send soldiers to make sure everyone has an equal chance to ask for help. No matter what country they're from."

She turned her horse off the path and moved back in the line, calling orders to her wagon drivers and guards. In a few minutes, she caught up with Ivy and Taran again.

Ivy kept the woman busy with questions. Taran was content to let the horses take them down the road while she studied the landscape around them. Bard dropped back to watch their rear.

When their band came over the top of the last hill and started down the long, shallow slope toward the border crossing into Westerland, Taran could hardly believe it. The border itself was a long stretch of wall, with flowering ivy growing all over it, of all things. The gate had been removed and a tall arch of iron strung with flowering vines stretched over the highway, with no impediment for crossing. The towns on either side of the border appeared to have merged into one town. As she grew closer Taran gaped at the sight of little footbridges going up and over the wall in various places.

"I find it hard to believe King Maddix encourages this," she said to Maeve, when she pointed out the bridges to her and the merchant woman laughed.

"Doesn't matter what he wants or doesn't want, likes or doesn't like. He tried to padlock the gate shut permanently. The people wouldn't stand for it. It's said the ghost of Healer Ambrose comes in the night every time someone does try to shut the gate and opens it again. They're one big happy town here on the border, and King Maddix pretends nothing is wrong."

"I almost feel sorry for him," Taran murmured.

Maeve just chuckled.

Taran! Bard's voice was loud and harsh in her mind, and Taran saw Ivy wince and hunch her shoulders. *Look ahead. Danger!*

She looked, and moaned as the traffic heading toward the gate cleared enough to reveal three mounted men sitting squarely in the middle of the road, maybe fifty paces from the gate, blocking it to all comers. King Maddix, with Clancy and Baethon, on either side of him. Taran knew they probably couldn't pick her and Ivy out of the long line of wagons and riders yet, but every step brought them closer to capture.

"What's wrong, lass?" Maeve looked ahead, following Taran's line of sight. "You know them?"

"That's King Maddix and two bad men who work for him," Ivy said, scowling. "When Mama and Papa died, he hid me so nobody could find me. Until Taran and Bard came to find me. They're my new mama and papa now."

"King Maddix." Maeve's mouth twisted as if she had tasted something foul. Taran wondered if she had heard anything else that Ivy had said.

A moment later, Maeve split the air with a string of shrill whistles. The guards on her wagons galloped up front and surrounded her and Taran and Ivy. And still they kept riding closer to the meeting point.

"Lads, see the fancy-dressed man on the white horse, and the two uglies on either side of him on the roans? We have the distinct pleasure of meeting the king of Stonemount." Maeve paused while several of her men spat curses. She slapped the two closest to her and made them apologize to Ivy. "Got that out of your systems, have you? Now, we need to get our friends past those three. Without tearing apart the border town," she added when several of her men laughed with boyish, mischievous eagerness.

"Disguise," one said, and whipped off his coat, to toss it to Taran.

Another pulled off his hat. It was large enough to tuck up all her hair and the cap she had been wearing all day. A third man leaned out from his saddle and down to the ground, hanging nearly upside down while they kept up their pace, and scooped up dirt from the road.

"Ah, good idea, Rickard." Maeve grinned. "Hide that pretty skin under a layer of dirt. Now, what about our little one, here?"

"Easy enough," a man Taran's age said with a grin. "Put her in the wagon under the canvas. Just the three of them can't make us stop to be searched. Not without papers."

"Didn't you hear me say that was Maddix? Since when does he care about legalities?"

Chapter Twenty-Two

"We just keep moving until we're over the border, and we promise never to come back." He shrugged, then winked and held out his hand to Ivy. "Ready?"

In moments, with Ivy giggling at the adventure, the men passed her from her saddle to the back of the first wagon. From there she scrambled to get under the canvas cover that hid Maeve's merchandise from the elements and discouraged thieves.

It smells yummy! Ivy reported.

"What do you have under there?" Taran asked.

"That wagon has all the herbs and spices and first-rate honey, for Princess Arden's healers to make into potions." Maeve grinned wickedly. "The lad's right. I dare anyone to try to interfere with *that* getting through the border." Then she looked at the riderless horse next to her, and the one behind them with their sacks of supplies. "I suppose they know what your horses look like?"

In moments, Taran found herself passed from rider to rider until she sat in the seat of the first wagon with the driver. Maeve's men loaded bags onto the saddles of the silvery-gray horses, then smeared their coats with dust, so they looked like they had been carrying packs all day. Just in time. Their group came around the last bend, emerged from the trees, and started through the town. Taran repressed a moan when she saw that Maddix and his two henchmen had left their ambush spot and came further down the road, so they were practically in front of the merchant band.

I'm almost there, Bard called.

We're safe so far. Ivy, are you all right? Taran thought a quick prayer of thanks that they could communicate in the privacy of their thoughts. It saved the trouble of explaining so much to their new allies.

This is fun. Like playing Hide'n'Seek, the little girl responded. A soft giggle filtered up from the back of the wagon.

Taran tried not to watch as the band came up to the three men. Miraculously, Maddix moved aside without challenging them. She kept her head bowed, praying the wide brim of the hat cast enough shadow to hide her features. Taran's heart leaped up to her throat when Maddix nudged his horse closer and he stared, frowning, at the newly loaded pack horses. Their silvery coloring seemed all too evident, despite the quick disguise. She counted her heartbeats once the merchant band had completely passed the three men. Forty. Sixty. Eighty. One hundred.

Bard, where are you?

I took the long way around. I'm ahead of you now. I couldn't come up the main road and let Maddix see me. That would ruin all your hard work. He chortled. *You take the high road and I'll take the wild, and I'll cross the border a'fore you,* he half-sang, which earned giggles from Ivy and a grin from Taran.

She looked ahead, where the cluster of buildings spread apart so there was a wide open space around the border and the unblocked gate. Sure enough, in the lengthening shadows as sunset streaked the sky, she saw a thick black shadow come to rest. Taran counted more steps. Then suddenly Bard leaped out from his hiding place so he stood in the open, in the last streaks of bright sunlight. What was he doing?

Please, blessed Yeshen, let no one —

A shout told her she hadn't begun her prayer soon enough. Despite telling herself not to look, Taran leaned out of the wagon seat and saw Maddix turning his horse away from the big gelding that he had obviously been studying. He pointed at the gate, and the black wolf, sitting and waiting calmly.

Bard, run!

No. As long as they see me, they won't see you.

Taran watched, helpless, as the two henchmen thundered past the wagon and then past Maeve and her riders. The three mounted men surrounded the black wolf. Their horses neighed and pranced sideways, fighting their riders, who yanked on the reins and shouted. The inhabitants of the border town gathered but stayed well back from the battle. The path to the gate and across the border lay clear and open while Maddix and his men were distracted.

"What are they doing?" the driver next to Taran muttered.

"Go." Maeve dropped back to ride beside the wagon. "I don't know why that wolf is there, but it's a blessing from Yeshen."

"That's Bard." Taran choked on a giggle when the merchant woman gave her a confused look.

"Whatever happens," the woman continued, "get these two over the border."

Bard snarled and snapped and lunged at the legs of the horses. He took ridiculous chances to force the horses and their riders further back from the gate. But Taren knew if she realized what he was doing, then Maddix would too. And he would target the people trying to pass through the gate.

"We're never going to be safe," Taran murmured.

"Yes, you will. Once you're over the border, you're free of

Stonemount," the driver said. He patted her knee and gave her an encouraging grin. It would have been more comforting if he hadn't been missing an eye, and if his patch didn't have a spiral sewn into it.

"What's to stop him from sending people over the border to capture us?"

"Well, now, you'll just have to trust that no one gets away with much at this particular border crossing." He nodded. "Don't worry about yon beastie and those men. Just a few more minutes, and it's all said and done."

Taran barely heard him. She hung over the side of the wagon, watching Bard dart and leap, terrorizing the horses and neatly evading the swords the men swung at him in time with their shouts and curses.

Clancy sheathed his sword and leaped off his horse, dragging a length of rope behind him. Taran saw the shadow of the gate arch pass over the wagon. She looked up, unable to believe they had reached that point without being recognized and stopped. When she looked back, Baethon had dismounted with a rope in his hand. The two men made loops and flung them at Bard, trying to entangle him.

Bard, run!

Not yet. They'll know.

Maddix leaped off his horse and charged, sword held before him like a lance. Bard leaped aside. A loop settled over his head. Clancy let out a shout and flung his rope on top of the first. Bard dodged it and stumbled when Baethon yanked on his rope. Snarling, Bard leaped on the man. Clancy flung his loop of rope again and this time it landed. He yanked hard. A yelp broke the air.

Taran shrieked and leaped off the wagon.

"Bard!" Ivy tumbled out of the back of the wagon, her face pale, her eyes wide in shock.

"No!" Taran caught up the little girl and put her back in the wagon. "Whatever happens, you have to get to Princess Arden, do you hear me? She will protect you. Ivy, we don't matter. Nothing matters if you are hurt. Do you understand me?"

Bard howled and Taran turned to see Maddix advancing on him, sword raised high in both hands.

Taran screamed, lunging forward onto all fours. Before she touched the ground, her hands became paws and her scream became a furious howl. People shrieked as she darted back through the gate toward the three men and the wolf.

Clancy and Baethon held the ropes, standing far back, slowly choking Bard as they held him still, helpless, unable to attack either of them. Maddix approached, his face alight with vicious eagerness. He swung down. The wolf yelped. The copper, hot tang of blood filled the air.

No one saw Taran fly over the black wolf, to hit Maddix square in his chest. She snarled and dug her claws in before they hit the ground. Maddix grunted on impact, the air knocked out of him. The sword dropped from his hand and his face went white. The sweet stink of pain battled with the scent of Bard's blood.

Taran leaped off him and lunged at the closest man. He screamed and let go of the rope to scramble for his sword. She knocked him down and slashed his chest with her front paws before turning on the other man. He fled, the stink of fear marking his trail. She shifted to human and turned to go back to Bard.

Maddix bubbled curses and blood as he stood over Bard. He tottered but managed to hold his sword poised over Bard's bleeding throat.

"One more step and I'll kill him." He laughed, spattering blood, when Taran skidded to a stop only three steps from Bard. "Just try to kill me. I'll fall on him before you can take your second step."

"Maddix!" a man called.

From over their heads.

Despite herself, Taran looked up. A white-haired man floated down from the sky, to hover at knee height above the ground. He looked hearty and vital, a man in his prime. But he was transparent.

"No, Uncle Ambrose. You're not here. It's a trick," Maddix said through gritted teeth.

"You're the healer, Ambrose?" Taran gestured at Bard. "Help him, please!"

"So you can see me ... Hmm, interesting." Ambrose nodded. "Help is coming. Maddix, haven't you learned anything yet?"

"No. No. No!" Maddix turned his back on them and raised his trembling arms as he faced the onlookers. "I am Maddix, your king! Obey me. Kill this wolf. This woman is a kidnapper. She stole a child entrusted to my care. Capture her. Find the child. I command you."

Silence rang with deafening clarity across the open ground around the gate. No one moved. Taran went to her knees and fought the tears that threatened to blind her as she carefully lifted the ropes from around Bard's neck. Ambrose settled down next to her.

"I'm sorry," he said. "There's not much I can do, except offer advice."

"Bard." Taran shrugged out of the borrowed coat and yanked the cap off her head. She tore it into crude bandages to try to stop the bleeding.

"Over here!" Ambrose shouted. "Quickly, children. There's not much time."

Taran ignored the sounds of running feet, the shouts of people, the clatter of weapons as Maeve's guards gathered around her.

She's safe, Bard said. His voice brought her the weakness from blood loss, the chill creeping through his body, the pain that ate at the edges of his mind. *That's all that matters. The child is safe. And you will be, too.*

Around them, the scarlet and gold spill of sunset began to fade into twilight.

"Here, let me help," a woman said.

Taran had an impression of a long spill of golden hair and vibrant, green-blue eyes, then a man caught her by her shoulders and tugged her away from Bard. She tried to fight, but the shuddering sobs seemed to take away all her strength.

She blinked away tears and choked, startled as a silver haze surrounded Bard. Taran stopped fighting, and the man holding her back gently settled her on the ground only a few steps away. She knuckled her eyes clear of tears. Yes, the woman had cast a strong healing haze around Bard.

This had to be Princess Arden, the Gifted healer.

"Will he be all right?" she asked, directing her question to Ambrose, who hovered at man-height above the two people kneeling over Bard.

The dark-haired man with the princess glanced over, opening his mouth to answer. Then he glanced upward. He flashed a grin at Taran.

"You can see Grandfather, can you? We'll do everything we can for your friend, but—"

"Grandfather?" Arden sat back on her heels. "There's something strange about him. Magic wound all through his being. One moment he's a wounded wolf, the next he's a man. I don't understand."

"He's under a curse," Taran blurted. Quickly, she related what Nueroch had done.

"The curse is fighting to keep its hold on him," Arden said, nodding. "It's interfering with my healing magic. What triggers the transformation?"

"Moonlight."

"I suspect when moonlight touches him, the curse will be broken," Ambrose said.

"That might be too long a wait," the dark-haired man said. Taran guessed since he addressed Ambrose as Grandfather, this man had to be Dylan, a talented healer in his own right.

"I can at least stop him from bleeding to death," Arden declared, and pressed her hands against the bloody wound once again.

The minutes trickled by, as slow as honey in snow. Taran crept close enough to rest her hand on Bard's head. The enveloping haze of magic tickled against her skin.

Taran, there's something happening, Bard whispered.

"What's happening to him?" she asked, fighting more sobs. He sounded as if he were a thousand leagues away and moving farther away with every labored heartbeat. Was that what it sounded or felt like when someone died?

A thin sliver of moon peeked above the roofs on Stonemount's side of the border. Taran felt the first cold, searing touch of moonlight on her skin. She leaped out of the way, letting the light touch Bard. The wolf shuddered, legs kicking out in all directions.

"Stand back!" Ambrose shouted. Dylan repeated the order, and he leaped over Bard to wrap his arms around Arden and drag her away.

Black and purple and bloody red streaks of magic appeared from a tear in the air just above Bard and enfolded him. Light flared out from him, bright enough to blind.

Bard shouted, echoed by a whimper. When Taran blinked the spots out of her eyes, she saw Bard and the wolf lying in a tangled heap. Fighting sobs, she scrambled the last few steps on her hands and knees and flung her arms around Bard.

"Torn for love," he rasped, and held her tight against him, hard enough to threaten her ribs. "It broke the curse. We're free."

"And just in time, too," Arden said.

Taran sat back and Bard let out a groan as they both saw the wolf lying too still in the dirt, bleeding freely. How could the wolf still bleed, when so much blood already stained the ground?

"There's nothing I can do for him," Arden continued. "Maddix, come back to the healer hall with me and I'll —"

"No." Maddix's voice cracked.

Taran turned, startled to hear his voice. She stared at the muddy, bloody, hunched figure that swayed before them. Maddix would have several wide scars across his face. Had she done that to him, in her furious defense of Bard? She tried to feel something, but neither pride nor remorse would emerge.

"You're bleeding badly, cousin," Dylan said. He reached out a hand and crossed the open ground to Maddix's side, but the king hobbled away from him.

"Only an idiot would cross the border into your territory and put himself into your hands. It's just the opportunity you've been waiting for, isn't it?"

"And I'm idiot enough not to want to hurt you. Come. You won't make it home. I don't have to touch you to know you're torn inside. You have broken ribs, and they've punctured you in too many places. The ride will kill you."

"Ha." Maddix's mouth twisted in a pained rictus. "I finally caught you in a lie." He shook his head. His gaze fell on Taran and Bard, still holding onto each other. "Don't think I'll forget how you betrayed me."

Taran knew, any other time, she might have argued. No one had made any promises, no one had betrayed Maddix. She was simply too tired to fight. She rested her head on Bard's shoulder and closed her eyes.

"He's almost gone," Arden murmured.

"Can you save him?" Bard said. "He—" He choked on bitter laughter. "He loves Taran as much as I do. I didn't ask him to fight. He chose it. He understood what was happening."

"I'm sorry," Arden said.

"Can't you put us back together?" He slid Taran off his lap and hobbled over the few steps to the wolf's side, to kneel over the dying beast. "Taran's mother combined a dying cub with her dying child and saved both lives. Can you rejoin us, so my life will save his?"

Arden and Dylan looked up and Ambrose floated down, and the three murmured together for only a few moments. Taran sat where Bard had left her, stunned, trying to comprehend what was happening. What shocked her more? That Bard said he loved her? That the wolf loved her? Or that Bard was willing to return to his bound existence to save the wolf's life?

"I saw how the magic unraveled." Ambrose gestured for Taran to join them standing around the wolf. "Taran, I need to examine the magic your mother wove, to copy it. What talisman did she bind it into?"

"My—" She stopped with her hand pressing against her bare skin. Taran fought the need to sob. "Mother bound the magic into an amulet, but Ivy made the amulet part of me, so I could have control over the transformation." Her eyes ached and burned, as if she would burst into tears at any moment, but they stayed dry.

"Interesting." Ambrose nodded and smiled. "Close your eyes, dearheart, and imagine a door opening in your innermost being, and let me in. Quickly, now. Our friend only has a few more breaths left to him."

Taran had never let anyone touch her mind other than her mother, and the thought of anyone else touching her soul and mind made her cringe. She fought down that hesitation before it could impede her, and ruthlessly called up the imagery Ambrose had asked for. In seconds, she sensed him moving through that door.

Then she fell. Through the years. Backward. To her childhood, to her infancy. To the pain of the illness that melted her flesh from her bones and paralyzed her lungs. The blackness pressed down on her, hot and thick and smothering. It wiped out all sound and color and light. And then the air was gone.

Taran gasped and nearly shrieked as light and sound and color and air burst upon her, shattering the blackness into sharp-edged shards. She found herself sitting on the ground with Princess Arden's arm around her shoulders to hold her upright. Bard lay spread-eagle on his back on the bloodstained ground. Maddix was gone. Full night had fallen and the moon hung high overhead. Most of the townspeople had left.

Of the wolf, there was no sign.

"Bard?" she whispered.

"He's fine. Well, maybe not fine," Ambrose said with a chuckle. "They'll both live. A word of warning. They are fully bound together now. What affects one body affects the other, just as it is with you. There can be no separating them a second time."

~~~~~

When their small party reached the healer hall, Taran found Maeve had kept her word and brought Ivy to safety. Keeping the little girl there was the hard part, but the three horses had refused to cooperate and take the child back to the border gate. Taran was busy reassuring Ivy that everything was all right and the bad king couldn't catch them, so she didn't see where they put Bard. Arden offered to take Ivy into her own quarters. Taran thanked her, then she ran. When she reached the long room full of two rows of beds where Bard had been settled, he was already sitting up, looking around. He saw Taran and held out his arms to her. She nearly shifted to wolf to cross that much more quickly to him.

Bard snatched her into his arms, pulling her down into his lap, and kissed her long and hard and deeply, taking her breath away. Taran swore she saw green and silver sparks dancing behind her closed eyelids.

"Now, that does my heart good," a woman commented in a loud whisper.

"Hush, dearest," Ambrose said. "They both have enough magic to see and hear us."

"Oh, good, more people to talk to." The woman chuckled when Taran raised her head to look around. "Later, my dear child. I think the two of you have a great deal to talk about." Two transparent figures hovering by the ceiling faded away before Taran could make out any details.

"Torn for love," Bard whispered.

"You were free." The words clogged in Taran's throat. She was afraid to question the decision he had made, and unsure of what she felt.
~~~~~

Chapter Twenty-Three

"I found out that what I wanted really wasn't what I wanted." Bard sighed and tugged down the collar of his torn, dirty shirt. "We aren't fighting each other, and I think I can shift shape by my own choice now."

He laughed when Taran stared at the triangular black mark that matched hers, just under the dip in his collarbone. She touched it lightly with the tip of her finger, and a green spark of magic shot out to nip at her fingertip. They laughed together.

"That makes all the difference, you know. Choice." Bard released her and nudged her to get her off the bed. "I am not sick, not injured, and while I pity these sick folk, what we have to say is none of their concern." He took her hand and led her to the door.

A short time later, a black wolf and a white wolf darted through the forests of Westerland, racing to the top of a small hill that let them look down over the border town valley. They raised their voices in a duet of happy, haunting song.

~~~~~

"Wrong, Dylan," Maddix rasped, as his horse limped through the gate of the palace in Stonemount. "I'm still alive, and I'm home. You didn't win." He whimpered as he turned to dismount, and fainted when searing pain tore through him.

He woke to find himself in his own bed, washed and bandaged, and his personal healers looking grave. They were fools. He knew Durmad would send one of his healers to tend him and make him well in no time. Durmad had invested too much in Maddix and Stonemount to let him die now. Maddix laughed, but in moments his laughter turned to gasping coughs that brought up spatters of blood. He snarled at his healers when they warned him to not exert himself. He had proven his famous healer cousin wrong, so these lesser healers without a touch of magical power were wrong as well. He fell asleep with a smile on his pale lips.

And never woke again.

~~~~~

Taran and Bard were still trying to decide what to do, where they should go with Ivy, who they should turn to for training the child, when the news came that King Maddix had died. Dylan was required in Stonemount. Already the tide was turning, and the nobles of Stonemount didn't want the throne to go to Maddix's son. Auntie Glynna, the plantwise woman who had Gifted herself to Arden, expressed some pessimism. She fully expected Dylan to be ambushed on the way to the capitol. After all, Maddix's two henchmen hadn't been seen anywhere near the palace, so they could be lying in wait. That problem was resolved when the guards from both sides of the border crossing volunteered to accompany him as an honor guard.

Bard and Taran promised Dylan they would stay with Arden and her daughter, Violet, until he returned, despite their eagerness to report to Kalista and ask for guidance. Glynna and Ambrose went ahead of Dylan to Stonemount, to scout out the situation. They returned two weeks later, before Dylan, with joyful and somewhat confusing news.

He was to act as regent until Maxin was an adult. Princess Fiera announced to all the nobles her intention to take the little prince home to Brentonwald with her and raise him as her son, and train him to be a king like his grandfather and great-grandfather. No one raised any questions or objections when she stated what many of them had likely been thinking: in Brentonwald, Maxin would be safe from the influence of Durmad's spies and envoys. Even if someone wanted to object to Fiera's plan, they had no authority to do so, because Maddix had made her guardian for his son.

Dylan returned to the healer hall, with plans to make the border crossing town the center of the government until his duties as regent ended. Taran and Bard were married in a simple, quiet ceremony, with Ivy and Princess Violet as their attendants. Then they left, traveling in wolf-shape, to consult with Kalista, while Ivy stayed with Arden, Dylan and Violet.

~~~~~

"Torn by love," Kalista greeted the two wolves as they approached the mouth of her cave home. She smiled and beckoned for them to follow her inside.

Taran and Bard shifted back to human and held hands as they stepped into the cave. It was no surprise to them when Kalista led them to the vision pool where Taran had first seen the white wolf staring up at her from the silvery surface. This time, when they knelt, the clouds of vision cleared to show them a vast landscape, rolling plains and thick, untamed forests, teeming wildlife, hundreds of rivers and streams that watered the land and made it fertile, and not a single person in all the many images that flickered and shifted before their eyes.

"What is it?" Bard whispered, when the images faded back to silvery water.

"Untamed land. Untamed magic land," a man said, startling them. He stepped from the shadows of a room deeper into the string of caves.

The magic humming over him and the light in his eyes told Taran
~~~~~

who he was before Kalista introduced him. This was Steward, Yeshen's hands and eyes and voice.

"Do you know the history of the Stewards?" he asked, when the four had settled down around a low table set with a simple meal of bread and preserves and cheese.

"They tamed magic and helped the first magic wielders find the land that called to them. They protected the land from the geysers of magic that would have destroyed all life." Taran nodded. She had read it in the journals of her ancestors.

"There is another land, over the sea, full of untamed magic. The power has slowly pooled there over time, like the water that formed my seeing pools. The time is coming, and soon, when that pool of magic will begin to overflow and harm the land," Kalista said. "Ivy was born for that time and place, to hold the reins of all that power. That is why Durmad wanted to control her since before birth."

"But Ivy is just a little girl. Even with her magic, she can't go into a wilderness like that and—" Bard stopped with an audible click in his voice. He bared his teeth in a fierce grin. "This is the need you said we were born to meet. Not just to find and rescue her, but to protect her in the wilderness of the untamed land. Man-wolves are the best guardians possible."

"Such clumsy names." Kalista clicked her tongue in teasing distaste. "You need a new name for a new race of folk. You will be part of the history of the new land, and you want a good name to be written in the histories and legends."

"What should we be called, then?" Taran asked, and mirrored Kalista's smile. She suspected the seeress already had a name chosen. Or perhaps more accurately, she had looked into the future and knew the name?

"I name you Werelings. The people of the wood. Fierce and fleet and strong. Loyal until death. Bound to Ivy and her descendants, you and your descendants." Her voice dropped to a whisper. "The descendants of Nueroch will come to you and earn healing and forgiveness and the restoration of power, and it will be a happy time for all."

"Huh," Bard grunted. "I doubt that. Nueroch, asking for forgiveness? No child of mine will ever speak love to any child of his, I can guarantee."

"Can you?" Kalista laughed and waved her hand, brushing away his response. "Trust in Yeshen, my friends, and let the future take care of itself. You have earned your happiness. May all the generations to come call you blessed."

THE END

About the Author

On the road to publication, Michelle fell into fandom in college and has 40+ stories in various SF and fantasy universes. She has a bunch of useless degrees in theater, English, film/communication, and writing. Even worse, she has over 100 books and novellas with multiple small presses, in science fiction and fantasy, YA, suspense, women's fiction, and sub-genres of romance.

Her official launch into publishing came with winning first place in the Writers of the Future contest in 1990. She was a finalist in the EPIC Awards competition multiple times, winning with *Lorien* in 2006 and *The Meruk Episodes, I-V*, in 2010, and was a finalist in the Realm Awards competition, in conjunction with the Realm Makers convention.

Her training includes the Institute for Children's Literature; proofreading at an advertising agency; and working at a community newspaper. She is a tea snob and freelance edits for a living (MichelleLevigne@gmail.com for info/rates), but only enough to give her time to write. Her newest crime against the literary world is to be co-managing editor at Mt. Zion Ridge Press and launching the publishing co-op, Ye Olde Dragon Books. Be afraid … be very afraid.

And please check out her newest venture: Ye Olde Dragon's Library, the storytelling podcast. Interspersed between the chapters will be interviews with authors of fantastical fiction. Listen to the podcast on your favorite podcast app or listen on the website: www.YeOldeDragonBooks.com, and click on the Ye Olde Dragon's Library link.

www.Mlevigne.com
www.MichelleLevigne.blogspot.com
www.YeOldeDragonBooks.com
www.MtZionRidgePress.com

NEWSLETTER:

Want to learn about upcoming books, book launch parties, inside information, and cover reveals?
Go to Michelle's website or blog to sign up.

Thanks for reading!
If you enjoyed this book, would you help Michelle by posting a review on Goodreads?

Are you a member of Book Bub? If so, please follow Michelle on Book Bub, and you'll get alerts when new books are coming out.

As a way of saying thanks, Michelle invites you to the Goodies page on her website. It will change regularly, offering you a free short story, a sample audiobook chapter, sneak peeks at new cover art, inside information on discounts and new release dates, etc.

Please go to: Mlevigne.com/good-stuff.html

Also by Michelle L. Levigne

Guardians of the Time Stream: 4-book Steampunk series
The Match Girls: Humorous inspirational romance series starting with **A Match (Not) Made in Heaven**
Sarai's Journey: A 2-book biblical fiction series
Tabor Heights: 18-book inspirational small town romance series.
Quarry Hall: 11-book women's fiction/suspense series
For Sale: Wedding Dress. Never Used: inspirational romance
Crooked Creek: Fun Fables About Critters and Kids: Children's short stories.
Do Yourself a Favor: Tips and Quips on the Writing Life. A book of writing advice.
To Eternity (and beyond): *Writing Spec Fic Good for Your Soul.* A book defending speculative fiction.
Killing His Alter-Ego: contemporary romance/suspense, taking place in fandom.
The Commonwealth Universe: SF series, 25 books and growing
The Hunt: 5-book YA fantasy series
Faxinor: Fantasy series, 4 books and growing
Wildvine: Fantasy series, 14 books when all released
Neighborlee: Humorous fantasy series
Zygradon: 5-book Arthurian fantasy series
AFV Defender: SF adventure series
Young Defenders: Middle Grade SF series, spin-off of *AFV Defender*

Magic to Spare: **Fantasy series**
Book & Mug Mysteries: **cozy mystery series**
Quest for the Crescent Moon: **fantasy series**
Steward's World: **fantasy series reboot and expansion**
The Enchanted Castle Archives: **fantasy series**